The

Painted

Sky

Murray Pura

for the cowgirls

Diana Flowers, Diana Montgomery, Noela Nancarrow,
Joy Ross Davis & Marian Baay

long may you ride

First Edition

Published by
High Noon Press

ISBN: 978-1-62208-525-5

Printed in the United States of America

Other titles by Murray Pura

The Rose of Saratoga County
> Volume 1 – The Thirteen Colonies

The Rose of Lancaster County:
> Volume 1 - The Rose Garden
> Volume 2 - The Covenant
> Volume 3 - The First Frost
> Volume 4 - A Rose Among Thorns
> Volume 5 - The Trial
> Volume 6 - The Kiss
> Volume 7 - A Rose in Winter
> Volume 8 - Resurrection
> Volume 9 - The Execution
> Volume 10 - The Wedding Quilt
> The Complete eBook

Remington Colt's Revolutionary War Series - The Declaration of Independence
> Volume 1 - Thomas Jefferson

Preacher Man
> Volume 1 – The Devil to Pay

American Civil War Series - Cry of Freedom:
> Volume 1 - Return To Shirley Plantation
> Volume 2 - The Last Waltz
> Volume 3 - Bachelor Buttons
> Volume 4 - Olivia's Wedding
> Volume 6 - Gettysburg's Chosen Sons
> Volume 7 - Sheltering Arms
> Volume 8 - Safe House
> Volume 9 - A Gettysburg Vignette [
> Volume 10 - To Paint a Sunrise
> Volume 11 - Sweet Child of Mine
> Volume 12 - Kentucky Rain
> Volume 13 - Soldier's Heart
> Volume 14 - Black Rain
> Volume 15 - The Star

The Name of The Hawk series:
> Volume 1 - Legion
> Volume 2 - The Land Beyond The Stars
> Volume 3 – Flame

The Painted Sky:
Volume 1 - Rio Oro
Volume 2 - The Widow & the Preacher
Volume 3 - The Australian Way
Volume 4 - A Church Called Lazarus
Volume 5 - The Fight
Volume 6 – Betrayal
Volume 7 - The Shadow of the Almighty
Volume 8 - All the Colors of Heaven
The Complete eBook

The Blue Heaven Romance Series:
Volume 1 - Emalyn's Treasure
Volume 2 - Blister Creek
Volume 3 - Do No Harm
Volume 4 - Heaven Is Not Far
Volume 5 - The Whispers of Angels
Volume 6 - A Dragon's Kiss
Volume 7 - The Bar Maid of Dodge City
Volume 8 - Jolly Angel
Volume 9 - Love's Eternal Flame

The Wells Fargo Express Series
Remington Colt - Volume 1 - The Desperate Road

Seven Oaks:
Volume 1 - The Plantation
Volume 2 - Stonewall
Volume 3 - The Storm
Volume 4 - Firebrand
Volume 5 - A Wedding In Virginia
Volume 6 - Raindrops
Volume 7 - A Seven Oaks Christmas
The Complete eBook

Marsha Hubler's Heart-Warming Horse Stories
Volume One - All the Pretty Little Ponies

Streams: Seeking God in the Waters of Scripture

Rooted: Finding God in the Gardens of Scripture

Mark Miller's One 2013
Volume 5 - White Man's God

Connect with Murray:
www.murraypura.com

Rio Oro

April, 1866, the New Mexico Territory

Marianne pushed her black curls out of her eyes as the wind came up and then pulled her long hair back and twisted it into a bun. The clouds moved away from the sun and a copper light covered the miles of green grass in front of her that bent and flowed. Cattle lifted their heads, turned their backs to the south wind, and kept on grazing. Her stallion rubbed his head against her arm and she smiled and kissed him between the eyes.

"Hey, Arquero, how's it going?" she asked the bright reddish brown paint.

A splash made her look to the right. Her daughter had tossed a stone into the river.

"So is that why it has the name it does?" The girl was staring at the body of water that rolled past them as they walked their horses along the bank. "Because when the sun hits it just so it looks like gold?"

Marianne smiled at her tall daughter who was holding her black and white paint loosely by the reins and tugging the mare away from a clump of clover.

"Well, perhaps there was gold here once, Selah, and the Spanish took it all. Or maybe you're right and they called it Rio Oro because of what happens when the sun and water come together in the early morning and evening. Who knows?"

"La Flecha doesn't have this kind of color."

"It's a day or two's ride north. It's a different river altogether. And they call it the Cimarron River now. After the town."

"Hm." The wind took Selah's hair out from under her wide-brimmed hat, hair that was dark like her mother's but with even more curl, and swept it over her face. She laughed.

"Do you want me to tie it back for you?" asked her mother.

"No! I love this! It's like the sky is playing with me!"

"Some days I think you are twenty. Then you're my twelve year old buttercup again."

"I'm not a buttercup. I'm a rose." She tugged at her mare again. "Oh, come on, Chica. And you never told me why our town is called Cazadora."

"Why are you full of questions? Did you just wake up?"

"I don't know."

"I've told you what the name means."

"A woman hunter. All right. But why?"

Marianne lifted both her dark eyebrows. "I cannot go back three hundred years to ask the Spanish explorers. Perhaps they met a woman here who was hunting a bear or a puma. Or maybe a deer for supper. An Apache huntress."

"Is that what you really think?"

"*Si*, that is what I really think."

"Do you think a Spaniard fell in love with her? That our town is all about romance?"

Marianne reached over and mussed her daughter's hair. "Romance. Yes, I am sure it is about romance. *Un bello romance del Corazon. Con un monton de besos.*"

"Oh, ha ha. For all you know there really were lots of kisses."

"For all I know. But I don't know much, do I?"

Selah was about to reply when she saw the three graves surrounded by a white picket fence and shadowed by half a dozen large cottonwoods. "Here's papa."

Marianne reached over to the back of the saddle as she walked. A bouquet of spring flowers was tied there. She brought it down and gave it to her daughter.

"Here. You place them. And take away the old ones."

Selah dropped her horse's reins and let the mare graze freely. She opened the small gate and bent by a white cross in the middle of three crosses. The dried and dead flowers in a pottery jar she picked up with one hand while putting the fresh

2

flowers into the jar with the other. Then she knelt and folded her hands.

"*Padre nuestro que estas en los cielos. Santificado se tu Nombre. Venga tu reino. Hagase tu voluntad en la tierra como en el cielo.*"

She paused and looked up at her mother. "And what is his will for those of us still here on earth?"

"You just prayed it, didn't you? Whatever is good for heaven is good for earth – peace, joy, kindness, light."

"But it's not that way."

"That is why we pray for it to be that way. That is why we fight for it to be that way."

"Are we going to fight?"

"If we must." Marianne shielded her eyes from the sunrise in the east. "There are riders coming."

Selah scrambled to her feet, her face pinched in fear. "Who?"

Marianne put an arm around her daughter's thin shoulders. "Don't be alarmed. It is our friends. The other two widows."

"But there are four riders."

"They have men with them."

"What sort of men?"

"Hired hands from their *ranchos*."

"For protection?" asked Selah.

"Yes."

"We do not have men riding with us."

"Well, we don't have ranch hands anymore, do we? Now it is just you and I living in town together."

"Will Mrs. Dianna's stallion be all right with your stallion?"

"They are usually fine."

Selah gave a crooked smile. "So long as my mare is fine, you mean."

Marianne smiled as well. "Certainly that helps."

The four riders drew up in front of the fence. Both men tugged on the flat brims of their brown Boss of the Plains hats. The hats had distinctive round crowns.

"Ma'am," said the one.

"Mrs. Freeman," said the other. "Miss Freeman."

Marianne nodded. "Mr. O' Shea. Mr. Cook."

3

A tall woman with blond hair tied up under a wide-brimmed black hat with silver conchos dismounted from her black horse, smiling at Marianne. "How are you, my dear?"

"Well enough, Dianna. It's a perfect spring morning."

"And a warm south wind makes it even more perfect." Dianna was wearing a black riding jacket and pants. "Those irises and tulips look lovely."

"They come up on the side of the house that faces west and south."

"How did you get the tulip bulbs?"

"My mother sent them from New York."

Dianna pulled off her black riding gloves. "So has she given up on the idea of you going back east with Selah?"

Marianne's face took on the look of stone. "Selah and I aren't going anywhere. We intend to move back onto our land in a few weeks. As soon as the judge rules and the squatters are removed from the ranch my husband and I built."

"Ahab Hawthorne calls it his land."

"The Freeman deed is legal. Do you think the courts will side with Hawthorne and turn the law inside out?"

"I'm on your side, Marianne. But Hawthorne has politicians and lawmen in his pocket."

Marianne tilted her chin. "Not God Almighty he doesn't."

"No." Dianna came through the gate and embraced Marianne. "God is definitely on the side of the stubborn Dutch."

Marianne cracked a smile. "Oh, we never left him with any choice."

"I like your outfit. Riding skirt and blouse and tall leather boots with a wide leather belt. It suits."

"Thank you."

"And the pistol goes right along with it."

Marianne put her hand on the revolver tucked into her belt. It had a frame engraved with scrollwork and its cylinder was etched with sailing ships. "Peter always carried his Colt Navy. He taught me how to shoot it."

"You didn't have it at our last meeting." Dianna continued to look her friend over from head to toe. "Where's your hat?"

Marianne tugged at a cord around her neck. "Hanging off my back."

Dianna smiled as Marianne turned in a circle. "Where did you get that one?"

"A trader from Texas."

"You are looking more and more like a *vaquero* every time I see you."

"*Mujer vaquero*. Yes, that's me. It's the look Peter always liked."

Dianna looked at Selah. "I didn't mean to ignore you, my dear. How are you?"

"I'm very well, Mrs. Dianna, thank you."

"Do you grow a foot every month?"

Selah grinned. "Soon I'll be taller than mom."

"Well, your mom's pretty tall. That'll take a lot of oats."

Selah laughed. "Mom says I drink a cow dry every day."

"I'll bet you do." She admired the girl's tweed riding skirt and matching jacket and her embroidered white blouse. "My, my, you must sit pretty on Chica in that. Where did you pick it up?"

"Grandma and Grandpa Van Brewer sent it from New York."

"Lucky girl. It fits you to perfection."

"Thank you, Mrs. Dianna."

"You're most welcome, my dear. I'm only telling the truth without an ounce of embellishment."

Dianna turned and put her hand on top of one of the crosses and was silent a moment.

"Bless you," said Marianne softly.

"And you," replied Dianna quietly.

The other woman had remained on her horse. So had the two men. All three removed their hats. The wind blew over the six of them and was gone.

Dianna looked up at the woman on the horse. "You plan on getting down off that old sorrel of yours anytime soon, Dana?"

"I guess I will." She put her hat back on and dismounted. "Time to join the party."

Dianna put her hands on her hips. "Well, Dana, I reckon we've mourned enough. It's going on two years now. Hank wanted to turn this into a picnic spot my lady friends and I could ride out to, a place we could spread a blanket and gossip

5

and laugh. So that's what we're going to do today. It's high time we did more of it to honor our men."

Dana grinned, the smile large and white in her tiny weather-browned face. "I agree with that. I'm not arguing." She took off her slouch hat again and tossed her head so that her brown hair fell in waves and ringlets to the shoulders of her long light-colored duster. "The last thing my Jack would want me to do is lie down and die here beside him."

She hugged Dianna and then put her arms around Marianne.

"You look younger," said Marianne.

"April is one of my best months."

"Did the winter seem long to you?"

"It's the first time since December I've been able to meet up with you two here. We lost some calves and foals last month with that snowstorm. Yes, it sure did seem long." She hugged Selah. "Such a beauty and so young."

"Thank you, Mrs. Dana," Selah replied, hugging her back.

"You get your new hat from that Texan too?"

"Yes, ma'am."

Marianne smiled at her friends. "I'm in town waiting for the law to clear up the title dispute over my acreage. What's going on with you two?"

Dianna's blue eyes slid to gray. "My ranch is fine. The men are loyal. But cattle have been rustled. And our best bull was butchered and left to rot last week."

"No!"

"It's Hawthorne's way of letting us know it's time to move on before his men burn us out like they did you. I guess he figured that when he had his killers from Texas gun our men down here by the Rio Oro that would be the end of it." Her eyes turned a darker gray. "He was wrong."

Marianne's lips were set in a thin line. "He was." She looked at Dana. "And you?"

Dana took a loaf of bread out from under her duster. "I know this seems crazy but bread and soup were Jack's favorite foods." She went to one knee by one of the crosses. "I expect the birds will eat it up in no time. Or a coyote hop the fence. That's all right. Jack wouldn't begrudge them a meal." She stayed on her knee a long minute and her friends waited, bowing their heads. Then she got up. "Hawthorne's boys have left their calling cards. Burned a haystack two weeks ago. Poisoned a slough the cows drink from the week before that. Thank goodness we have the fresh grass now and don't need the hay. And spring rains have pretty much filled up a new waterhole we've dug." She shrugged. "The crazy North and South war's been over for a year. I count on the army to give us some extra protection this summer."

"Unless Hawthorne's got them wrapped up too," muttered Dianna.

Dana's eyes darkened. "He can't run everybody and everything the way he wants. He can't call every settler or small time rancher a squatter or rustler. I don't care how many sheriffs and lawyers and courts and senators he crams under his vest. There'll always be a few who won't knuckle under to the likes of him. That's all we need. A few." She put her slouch hat back on her head. "And when I meet a real man that'll be the day I marry again. So far no one's turned up."

Dianna narrowed her gray eyes. "Are you already thinking about that?"

"Already? You said yourself it's almost two years. I want some children. For Jack and the ranch as much as for myself."

Dianna sniffed. "The sun'll never rise on such a man for me. I reckon I'll wear widow's black till the day I meet Hank again."

"Suit yourself. Seems like a waste to me."

"What's a waste?"

"There you are all tall and blond and beautiful and no one to give it too."

Dianna reddened.

Dana walked back to her horse. "To say nothing of the love you have in your heart. Why, you are one of the most loving women I've ever met. Who are you going to give all that to?" She rooted around in one of her saddlebags. "You and Hank didn't have kids either."

"We had one boy. We lost him."

"I know. And I'm sorry. But it doesn't have to end there."

"Yes, it does."

7

Dana unrolled a tablecloth and went over to spread it under the cottonwoods. "God tell you that?"

Dianna said nothing in response.

Dana laid the green and white-checkered cloth on the grass and looked up at the branches full of leaves just opening up. "God and the cottonwoods know when its time for new life, don't they? I guess he's told you some things and you've ignored them. The way people ignore the preacher at church when he's hitting home."

"So are you preaching at me now?"

Dana's smile came to her tanned face again. "Yes, ma'am, I am. Come on over here, will you? I'm about to pass the plate."

Dianna tugged down on the brim of her black hat. "Do me a favor, will you, Dana?"

"You bet."

"Y'all tell me when this man I'm supposed to marry comes along, all right? Because I might miss him. Seeing as I won't be looking for him."

"It would be a real pleasure to point him out to you."

"What makes you think I'll agree with you? You going to argue me into falling in love with him?"

Dana's smile had not left her. "I won't have to argue. You'll come running."

"Ha."

"You said yourself the time for grieving was over."

"But not for forgetting."

Dana's smile was gone. "I'll love Jack till the day I die. Just like you'll love Hank and Marianne will love Peter. But the grass is greening and the trees are opening and the rivers and creeks are running. Winter's long over, Dianna. It's time to start again. God help us."

"He will have to." Dianna took off her hat and removed the band with the silver conchos. "Hank always liked me in black and silver." She hung the band from the top of the cross. "If it's here a month from now I'll know there's still some hope for this country."

Dana came over to the horses again. "Since I haven't been here for a while I brought some food. Cold beef."

"Why, I brought some greens," said Marianne. "Onions and radishes and early lettuce."

"And I have potato salad and fried chicken." Dianna smiled at the two men who were still mounted. "You boys going to join us?"

"Well – "

"Mr. O'Shea. Mr. Cook. You must be starved."

O'Shea, who sported a long dark handlebar moustache, peered around them. "Mrs. Charming, I could eat from my saddle."

"Don't be ridiculous. You can see other riders coming for miles without sitting on your saddle. Please join us. Mr. Cook?"

Cook tilted his Boss of the Plains Stetson back on his head. He was younger than O' Shea and freckled with a generous amount of red to his hair. "She's right, Bob. No one can sneak up on us here. Not even Apache."

"Yeah? Those cottonwoods could be Apache for all you know."

O'Shea grumbled a bit more and finally dismounted. He drew his long Spencer repeating rifle from its scabbard on his saddle. It had the look of the muskets soldiers had used in the war but under the trigger was a lever that moved fresh cartridges into place for firing. He carried it with him to the picnic spot and leaned it against the trunk of the largest cottonwood. Cook followed him. They both sat so they could see past the trees.

"Mrs. Freeman." Cook smiled at Marianne as she gathered her skirt and sat by the tablecloth, setting out her wooden bowls of radishes, green onions, and lettuce. "I couldn't help but notice you have yourself a pretty thing on your saddle there."

"Oh?" Marianne glanced back at her horse. "Do you mean the Henry rifle?"

"Yes'm."

"Well, I don't have ranch hands anymore. I have to take care of myself and my daughter."

"Have you fired it?"

"I have."

"Where did you pick it up if you don't mind my asking?"

9

"I have a friend." Dianna and Dana brought their food and dishes and Marianne made up a plate for Cook and handed it to him. "He used to be a lawman. Now he's a circuit rider. He gave me the rifle and taught me how to shoot it."

"I had my hands on one once. Pretty slick. The Henry fires .44 rimfire cartridges, am I right? Fifteen or sixteen at a time?"

"Yes."

"How'd you meet him?"

"Marco Vogelaar? He's a friend of the family. Dutch. Came over on the boat the same time we did. He was the minister who started the church in Cazadora after he put away his badge."

"Is that a fact?"

"He's come by the ranch, Tim," Dianna said to Cook. "Tall. Slender. White gelding. Short beard. Always in a hurry. But you told me you liked his preaching."

"Him?"

"Him."

Cook grinned. "He's got nerves of steel, I'll say that. I do admire his pluck. Yes, I do admire that. Riding around among the Apache with nothing but a Bible and a white collar around his neck." He nodded at Marianne. "There's someone who'll never knuckle under to Ahab Hawthorne and his cutthroats."

"No, Marco wouldn't, Mr. Cook. He fears God more than he fears man."

Dana slapped her hands down on her knees. "We best pray. Then we can talk about preachers and Hawthorne and clerical collars. The food's getting cold."

"It's already cold," responded Cook.

"Well, it's getting colder. Will you say grace, Bob?"

Hats were removed while Mr. O'Shea thanked God for their food and their safe journeys. Then they all began to eat. After Dianna had helped herself to some potato salad and fried chicken she took a swallow from her canteen and patted Marianne on the shoulder.

"The church Reverend Marco started. Does it still have the same preacher?"

Marianne finished chewing and swallowing before she replied. "Hawthorne didn't like his preaching. So his men started coming to the services and heckling him. One shot out the corners of his pulpit. That pretty much did it for him, I'm afraid. He packed up and left the next morning."

Cook frowned. "The preacher let Hawthorne's boys hoorah him?"

"Six of them to one of him, Mr. Cook. If you consider that hoorahing then I suppose he was hoorahed."

"No one helped him out?"

"The men that would have are dead. Men like my husband."

"I'm sorry, ma'am."

"How long ago was this?" asked Dianna.

"Three weeks."

"Was he Methodist?"

"Yes."

"Will they send another?"

Marianne shrugged. "The mayor wrote them a letter. We haven't heard anything."

"Hm." Dianna stood up and dusted herself off. "All our towns and settlements could do with good ministers but they are in short supply this side of the Mississippi. Men like Marco would be wonderful if only they had an itch to settle down rather than an itch to keep moving on."

Marianne also got up. "He wants to take the Word everywhere. That's his calling. The settled down types have settled down in nice cities and towns in the east."

Dana remained under the shade of one of the cottonwoods. "So soon?"

O'Shea picked up his rifle and headed over to his horse. "Days are still short, Mrs. . And no one wants to be caught out in the open after dark. Not with Hawthorne's owlhoots out looking to cause any sort of mischief they can."

"They wouldn't lift a finger to a woman, Bob."

"Don't count on it."

She glanced at the small cemetery. "I see the squirrels have already made short work of the bread." Then she looked at Marianne and Dianna. "If they meant to catch those killers they'd have caught them long ago."

"The sheriff said they're still holed up in Mexico," replied Dianna.

"The sheriff. He'll say whatever Hawthorne tells him to say. The gunmen are probably working on his spread out by Cimarron."

Marianne bent to gather up her bowls. "Yes, well, if only we knew what they looked like I would ride up to Cimarron and get them myself."

Dianna put her black hat on her head. "I hope you're not serious."

"After what Selah and I have been through I think I'm capable of almost anything when it comes to Hawthorne and his cronies." She straightened and held up a finger. "One more inch. One more straw. One more match. And he will have gone too far with me."

Dianna shook her head. "Don't even begin to think that way, my dear. He's not afraid of you."

Marianne's dark eyes flashed. "So maybe he should be."

Dana got up and grasped Marianne's hand. "We all feel as you do from time to time. But these are rough men."

"I don't care."

"Let other rough men take care of them."

"Rough men won't take care of them. Rough men are just like them. We need good men to take care of them. And they've killed all the good men or bullied them out of the county."

"Others will move in."

Marianne stared into Dana's brown eyes. "When? When will the good men come? And how long will they stay alive after they arrive?"

"There are plenty of good men in the New Mexico Territory, Marianne," insisted Dianna. "My hired hands are good men. So are Dana's. So will yours be if you get back onto your land this summer."

"Spring! I will be back on my land this spring, thank you!"

"And you will have good men working your ranch when y'all do. But they can't stand up to gunslingers without a leader. Neither can you."

"I don't require a leader. I know my own mind. I know what needs to be done."

"You aren't Joan of Arc are you? A woman who can command an army of men?"

"No, so maybe I am Deborah in the Bible, *ja?* She headed up an army of men."

The angrier Marianne grew the more heavily accented her English became.

"Take it easy," Dana soothed. "We just don't want a fourth grave here, that's all."

Marianne was trembling and her face was dark with blood. She glanced at her husband's cross and looked back at her friends. She covered her face with her hands.

"I ask God to do something. I ask him to make things right. I ask for our land back that Peter and I prayed over. I ask for justice. Nothing happens. Nothing, nothing." Her hands curled into fists. "There is so much evil and no one is going to stop it."

Dana and Dianna reached out carefully to put their hands on Marianne's shoulders, unsure of how she would react to their touch. When she did not pull away they both gathered her into their arms as tears cut across her face. Tears burned in Dana's eyes too, and in Dianna's, and in moments the three young women were clinging to each other and letting the pain of their husbands' murders and the sharp loneliness of their widowhood pour out of them. When they were done Dianna kissed Marianne on the cheek and walked quickly, head down and hat brim pulled low, to her tall black horse. The stallion tossed his head. She put a hand to his cheek. Her ring finger still carried her wedding band.

"Shh, Trueno, it's all right. Shh. We are calm now. We are quiet." She pulled herself up into a black saddle that flashed with silver conchos. "Do we have everything, Mr. Cook?"

"Yes, ma'am."

"Are you coming, Dana?" she asked.

Dana gave Marianne a final hug. "I am." She went to her sorrel and put a booted foot in the stirrup. "In a month, Marianne? May 14th?"

Marianne stood with her hands at her side. "Yes. I will be here."

"God bless you," Dianna said. "We love you. Please be careful."

"Thank you. I love you both as well. Yes, yes, I will be careful. I'll pray more. That always makes me stronger."

"*Vaya con dios.*" Dana reined her mare to the right. "Come on, Juniper. Let's get you a drink at the ford and head for home. Bob?"

"Right behind you, Mrs. Fleming," said O'Shea, the Spencer in one hand, reins in the other.

Dianna tugged on her hat brim and swing Trueno around. The four of them rode swiftly along the riverbank to the east.

"You okay, mom?" asked Selah.

Marianne put an arm around her daughter. "Not really. Maybe one day I will be."

"I can pray for you a bit."

"Yes, please, I'd like that."

The girl took off her hat, held her mother's hand, and prayed in a mixture of English and Spanish and Dutch. Then they planted their hats firmly on their heads, mounted their paints and walked them upstream to a small eddy where the horses could drink. After that they carried on along the riverbank, passing clusters of cottonwoods every now and then, eventually making it into open country that began to slope upwards with every mile.

"Oh, mom, I never get tired of this!" Selah said, a smile splitting open her face.

"Neither do I."

"Thank God!"

"Yes. Thank God."

"How far apart are Mrs. Dana and Mrs. Dianna?" Selah asked.

"About two miles."

"That's not much."

"No, it isn't."

"When we go back to our ranch we'll be much closer to them again, won't we?"

Marianne nodded. "Indeed we will. Something to look forward to."

"Will we – will we always leave papa back there under the cottonwoods?"

Marianne did not reply for a long half minute. Eyes straight ahead she finally said, "It was where the three men liked to meet. It's where they prayed and read the Bible together. And went hunting and fishing. It's where they died together. He is at peace there, darling. We will leave him with his friends by the Rio Oro."

"But." Selah's forehead was a thatch of deep lines. "He's not there, is he?"

"No. Not really. But we will keep what was of the earth in the earth and remember him by the river under the cottonwoods."

Tall rugged mountains with snow on their peaks came closer and closer. Foothills rolled and surged and groves of evergreens appeared. The south wind continued to blow and Selah put one hand on the top of her hat to keep it in place. She smiled and closed her eyes. The soft air and warm sunshine slid over her face like a silk scarf and wrapped itself around her neck.

"Six things always meant New Mexico to your father," said Marianne. "The light that fastens itself to everything. The land, so dry and rugged down south, so verdant and rugged up north by the Rio Grande. The mountains, the Sangre de Cristos, that reach to heaven. And the sky that beats with such color and such vastness it's as if it has its own heart."

"What are the other two things?"

"The people. Your father loved the mix of people from the desert country and from all over the world."

"And?"

"God. He called this God's front door."

Selah continued to smile, her eyes still closed as she felt the wind and sun on her face and listened to her mother talk.

Kreeeeee. Kreeeeee.

She opened her eyes and spotted the hawk. "Look at him, mom. Just gliding and having fun."

"And hunting."

"Oh, I suppose. But I think he's mostly just fooling around." The hawk swooped and Selah followed it with her eyes.

"Hey." She pointed. "Mom, look."

"Mm?" Marianne had been watching the banks of the river rise as they approached the mountains so that parts of the Rio Oro looked like cliffs. "What is it?"

"See the hawk diving?"

"*Ja.*" Marianne spotted the long dark wings of the bird. Then she saw what was on the ground beneath it. "My goodness!" She dug the heels of her leather boots into the flanks of her horse. Arquero sprang ahead. "Go, boy, go!"

A figure was sprawled on the ground while a small animal darted back and forth trying to avoid the hawk. As soon as Marianne galloped up the hawk screeched in fury and flew off over the river. Marianne jumped from the saddle and knelt by the body.

"Are they alive?" Selah rode up and dismounted, her hand on her hat.

"*Ja, ja,* but it's not good. She's been shot."

"Apache?"

"I don't know."

Selah saw the animal cowering by the woman's head. "A puppy!"

"The puppy is safe now, the hawk is gone. Get me some of that clean cloth we use for bandages. And the canteen on my saddle. Hurry."

Selah ran to Arquero and rushed back with the cotton cloth and canteen. Marianne began to tear the cloth into strips.

"Wash the wound, please, Selah."

"Where is it?"

"See here? On her left shoulder? Cut the sleeve of her blouse away with your knife and make sure you get out all the dirt and bits of cotton. You understand? That is very important. Otherwise we will wind up with an infection. "

"Yes, mother."

Marianne gently turned the shoulder over as her daughter worked at the wound with a clean cloth and water. "The bullet went straight through. That is something to thank God for." She carefully reached out a hand and stroked the trembling puppy. "You will be all right, little one. No one is going to harm you now." She leaned over and kissed its dark red head. "An Irish Setter, Selah."

Selah smiled as she dabbed at the bullet hole. "It's very sweet. But what was she doing out here all by herself with a little puppy? No horse, no gun, no jacket."

Marianne made a movement with her head. "Look there. Hoof prints. Big ones. All around her body. I'm sure that was her horse and she fell from the saddle."

"Then where is it?"

"I don't know. We don't have time to track it right now."

Selah began to look at the hills and forests just ahead of them. 'That's where I would go if I were a horse."

"Sometimes I think you are half horse. We will take a quick look once we have bandaged her up. Arquero will carry the two of us easily. Are you done yet?"

"Yes, mama."

"Lift her arm a bit so I can get the bandages right around the wound. Good." Marianne made seven or eight wraps and tied the bandage off. Then she placed her palm on the woman's head. "There's a bit of a fever. We're still an hour from town. Help me get her up on my saddle. She's not very big so it shouldn't be hard."

"What about the puppy?"

"You carry him. But help me first."

They picked the woman up. She wore a dark riding skirt and boots along with her cotton blouse. Barely five feet in height and light as a sapling, it was not difficult to haul her up onto Marianne's saddle. Marianne quickly climbed up behind the woman and put an arm around her waist.

"She has lovely long hair," said Selah.

"Yes, like rubies hm? Pick up the puppy and let's be on our way."

"Is she going to make it?"

"If there's a God in heaven."

Selah cradled the puppy with one arm as they rode, holding it close to her chest. "It's not shaking anymore."

"*Goed.*"

"Where do you think her horse is?"

"The trail takes us past the Ponderosa pines over there. The horse may have gone in among the trees to get out of the wind." She pointed with her chin. "Some hoof prints. You can take a look but don't go in too far. We have no idea where the persons are who shot this woman."

"I'll be careful. Come on, Spurs."

"Spurs?"

"That is the puppy's name."

Marianne half-smiled. "Oh, yes? You asked it?"

"Well, not exactly, but it suits for now. I suppose the woman has her name for it."

"I would think she does. Stay where I can see you, please."

Her daughter clicked her tongue and Chica trotted off the trail into the first stand of young Ponderosa pines. Marianne watched Selah and her paint move through the trees. As the forest grew thicker and the pines taller she lost sight of her daughter several times but only for brief periods of time. She had turned her head to glance at the white face of the woman in her arms when she heard the loud shout.

"Hey!"

There was a pounding of hooves and a snapping of branches and a huge horse hurtled out of the forest at Marianne. It swerved at the last moment and roared past, long black mane and long black tail flying, the long hairs or feathering just above its hooves streaming back like dark smoke. Marianne was afraid it would plunge over the cliff into the water but it ran along the bank and behind them. Selah galloped out of the pines after it.

"Stop!" cried Marianne. "The poor beast is frightened enough to run all the way to Boston! Leave him be!"

"But we can't leave him here all alone, mama."

"Well, we can't make a big gelding like that come along with us either. He's over seventeen hands and heaven knows how much he weighs. He looks like one of the workhorses we used in Holland, a Shire, see the muscles in his legs and shoulders? Let him be. We must get this woman to Doc Bartley."

"But mom – "

"If he wants to follow, he will follow. We can't make him. Perhaps he'll pick up her scent." Marianne urged her paint into a fast trot. "We need to put on some speed."

Selah's face twisted up with her mouth but she reined her mare around and rode after her mother. Glancing back she saw the large horse had stopped and was watching them head west on the trail as it led through the Ponderosa pines.

"Mom!"

"What?"

"He's watching us!"

"*Goed!*"

"Mom!"

"Yes? What?"

"He has the color of a strawberry roan and his mane and tail are gorgeous long!"

"*Ja, ja, goed!*"

They trotted through the pine forest at a quick pace and emerged on a part of trail that bent sharply upwards.

"Mom!"

"Yes?"

"He's not behind us!"

"There's nothing we can do! He must make his own choice! Perhaps he wants to go free and be a wild horse!"

Marianne wanted to add, *like you,* but bit her tongue.

The trail took them along a ridge for several miles, the high mountains to their left, the lowlands by the river to their right. Ten minutes went by with no sound but the horses' hooves and the creak of their saddles and stirrups. Marianne hoped she was right about seeing color coming into the woman's cheeks.

"Mom!"

"*Ja?*"

"We're being followed!"

"So good, good."

"But it's a man! It's not the horse!"

"A man?"

"Two men! Three men! Four!"

"What?"

"They are behind us on the ridge! They just showed up and are riding fast!"

Cold cut through Marianne's body. Her arm still around the woman she maneuvered her hand to the front of her belt and slid her Colt revolver loose.

"What do we do, mom?"

"Get ahead of me!"

"What? Why?"

"Don't argue! Get in front of me now!"

19

Selah moved her horse past her mother and Arquero. Marianne glanced back and saw the men were coming on at them one after another. There looked to be more than four and all of them were dressed in black and wore long black coats.

We can't outrun them, not with a wounded woman in my arms. Lord, help us.

"Selah!" shouted Marianne. "You ride ahead as fast as you can! We're only a half hour from town! Get some men! Get the marshal and the sheriff and bring them back here!"

"The sheriff and the marshal are no good!" Selah shouted back.

"Never mind! Just bring them! And whoever else you can find! The farrier, the blacksmith, Doc Bartley!"

"I'm not leaving you!"

"Of course you're not leaving me! You're going and coming back! The sooner the better!"

"Mom, no! I'm not afraid of them!"

"Well, I am! Stop arguing and ride! I know how fast Chica can go when she wants to!"

Marianne wheeled her horse around to face the riders. There seemed to be as many as six or seven of them now, raising dust and coming straight on. She cocked back the hammer on her Colt 1851 Navy and fired a shot into the air. Arquero snorted and reared but she gripped him tightly with her legs. The first rider was almost on top of her but he reined in sharply with the crack of the shot.

"Leave us alone!" Marianne aimed the Colt at the man's heart. "Go back where you came from and leave us alone or as sure as God is in his heaven I will shoot!"

The man stared at her with piercing blue eyes. Then he slowly pulled away the front of his black coat to reveal a white clerical collar at his throat.

"I'm pretty sure God is in his heaven, ma'am," he said. "But I'd rather you didn't shoot me just the same."

The Widow
and the Preacher

Marianne did not move her pistol away from the man even after he showed her his white clerical collar.

"Is it something I said?" he asked.

"No preacher packs iron like you do."

He glanced down at the six-gun on his hip and the rifle in a scabbard at the front of his saddle. "The West is a wild place, ma'am. All God's children are obligated to look after themselves." He glanced back up at her, his blue eyes like bits of the New Mexico sky. "And to look after others."

"I don't need your help."

"One of my brothers could carry that young lady for you."

"I told you, I don't need your help."

He touched his hand to the brim of his hat. "In that case, will you let us pass? We have business elsewhere."

"Where?"

"A town named Cazadora."

"That's my town. What sort of mischief are you up to there?"

He smiled, his eyes going to the softest blue she had ever seen. "We intend to put a pastor back in the church."

"Who?"

He flicked his head. "Maybe my brother Luke there."

A slender young man with brown eyes and brown hair touched the brim of his hat. "Ma'am."

"Or maybe Benjamin and Joseph. I'm still thinking and praying on it."

"They'll run you out like they did the last one. Ahab Hawthorne will run you out."

The man's eyes turned to hard blue ice. "No, he won't." He smiled again but his eyes retained their cold blue. "As sure as God is in his heaven, he won't."

Marianne kept her gun on the man. "Even if your friends shoot me out of the saddle I will put a bullet in you first."

He burst out laughing. "My friends shoot you out of the saddle? A lovely woman like yourself?" He leaned both hands on his saddle horn. "First of all, the men with me are my brothers, not my friends. Second of all, they are each and every one of them my blood brothers, not just my brothers in the Lord, though they are that too. Finally, the only thing they would like to do with you is court you, if I know my brothers. Pray with you, take you to church, and court you. In my family no one wastes the pinnacle of God's creation by shooting it."

"The pinnacle of God's creation?"

"Women." He bowed his head briefly in her direction. "Such as yourself."

Her face reddened quickly from the neck up. "Don't think you can flatter me."

"The farthest thing from my mind, ma'am. If I don't mean something I don't say it."

"There are nine of you."

"That's right."

"No man has so many brothers."

"He does if his mother and father had a habit of hitting the sack early every night."

The red in Marianne's face deepened. "What is your name?"

"Brett David. You've met my younger brother Luke."

"What are the others' names?"

"What, all of them?"

"*Ja,* all of them."

"*Ja?* You remind me of a Dutch girl I courted once."

"I'm not her. What are your brothers' names? If they are your brothers."

"You think I'm lying?" he asked.

"You wouldn't be the first man who lied to me. What are their names?"

Brett David nodded. "Hospitality is distinctly lacking in the New Mexico Territory. No wonder they need churches. Your husband must find you a hard woman to live with."

"My husband was shot out of the saddle by gunslingers. You'll pardon me if I don't spread a tablecloth on the grass here and set out my best china."

"I'm sorry to hear that."

"I don't need your sympathy."

"You don't need much, it appears."

Marianne tilted up her chin. "Not from hired killers I don't."

Anger darted across his face. Without taking his eyes off her, he recited the names of the men behind him: "Besides Luke there's Reuben, and Joseph, Benjamin, Bobby, Scott, Michael, and Adam. Satisfied?"

"All preachers?"

"All preachers."

"How can nine brothers be preachers? Why aren't some of you lawmen or soldiers or bankers?"

"Or butchers and bakers and candlestick makers? You might take it up with God. You can point your 1851 Navy at him and see what kind of response you get. As for me, well, I think you have just about worn me out with your good nature and your kindness. We're going to ride by."

She jabbed her pistol at him. "Jeremiah 19:20."

"What?"

"Don't you know your Bible, preacher? Jeremiah 19:20."

He stared at her for several long seconds. "There is no Jeremiah 19:20."

"Try 1st Samuel 19:20."

Brett continued to stare at her, his eyes like dark blue stones. "*And Saul sent messengers to take David. And when they saw the company of the prophets prophesying, and Samuel standing as appointed over them, the Spirit of God was upon the messengers of Saul, and they also prophesied.*"

"Micah 7:8."

"Rejoice not against me, O mine enemy – when I fall, I shall arise. When I sit in darkness, the Lord shall be a light unto me."

"Matthew 1:1."

"The book of the generation of Jesus Christ, the son of David, the son of Abraham."

She hesitated. Then lowered her pistol.

Brett nodded. "This son of David is about to head on to Cazadora. Thank you for the tea and jam."

"I'm sorry."

"No need. Considering what you've told us, I shouldn't be surprised. I wish you God's blessing."

"Wait. Reverend David."

He reined up. "How can I help?"

"Perhaps one of your brothers might hold this young woman. My arm is cramping up badly."

"Of course. Luke."

Luke walked his horse closer. "What's up?"

"Take the woman from this lady's arms."

"Please be careful." Marian loosened her grip. "She's been shot."

"Where? How?" Luke carefully took the woman from Marianne and cradled her against his chest.

"High on the left shoulder. You see I've dressed it. I don't know how she was shot. We found her on the trail." She nodded with her head. "My daughter and I. Selah."

Selah moved her horse out from behind her mother's, smiling shyly at the men, the Irish Setter puppy asleep in her arms. Brett and Luke smiled back. Luke lifted his hat.

"We'd best get moving," grunted Brett. "This woman needs care." He looked back at his brothers. "The road's clear. Let's go."

He put his horse into a fast trot. Marianne fell in beside him.

"My name is Marianne. Marianne Freeman."

He gave her half a smile. "Glad to make your acquaintance."

"I apologize again. I do not normally point my pistol at strangers. But nothing is normal about the New Mexico Territory these days."

"It's beginning to sink in. That's why the Methodist head office sent us out here."

"What is it you are expected to accomplish? You do not have badges."

"From what I've heard it wouldn't make much difference."

"No. It wouldn't. One man has the courts and lawmen and politicians in his pocket. What do you and your brothers intend to do about all that?"

"Plant churches."

"What? That's it? Plant churches?"

"A strong church makes people strong. They're able to resist evil and corruption and go about living good Christian lives. A church helps them band together and work together. Men and women and God shoulder to shoulder. *A threefold cord is not quickly broken.* It will be a lot harder for men like Ahab Hawthorne to break churches than to break ranchers or sheriffs or judges. Even some of his roughest men won't ride with him if he starts to do that. Especially when those churches are full of women and children."

"It sounds like you have it all planned out."

"Planned out, prayed out. Our circuit riders put the seed in the ground. We water it with new pastors. God gives the increase. One or two churches around Cazadora. Half a dozen more around the county. Make sure all the congregations get together once a month for worship and fellowship. Hawthorne will have a hard time wrestling that steer to the ground."

Marianne shook her head. "He will set fires that look like accidents. Burn the church buildings to the ground. He's done that with plenty of ranches."

"We'll be ready."

"How can you shoot back if you are a pastor?"

"Just by aiming and squeezing the trigger, ma'am."

"But you are – "

"I am sworn to uphold the Lord's righteousness by loving my neighbor as myself. Jesus used a whip to cleanse the Temple. I'll use the Bible and a pistol to cleanse New Mexico.

The one who rides the white horse in the Apocalypse is called Faithful and True and a sword from his mouth slays the wicked. God Almighty has used armies to humble evil nations. He can use our army to do the same."

"David and Goliath?"

"Something like that."

"What about loving your enemies?"

"I love them best by preventing them from doing deeds of wickedness that harm others and harm their own souls. Should I let them run wild and kill and destroy and in the end heap judgment on their heads? Love in my book means stopping them from doing wrong. It adds up to grace for them and grace for the people they intend to hurt. Anything less isn't love, ma'am."

"Hey, she's coming to." Luke spurred his horse up beside Brett and Marianne. "See?"

The red-haired woman was blinking her eyes. Then she stared at Luke. "Who are you?"

"I'm, well, I'm a minister of the gospel."

"Are you an angel then?"

"No, no, just an ordinary man."

"You don't look very ordinary to me."

"I'm just – I'm just here to take care of you, ma'am."

The woman tried to smile. "I like the sound of that. My shoulder and arm hurt so much. Can you do anything about it?"

"I'm getting you to a physician."

She smiled. "Sure, angels don't need to ask physicians for help, do they?" she patted his face. "Thank you." She glanced around her as they rode. "I was part of a wagon train. We were attacked."

"Apache?"

"Men with scarves over their faces. We fought them." She tried to lift her head but winced and let it fall back. "I went for help on one of our draught horses, a great wonderful beast. It was all I could do. I fell out of the wagon on top of him. Where is he?"

"I don't know, ma'am," replied Luke.

"Angels don't call women ma'am. My name is Joyeux. But Joey will do."

"Joyeux's very nice, ma'am."

"Whichever suits. I'm Irish but my mother had a fancy for French words and French things. Are you sure you haven't seen my horse?"

One of the other brothers heard her and brought his horse over as they went at a steady gait over the trail. "Reuben David, ma'am. We found a workhorse by the side of the trail but it was well nigh impossible to get it to come with us. We lassoed it and it near dragged two of us over a cliff."

Joyeux laughed, winced, and laughed a bit more. "That is Donegal. A gelding. Ardennes crossed with Shire stallion. A mind of his own."

Another brother rode up. "He's following us. Benjamin put some oats on the trail and now your horse is following us."

"A fourth angel. This is wonderful. A woman could be excused for thinking she'd died and gone to heaven. If only the angels would stop calling me ma'am."

"Sorry, ma'am." The brother touched the brim of his hat.

"And which angel are you?"

He smiled. "One of the shorter ones. Joseph."

"Ah. Do people call you Joe?"

"Not more than once."

She laughed. "Angels that bite. I suppose you have a sword, Joseph?"

"We all have swords."

Her face suddenly darkened. "I wish I knew how my friends have fared."

"Where was your wagon train?" asked Luke, his brown eyes soft and concerned.

"We had made our way down the Santa Fe Trail. We were headed for a town called Cazadora."

"What?" Marianne snapped her head around. "That's where we're going now. That's my home."

"We had purchased a parcel of land. Enough for several families."

"Smoke!" Reuben pointed. "Black as sin!"

A thick dark column was rising into the blue sky just ahead of them.

"You ride on." Brett David's eyes sharpened. "You and Joseph and the others. I'll stay with Mrs. Freeman and her daughter and with Luke and Miss Joyeux. Keep your wits about you."

"Yes, sir."

Reuben kicked in his heels and waved to his brothers behind him. They galloped past Marianne in a scattering of dust and stones. In five minutes she saw for herself the source of the smoke. Four burned out wagons on the outskirts of Cazadora. The brothers had already dismounted and were beating out the flames or cutting the horses free and trying to calm them. Bodies lay on the grass. A coldness swept through Marianne's body.

"This will be her friends," she said to Brett in a low voice. "This will be her wagon train."

"How do you know?"

"I'm sure of it. How many other groups of wagons would have been raided in this county today?"

Cradled in Luke's arms, Joyeux lifted her head as they approached the wagons.

"Why, those are my – those are my – " She stared at the panicking horses three of the brothers were fighting to control. "I know those horses. They're ours. They're mine. Oh, no." She saw the blackened wagons and the rolling dark smoke. "No! It's not them! It's not them!"

She began to shriek.

"Get her away," Brett ordered Luke. "Get her away from here and calm her down."

Luke reined to his right and headed for a cluster of trees.

A group of horsemen were approaching from the far side of the wagons.

"Who's that?" Brett asked out loud.

"I know them." Marianne's face fell into hard and sharp lines. "Sheriff Teddy Westcott and his deputies."

"Will he help? Or hinder?"

"Teddy Westcott is a rag in Ahab Hawthorne's back pocket."

Brett glanced at the chiseled look of her features. "I see." He put his eyes back on the sheriff. "He looks to be about six high by six feet wide."

"But less than six fingers deep. Scrape him just a little, Reverend David, and you've gone through skin, bone, and body and right down into the pit of hell."

Marianne shot a fierce glance at her daughter. "You stay right here beside me. No fooling around."

Her daughter's face was white as she looked at the wagons, the puppy in her arms. "All right, mom."

Teddy Westcott swung down from his horse. "Get away from there! Who are you? Get back from those wagons! I'm Sheriff Teddy Westcott and this is my business!"

"We were here ahead of you, sheriff," responded Joseph. "No disrespect intended, but we'll finish what we're doing before we back away. We've just about got the horses under control and one woman by the wagons is still alive."

Westcott glowered. "You a preacher? Or is that collar just for show?"

"I'm a Methodist minister. I'll be taking over the pastoral duties at the Cazadora church. My brother Benjamin and I."

"Is that a fact? First I heard of it."

Brett smiled and spoke so that only Marianne could hear. "First I heard of it too. I guess God told Joseph and Benjamin before he told me. I can live with that."

Westcott strode towards the scorched wagons with his deputies. "Apache."

Two of the brothers were helping a woman on the grass take water from a canteen. One of them looked up at the sheriff.

"I don't think so," he said. "This lady says they were masked men. Masked white men."

Westcott spat. "She's probably out of her head after this massacre." He glanced at the bodies in the wagons as well as the ones laid out on the grass. "I'll need to telegraph for troops to hunt down these murdering savages."

"She's pretty clear headed, sheriff."

The woman pushed herself to a sitting position. "I *am* clear headed. I may be a bit addled after what I've just gone through. I may think I'm in a nightmare I can't quite pull myself out of. But I know what I saw. Men who had bandanas over their faces. Tall men. Riding tall horses. Using English when they shouted to each other. Swearing in English when they shouted at us. *Get out of here! This ain't your land! You don't own nothing in New Mexico! Run! Run!* But they didn't give us a chance to run. Just shot us – men, women, and children. Shot us and threw torches into our wagons. Not Apache. White bandits, mate."

Westcott stared at her. "You *are* off your head, lady. I can't understand half of what you just said."

Even from where she sat on her horse Marianne could see the woman's eyes ignite.

"Then clean the dirt out of your ears, mate. They were white men. Not Apache. And they were running us off the land we have legal deed to. They're Someone's hired guns. Go track them and you'll wind up at that Someone's big ranch. That's pretty simple, isn't it? You can tell the difference between a boot print and a hoof print, can't you, even if you don't know the difference between Geronimo and Jesse James?"

Westcott spat again. "You're *loco*. Maybe a few slaps to the side of your head'll bring you out of it."

One of the brothers at her side stood up. He was, Marianne reckoned, at least six foot five.

"I don't think that's a good idea, sheriff," he said.

Westcott scowled. "I've had nothing but trouble from you boys since I got here. For all I know you did the damage and then pulled your scarves off. Now step aside and let me do my business."

"Perhaps another time."

"'Scuze me?"

"Don't talk to her. Don't touch her. She's told you what she saw. Her English is better than yours. Look for outlaws. Look for gunslingers. But let her be. She needs quiet. And she needs rest."

"Why, you two bit, snot-nosed, puppy-dog preacher. Don't think your dog collar protects you from me. I spat God out years ago along with Santa Claus and the Flying Dutchman and I ain't missed him or needed him since. So get out of the

30

way. I've got five deputies and I'll question the witness in the manner I see fit."

"You won't."

Westcott put his hand to the pistol on his right hip.

His deputies did the same.

The brother did not move.

"Try it," he said.

For the first time the sheriff realized the man he was facing off against had a gun.

"I ain't never seen a preacher with iron on his hip before," he growled.

"*For he is the minister of God to thee for good. But if thou do that which is evil, be afraid. For he beareth not the sword in vain. For he is the minister of God, a revenger to execute wrath upon him that doeth evil.*" The brother still hadn't moved a muscle but his white-handled revolver was plain for all to see. "Romans 13:4."

"You're not the law," sneered Westcott.

"I am. God's law. We all are."

The sheriff and his deputies saw that the man's brothers were on foot and facing them, hands at their sides, all except Brett David, who remained in his saddle but slid his rifle free of its scabbard.

"Watch your step when you come into town," hissed Westcott. "Yes, indeed, you all watch your step when you ride into Cazadora."

He turned and stalked back to his horse.

"What about the bodies, sheriff?" asked Reuben.

"You're preachers, ain't ya?" snarled Westcott, pulling himself into his saddle. "You bury 'em. I've seen all I need to see. Another Apache attack."

He wheeled his horse and galloped away followed by his five deputies.

The one brother knelt back down by the woman. "Are you all right?"

"I should be asking you." She offered him a half smile. "But you don't seem the worse for wear for someone who almost had a gun fight with six men. Thank you, mate."

"You're welcome."

"What's your name?"

"Adam. Adam David."

"That's a good solid name. I like it." She thrust out her hand. "I'm Noelle Saunders. From Brisbane."

Adam smiled. It was a smooth, easy, and friendly smile. Marianne felt the smile all the way from where she sat on her paint Arquero.

"Australia." His smile warmed up even more. "You're a long way from home."

"Not really. New Mexico's my home now." Her face suddenly paled. "These people were going to be my neighbors."

"I'm sorry. We'll do what we can to give them a Christian burial."

Her head drooped. "It's just sinking in, y'know?" She put a hand over her eyes. "Do you have any more of that cold water?"

"There's plenty."

"Could you put some on a cloth and put the cloth on the back of my neck? I don't feel all that well, Adam."

"I'm not surprised, ma'am."

"I feel worse when you call me ma'am. Noelle will do."

"I thought you might be married."

"I was married when I left Australia. When I docked in San Francisco I wasn't. He took ill and died at sea."

"I'm sorry."

"It was very hard. We were supposed to settle the land together. I met the people he and I planned to form a community with. All of us traveled here together in this wagon train. I thought their company would cheer me up. It did, y'know. Until now."

Tears were at edges of her eyes.

"Here." Adam put the cloth on her neck. "You won't be alone. We'll see you safe and settled on your ranch. Get buildings up. Help you with horses and cattle. You and everyone else who wants to live here."

"What are you? Preachers and deputy marshals and carpenters and cowboys all rolled into one?"

"It seems that way, ma'am."

"*Adam*." Head down, tears slicing through the grime on her face, her tone was still sharp.

"I mean, Noelle." He pressed down on the cloth lightly with his hand. "We're going to plant churches in this county. Churches that give people backbone, shore them up with something to believe in, fill them to the brim with hope. My brothers and I will pastor those churches. We plan to put up half a dozen or more. Places where people can worship and pray together and take strength from one another and from God. Once your heart is wedded to God's heart nothing can stop you. Not bullets, not hate, not all the wickedness in the world."

"Is this your sermon?"

"Why, no, I'm just warming up. The sermon's in a few minutes."

"Oh, Adam." She laughed a bit. "My heart's breaking but you put life in me despite my grief. How do you do that?"

"Excuse me."

Adam looked up at his brother Luke. "What is it?"

"The woman I was carrying. She was part of this wagon train."

Noelle sat up straight and the cloth fell in the dirt. "There's someone else alive besides me?"

Luke took off his hat. "Yes, ma'am. Her name is Joyeux McCain. She – "

"No ma'ams." Noelle got to her feet, staggered, was steadied by Adam's quick hand, and looked over Luke's shoulder. "The Irish widow."

Joyeux was standing with her red hair over her shoulders and falling down to her waist. Her eyes were dark and swollen.

"I thank God himself you're alive, Mrs. Saunders," she said in a weak voice. "Is there no one else?"

"No one," replied Noelle.

"No child? None of the men?"

"No."

"Do we carry on with our dreams? Do we try and make new lives for ourselves in this place?"

"Yes, Mrs. McCain. Yes, we do."

"And how is it we go about doing that? Two women on their own – how do we bring ranch houses and corrals and hayfields to pass?"

"We'll have to figure it out as we go. But the luck of the Irish and the pluck of the Aussie ought to count for something with God Almighty. At least, a few of these men have managed to persuade me it may be so."

Luke turned his hat over and over in his hands and looked at Adam. "I told Mrs. McCain we'd help her out. That she wouldn't be abandoned."

Adam nodded. "You did the right thing, little brother. I used the same words with Mrs. Saunders myself."

Noelle smiled. "So you see, Joyeux, it's settled in heaven and it's settled on earth."

Joyeux found a smile as well. "Aye, so it seems." Her eyes glimmered. "Oh, here we go again, Noah's flood."

They embraced each other.

"I'm glad you made it, Joyeux."

"Thank you. I feel the same way about you. I admired your humor and your feistiness on the Santa Fe Trail. And your faith."

"I could use exactly the same words to describe you, y'know."

"Is there a place for them in your home for the time being?" Brett asked Marianne.

Marianne's own eyes filled as she watched the women cry. "Of course. You don't need to ask. There is a place there for all of you."

"Things could get cramped, ma'am. Bunking down in the church would suit my brothers and I best."

"It won't suit me," she snapped with a touch of heat. "You will come to my house."

Brett thought she might yank out her pistol again. "Just as you wish, ma'am."

"And another thing. I don't like being called ma'am any more than the other women do."

Joyeux was reunited with her great horse Donegal and her Irish Setter puppy that she called Finnegan. But she liked

Selah's name for the puppy so much she decided to use it instead.

"Spurs is a fine name for a New Mexican pup," she said. "I must bear in mind I'm not in Ireland anymore. Ah, much as I love the green hills and the sea of the old country, this is home now. This great big sky and everything underneath it is home. I'm not sorry."

The brothers dug one large grave under the nearby trees and placed the bodies in it. The two women clasped each other's hands and wept as Reuben and Joseph and Adam prayed, read several chapters from the Bible, preached a few words, and put the souls of the dead in the hands of God and Christ. Brett and Marianne were concerned about Joyeux's wound and wanted her to move on to town with several of the brothers. But she had no intention of going anywhere until the grave was filled in and a wooden cross of tree limbs erected at the spot.

"Now I'm ready for Cazadora," she said when all that was done.

There was no saddle on Donegal. She climbed onto Luke's horse with his help and, as he held his horse and Donegal steady, slipped onto the great horse's back, gripping him tightly with her legs and wrapping his dark mane in her fists.

"Are you sure you don't want me to ride up there with you?" asked Luke. "That shoulder of yours must be hurting something fierce."

Joyeux smiled. "That is a sweet temptation and all the more surprising for the fact it's coming from a young preacher. But right now it's important I do this on my own. Did you say it was a mile from the town, Marianne Freeman?"

"It's less than that," Marianne replied.

"Then I must do this ride. Thank you all the same, Luke. Though I hope you won't abandon me."

He smiled and swung up on his horse. "I'll be right beside you."

"That's grand."

They headed towards Cazadora and entered the town with the nine brothers spread out all around the three women and Selah. Townspeople stopped to gawk at the tall, slender men in long black coats and black clothing who wore white clerical collars at their throats. Brett insisted on getting Joyeux to Doc Bartley first. After the doctor had cleaned her wound thoroughly, and put a fresh dressing on it, Brett asked Marianne to take them to the church.

"It is not much but here it is," announced Marianne when they arrived at the small white building.

Brett grunted. "It'll do for a start. Why isn't there a cross and a steeple?"

"Hawthorne's men tore it down."

"Do you have tools at your home? And lumber?"

"I have saws and hammers, yes, but not lumber."

"Would your general store have some?"

"Mr. Whittaker? Yes, I believe so."

"Bobby. Benjamin. Scott. Go buy us some wood and paint for a decent size cross and steeple."

"Yes, sir."

"I'll meet you back here in half an hour."

The three brothers went for the lumber and Marianne led everyone else to her house. It was a simple two-story structure with a small porch and tiny windows but Noelle and Joyeux *ooh'd* and *ahh'd* over it. The women set about brewing coffee and cooking a stew while Brett collected the tools he felt they'd need at the church, including a ladder. The brothers had time for a cup of coffee each before Brett hustled them out the door and back to the church to meet Bobby and Benjamin and Scott. The stew was ready to eat and simmering on the stove by the time the nine men returned. Brett smiled as the women told them where to sit and who to sit next to.

"I imagine we'd sit anywhere, even on our heads, just to get a bowlful of whatever's cooking in that pot," Brett laughed, taking his seat.

"But you would not sell your birthright like Esau," said Marianne, putting stew and a spoon in front of him.

"I'm pretty hungry, Mrs. Freeman. You never know."

On Saturday the brothers and the women canvassed the town and let people know there would be two worship services the next day and that the services would be safe and secure. In the morning about fifty men, women, and children showed up at the church, filling half the space. Some of the brothers were inside, some just outside the door, and others were not far off, watching from horseback, several of them unseen from the church or the road. That evening the church was full, over a hundred taking up seats in the wooden pews. Brett David preached both sermons and Reuben used a Martin guitar to lead the people in the singing of hymns.

"I thank God," Brett said over coffee that night at Marianne's home. "It's a good start. But there's a lot more work to be done. I'll be heading out in the morning. Where did you say your friends' ranches were, Marianne? We'll put up a church building nearby."

"What? You're all leaving?" Joyeux looked around at the faces in the kitchen. "Surely not all of you? The house will go from being just right to being not quite right enough."

"Well, we want to get you and Mrs. Saunders and Mrs. Freeman on your land as soon as possible now that it's spring. But before we do that we need the churches in place as a rallying point for the settlers, safe places where they can come for prayer and worship and teaching and get a fresh burst of faith in their hearts. Once the churches are up we get your ranch houses up. First the one, then the other."

"Aren't you leaving anyone?" asked Joeux, looking smaller and smaller in her chair. "Not even a tidbit?"

Brett finished his coffee and poured himself another.

"It's true that Westcott is bound to hit back pretty soon, especially if Ahab Hawthorne starts leaning on him," he said. "Joseph and Benjamin will be sticking around – the Cazadora church is theirs to pastor and this is going to be their flock to bless and defend. Luke and Adam will stay with them for now – four preachers are better than one and so are four guns. So you won't be alone, Mrs. Saunders."

She was suddenly sitting up straight in her chair and her whole face was a smile. "Bless you."

Noelle ran her finger around the rim of her coffee cup but did not look up. "That's good news. I hope you won't be gone long."

"We'll buy a wagon and mules and fill the wagon up with lumber and paint and whatever tools we need. I guess we'll be out of your hair for a while. But we'll be back. Count on it. I'd like to have all the churches get together in Cazadora in July or August."

"July or August?" Marianne set down her coffee. "But it's only April. That's months away. Will you be away that long?"

"I'm afraid so. Even at that we'll need help from the settlers as far as getting the churches up in good time, never mind the ranch houses. I suspect you ladies will need to live under one roof if you want to be out on your spreads before the snow flies. There won't be time to get more than one *rancho* on its feet."

He pushed himself away from the table. "Early to bed. Joseph, you keep an eye out till two. Benjamin, you spell him after that. If it looks like the good sheriff is up to something, let us know."

"You bet, brother."

Some slept in the kitchen, some in the front room, some in the parlor. Selah slept with her mother and gave her bedroom to Noelle and Joyeux. The Irish Setter snuggled up against her chest and stomach as puppy and child drifted off. Marianne listened to the whole house settle but for the scrape of Joseph's boots now and then.

What am I feeling, Lord? What is going on? You drop these men into my life and I don't know what to say; I don't know how to act. Yet when they speak about leaving I am suddenly empty inside. Especially when one particular man speaks about leaving. I am glad to have the new pastors, the brothers Joseph and Benjamin. I am truly happy to have two new friends in my life like Noelle and Joyeux. But Brett David, I don't know what I should think about him. His face is always there, his blue eyes are always there, his kindness is always there – and his strength. I don't want him to go. But I am afraid to ask him to stay. Because he will say no. He has the Lord's business to take care of. And why should he stay? I'm the woman who pointed a gun at him. He must think I'm a bit crazy in the head. Maybe I am. I have been so long on my own. Perhaps there is no future between a man and me. Perhaps I will never marry again. Oh, I wish I could forget his eyes and his voice. Once, when I poured him coffee, my hand brushed his. I felt such a shock go up my arm. But what did he feel? Did he feel anything?

In the morning she watched him and four brothers ride down the street to buy a wagon and mules and supplies. In a minute or two they were out of sight. She could not help herself from thinking about Dianna and Dana out on their land and close to where one of the churches was going up.

You will see him and I won't. Why, you will see more of him than I ever have. It doesn't seem fair to me and I am more than a little jealous. I hope you notice Reuben. I hope you take a liking to Scott or Bobby or Michael. Leave Brett alone until I can sort my heart and mind out. Will you do that for me? Dianna? Dana? Can you look somewhere else when they come riding up to your ranch?

But Dianna and Dana had nowhere else to look except to the west and pray for help they knew would never come. Hours after Marianne said goodbye to Brett David, gunfire crackled back and forth between the outbuildings of Dianna's ranch. The two women crouched in the front parlor, both holding Civil War muskets they had never fired in their lives.

"Where's Tim Cook?" Dianna raised her head slowly and looked out the window. "I haven't seen him at all in the past five minutes."

"With Bob O'Shea. Somewhere around the barn."

A hut burst into flames.

"Our spare saddles and tack!" Dianna didn't know whether to cry or spit. "Oh, I wish I could get a clear shot at one of Hawthorne's men."

"Do you really think you can hit anything with that?"

"Well, they hit plenty during the war with guns like this."

Another hut went up.

"Those blackhearts!" Dianna almost screamed. "They'll burn the ranch down around our ears!"

Dana was praying with one part of herself and talking to her friend with the other part. "The gunmen didn't just pick this day out of their hats. They knew I was coming over. They knew we'd be here together. It'll look like one of us knocked over an oil lamp. That's how they'll set it up. An oil lamp in your tack hut spread to the other buildings. They'll leave our bodies in the ashes and Sheriff Westcott will chew and spit and say, *Yup. Pure carelessness. Those widows should never have been out here by themselves.*"

"Will you stop talking that way? You're making me nervous."

"I'm not just talking; I'm praying too."

There was a flurry of shots and the women watched in horror as one of Dana's hired hands, Bob O'Shea, staggered out into the open, fired wildly at a man behind a rain barrel, and flew backwards as bullets struck him in the chest.

"Bob!" cried Dana. "Bob!"

She fired her musket through the window, shattering the glass, and saw water splash upwards from the barrel. But the next minute the man hiding behind it fired at the house and bullets smacked against the wall behind her. Dianna grabbed her arm and yanked her down.

"Are you crazy?" she snapped.

Tears cut across Dana's face. "They've killed him. He's the best man I have. He's been a good friend for years."

"I'm sorry, Dana; I'm sorry."

Dianna hugged her friend tightly.

"We'll get out of this," Dianna promised. "And one day there'll be justice for Bob O'Shea."

"Justice? Who's going to give us justice? The judges are no good, the lawmen are no good, the politicians in Santa Fe are no good."

"But God is good. God is just. I don't believe it's going to end like this. I just don't, Dana."

Anger and pain covered Dana's face. "I won't give up. They'll have to kill me first. I'll still be praying when that happens. They'll never take that away from me."

"Come out and you won't be harmed!"

The man behind the rain barrel was shouting.

"All your men are dead! There's nothing more you can do! Come out! It's over!"

Dianna looked at Dana and grit her teeth.

"We're never coming out, you rat!" she hollered. "If you come any closer we'll blow your head off!"

"Don't be crazy! Don't die for nothing! A few torches on the roof and you'll be in a furnace! You run out, we'll shoot you dead! You stay in, you'll burn alive! Come out now and we'll spare you! What do you say to that?"

"I say you're a skunk!" yelled Dianna.

"You crazy women! Have it your way! Torch 'em, boys!"

Dana and Dianna poked their heads up and saw a man on the roof of the barn lighting a wooden torch dark with oil.

"I can get him," said Dianna in a low voice. "It's just like a squirrel hunt except he's bigger and he's a rat."

She aimed her musket and fired. The man cried out and fell, hitting the ground with a thud.

"Why, you wicked witch!"

Bullets blasted through the parlor smashing pictures and lanterns and china. The women ducked their heads as broken glass and splinters of wood showered their backs and shoulders.

"I have to reload," said Dianna.

"I'm still praying," responded Dana. "But I don't think you're going to get the chance to fire again."

More bullets tore the room apart. Blood shot down both their faces as bits and pieces of furniture and crockery cut the air.

"Torch 'em!" the man by the rain barrel shouted again.

"I guess this is it," said Dana.

"Are you still praying?" Dianna asked.

"Yes. Aren't you?"

"Without a break."

They raised their heads. Two men were on the roof of the barn and both had burning torches in their hands, waiting a moment for the flames to grow larger.

"Oh, it gets worse," moaned Dana.

"Burning alive is bad enough. What's worse?"

"We were going to slip out the back door, weren't we? Or a back window? Some place they weren't watching?"

"We were going to try. That was always the plan."

"They didn't have enough men to watch every way out of this house. That was our one chance. Now they do."

"What are you talking about?"

Dana flicked her head to the west.

Riders were tearing across the field towards the ranch house.

They were all dressed in black.

Dianna's face tightened. "That doesn't look like any posse I'd want to rescue me. I guess our luck's run out."

"Not our faith."

"No, not our faith, just our luck. We'll take our faith to the grave."

Shots cracked through the air.

They watched the men on the roof spin around and fall to the ground, their torches still in their hands.

"What?" exclaimed Dianna.

More shots.

The man by the rain barrel slammed against it and dropped to the ground.

He did not move.

"The riders are using rifles." Dana's eyes were wide. "But not on us."

The gunfire was loud, and furious, and fast.

The women put their arms around each other and lay flat on the floor.

"What is going on?" whispered Dianna.

"I don't know," Dana whispered back.

"Have you stopped praying?"

"Are you kidding?"

It was quiet.

As if a twister had roared through the ranch and was gone.

Or a hailstorm had ended.

Or thunder had stopped.

They both heard the sound of horses' hooves. The crunch of boots on stones and pebbles. The creaking of boards as men walked through the house.

"I won't open my eyes," said Dianna.

"Neither will I," said Dana.

A minute went past.

There were no more sounds.

They both felt that someone was standing over them.

After a long moment Dianna risked opening her eyes about the same time as Dana.

Three men with strong chiseled features and deep green eyes and dusky tanned faces were looking down at them. They were in black with white clerical collars. One of them knelt and touched Dianna's face where there was a streak of blood. Heat shot right through her. Another put a hand gently on Dana's shoulder, a warm smile spreading over his handsome face. She was sure her mouth had fallen partly open.

"Ma'am," he asked her. "Are you all right?"

The Australian Way

"My name's Michael, ma'am."

The man in black with dazzling green eyes knelt by Dana, a canteen in one hand, a damp cloth in the other, and began to wipe away the streaks of blood and tears on her face.

"Always Michael," he added with a smile. "Never Mike."

"I'm Dana," Dana finally replied. "Dana Fleming."

"Sorry to meet you under these circumstances, ma'am, but it's a pleasure to have your acquaintance just the same."

Another one of the men knelt by Dianna.

"I'm Reuben David," he told her as he removed his black hat. "We're all brothers here. And preachers. May I take a look at those cuts on your face?"

Dianna stared at his white clerical collar. "What are preachers doing way out here? And how is it you happened to show up when you did?"

"We're putting up churches, ma'am. A bunch of 'em. To bless the people here abouts. Get 'em to pull together. Give 'em heart." He sloshed water from his canteen onto a red scarf he pulled from his pocket and gently touched Dianna's cheeks and forehead with it. "The Methodist Church has purchased small parcels of land all through this county. The first church we're building is not far from here. On a small hilltop. I'm pretty sure you can see the hill from here."

"Lazarus? Is that the hill you mean?"

"I'm not sure, ma'am." He held her chin with several black-gloved fingers. "Steady now. How'd you get all these cuts?"

"The bullets they fired in here. Glass and bits of crockery were flying everywhere. And splinters of wood. My name is Dianna Charming, by the way."

Reuben smiled into her eyes. "And charming you are. Am I hurting you at all?"

Dianna was caught up in Reuben's green eyes, darker than his brother Michael's, and the soft way he was rubbing the wet scarf over her skin. "No, you're not."

Two more men walked into the room, rifles hanging down from their hands.

"How are these two ladies?" asked a tall man with piercing blue eyes.

"As well as can be expected, Brett," replied Reuben. "Bits of glass cut them up some but neither of them have bullet wounds, so far as we can see."

"We don't," Dana and Dianna said at the same time.

Brett lifted his hat from his head. "I'm Brett. This fellow with me is Bobby. I expect the others have introduced themselves."

"All except me." A young man with a bright grin lifted his hat. "There weren't enough wounded ladies to go around so I was left out. Name's Scott David."

"Are you all brothers?" asked Dianna.

Scott nodded. "We sure are. And there's four more of us back in town."

"Nine? What are nine brothers doing in our county? Don't tell me you're all preachers?"

"We are."

"From one family? How can that be?"

Scott's grin grew wider and the freckles on his face spread out at the same time. "The call of God, ma'am. It just never let up on the David household."

"Was your father a preacher?"

"No, ma'am. A lawman. And after that a lawyer. Now he's a judge back east."

"My goodness. Doesn't he ever plan to retire?"

"Papa David? When we all gather at the river of God, I reckon, but not a minute before."

Brett's hat remained off his head. "We put out the fires. But I have to tell you that there is no man left alive out there."

Dana hung her head but Dianna jumped to her feet.

"What?" Dianna exclaimed. "I had five hired hands!"

Brett nodded. "I'm so sorry, ma'am. We have laid all the bodies out in the shade of the barn. I know it is a difficult task but if you could identify your men we would bless them and give them a Christian burial."

"One of the men is mine," Dana said in a low voice. "We rode here together from my ranch before the trouble started."

"Where is your ranch, ma'am?"

"About two miles north."

"I expect a few of us had better ride out that way to make sure everything is all right. We'll do that as soon as we've identified your men and laid them to rest."

Tears spilled over Dianna's face. "This is a hard thing to do and to do it so quickly."

"The heat is not in our favor, ma'am. And there is the possibility of another attack. I'm sorry."

"Someone coming," announced Bobby, glancing out the broken windows. "One rider."

The men went outside and Dana and Dianna followed them. The rider had stopped by the barn and was looking at the bodies laid out there.

"I heard there was a ruckus," the man said in a loud voice. "Looks to me like you had more of a war."

It was Sheriff Teddy Westcott.

"How'd you hear that?" asked Brett.

"A rider told me."

"The shooting only stopped fifteen minutes ago and it's a two hour ride to town."

"I happened to be in the neighborhood." Westcott glanced at the bodies again. "There are six of Ahab Hawthorne's men here. Each of them as full of holes as a saltshaker. How'd that happen?"

"They attacked the ranch and these two ladies," answered Brett.

"I find that hard to believe."

"They burned down those two outbuildings."

"More'n likely you boys caused those fires. Or the women did, being naturally careless. My sense of it is, Hawthorne sent his employees to serve notice on this ranch because it's an illegal settlement and that you all shot them out of their saddles. I'll have to arrest you for murder." He waved his hand over them as if he was casting a spell. "You five men and two ladies. You need to ride back with me to town."

"Murder?" Brett's eyes went ice blue. "They were the ones trying to murder these two women when we intervened."

"More'n likely the women had you five waiting in ambush and you opened fire once Hawthorne's employees delivered their ultimatum."

"Employees?" spat Dianna. "Hawthorne's men are nothing more than a pack of gunslingers and cutthroats!"

"I think you have that shoe on the wrong foot, ma'am. You and your hellfire preachers answer best to that description. Are you going to come with me easy or are you going to come hard?"

"We're not going to come at all," said Scott. He was still grinning. "But you can try your luck. One man against five."

"Oh, I got my own five. Their guns are on your backs." Westcott grinned back at Scott. "I never go anywhere without my five deputies."

The brothers whirled, Brett and Bobby lifting their rifles, the other three yanking revolvers from their holsters.

"There's no one," said Reuben.

Westcott continued to grin. "You'll see." He whistled. "Drop your guns or you're all dead men."

None of the brothers dropped their guns and none of Westcott's deputies appeared from behind farm buildings or up on rooftops.

"Looks to me like you're bluffing, Mr. Westcott." Scott's grin was bigger than ever. "I reckon you're playing poker with an empty hand."

Westcott's grin was gone and a scowl was in its place. He whistled again. Nothing happened. A third time. And then a line of men appeared from behind the farmhouse, hands over their heads.

"What in tarnation are you boys doing?" Westcott exploded. "This is no time to be playing games!"

A tall woman in black, riding a black horse, a rifle on the five deputies, herded them out into the open.

"I was out looking for strays and I found these rustlers instead," she said.

"Those are lawmen!" cried Westcott. "Take your gun off them! They're here to apprehend a pack of murderers!"

"Murderers?" The woman smiled at Brett and the others. "Well, I've called you a lot of names, dear brothers, but never that."

"What in blazes are you doing here?" demanded Brett.

"Saving your neck, as usual, big brother."

"You have no business being out here in harm's way! You turn around and head back to New York as soon as you've watered your horse!"

Her blue eyes, even more brilliant a blue than Brett's, turned to flame. "I have as much business here as any of you so don't start giving me orders." She pulled away the flap of her coat to reveal her white collar. "I'm a licensed minster with the Methodist Church now."

Brett's eyes had a fire of their own. "Says who?"

"Says the Methodist bishops who prayed over me two weeks ago and sent me here to help you out. And I intend to follow their orders and God's, not yours, Brett Daniel David!"

"You turn that horse around!"

"I won't! I already had this argument in town with the rest of you misfits and I'm not going to go through it again out here! I just saved your lives, you can thank me later, but for now you can just get used to the fact that your baby sister is as much a minister of the gospel as any of you! I was sent here to make sure four new churches went up before the snow flies and that's what I'm going to do!"

"I don't think so!"

"What you think doesn't make one whit of difference to me! No more than it did the time you stole my pony and lied about it!"

"I never stole that crazy pony!"

"Yes, you did!"

Scott laughed and held up his hands. "I surrender too if it'll mean stopping this shootout between the pair of you. Sheriff, I guess these are your employees, since you're fond of the word. I reckon you can skedaddle back to Cazadora with them right about now."

Westcott's face was like a thunderhead. "You preachers are making the biggest mistake of your lives. Hiding behind a bunch of women and your collars won't save y'all from what I'm gonna unleash on you."

"What's your plan?" Scott laughed. "You gonna turn the United States cavalry loose on the Methodist Church? Somehow I don't think that'll go over well in Washington."

"Washington? That's the least of your worries you snot-nosed spit of a preacher. In one day you've crossed more lines than the Apache and you're gonna pay hard for it. Heard of *Los Quinientos*? Use that for your pillow tonight." He pointed his finger at the woman on the black horse. "I don't know your name and I don't care to know it. Just turn my deputies loose and give them back their guns."

The woman smiled, her teeth a perfect white against her tanned skin and the black of her hat and coat. "My name's Tommy. Try to remember that for next time. And the guns stay back there in the dust along with their badges."

"What about the horses?"

"Start walking west. I'll send them along in about five minutes."

"You turn 'em loose and it'll take us an hour or more to round 'em up!"

"Better be on your way then, Sheriff. You're burning daylight."

His hand went to the gun on his hip.

She poked her rifle barrel at him. "Go ahead. A woman preacher can give you a Christian burial as good or better than any preacher man can."

His eyes were narrow and black. "I'll take great pleasure in dealing with you myself when the day of reckoning dawns."

"And I'll take great pleasure in returning the favor. The Lord hasten the day, Sheriff. I've got goose bumps I'm that excited just thinking about it." She prodded her large black horse forward, making the five deputies break into a run. "Go on, git. You're not real men anyhow. So make like the rattlesnakes you are and slither on out of here."

The deputies ran until they were sure she wasn't going to follow them, then slowed to a walk, cursing and glaring back at her, Westcott riding slowly beside them and cursing them as much as they were cursing her.

Tommy lifted her hat. Heaps of shining black hair were pinned on top of her head.

"My apologies, ladies," she said with her white smile. "I don't usually drop in on folks in such a rough and ready fashion. But my brothers do need looking after and that had to come first."

"I'm glad you did drop in on us in such a rough and ready fashion," said Dianna. "I'm Dianna Charming."

"And I'm Dana Fleming. Is Tommy your real name?"

"It used to be Tomboy, so this is an improvement. It's the name this pack of rascals the law calls my brothers gave to me."

"It suits," said Scott, the perennial grin on his face as he holstered his pistol.

She narrowed her eyes and stuck her tongue out at him.

"What name did your parents give you?" asked Dana.

"Teresina."

"What a lovely name. What does it mean?"

"Late summer. I reckon it'll be late summer in my life before anyone calls me by that name again."

"Oh, my dear, I wouldn't think so. A girl as lovely as you will snatch up a husband in no time."

"A husband? I might have had a dozen husbands by now if my brothers hadn't chased them all away."

She made a sour face.

"None of them were good enough for you," said Scott.

"Or us," quipped Reuben.

"I don't see too many wives hanging off your arm, Reuben Caleb!" snapped Tommy with a scowl.

He raised his hands palm outward as if she had pointed her rifle at him. "I'm a monk, remember? We 're all monks. Till the day we die. And you're the nun."

Tommy tossed her head at the same time as her horse. "As it happens I have very little interest in men. Perhaps living with nine brothers had something to do with that. Men seem to me to be very pale and helpless creatures. I'm better off on my own. Just me and God and my horse."

"Oh, the right one will come along," Dianna spoke up.

"Are you married yourself, ma'am?" asked Tommy.

"Not any more, no."

"Are you?" Tommy's eyes rested on Dana.

"I reckon I'm in the same boat as my friend Dianna. We're both widows."

"Well, it seems like I've landed in suitable company then. Not a few people have commented that my clerical attire looks like widow's weeds. *That's fine with me,* I tell them. *I don't mind being a widow for the gospel.*"

"I pray a good man comes along for you, Teresina, just as I pray one comes along for me and for my friend here," said Dana.

"I don't think there is such a man."

"Of course there is."

"Let me know when he shows up. I'll likely be too busy having a good time to notice."

"Now you sound like Dianna," grumbled Dana.

Tommy touched the brim of her hat with a black-gloved hand. "Excuse me a moment."

She walked her black behind the farmhouse. Half a minute later she was chasing five horses past the barn out into the fields. The deputies, two hundred yards ahead, waved their arms in the air as their mounts pounded past them. Westcott rode after a sorrel, swinging his lasso. He managed to loop it over the sorrel's head and an instant later he had been yanked out of his saddle and was rolling on the ground. Tommy and her brothers and Dana and Dianna laughed.

"It doesn't do much to brighten up the day," said Dianna, "but it helps."

Brett nodded. "We have graves to dig. We will be certain to separate the sheep from the goats first."

Dianna's laughter was gone in a moment. Her eyes went to the bodies on the ground by the barn.

"Thank you," she said to Brett.

"Reuben. Michael." Brett jerked west with his thumb. "You best bring the mules and wagon in now."

"Who are *Los Quinientos?*" asked Dana.

Brett turned to look at her. "The Five Hundred. A gang of desperadoes from Texas who spend most of their time hiding out in Old Mexico. When they're not hiding out they're killing and robbing this side of the border."

"I've never heard of them."

"Just as well. I don't believe they've brought their plagues to the New Mexico Territory yet."

"It sounds like the Sheriff and Ahab Hawthorne are going to change that."

"We'll be ready for them."

"Nine men?"

"Nine men and a tomboy."

Dana glanced at Tommy as she flared her eyes at her brother.

"That doesn't sound like enough," Dana said. "Ten against five hundred."

"Oh, there aren't five hundred. That's just a name they use to spook people. I doubt they have more than ninety gunmen."

"That still sounds like a lot to me."

"I suppose it is. We may have to ask some friends of the family to join our ministry here."

"And who would that be, brother?" asked Tommy.

Brett glanced up at her. "Climb down off your horse and we'll talk about it."

"I'm quite happy up here, thank you. I like being over your head now and then."

"We still haven't settled on whether you're staying or not."

Tommy patted the pocket of her long black coat. "Your opinion on the matter is neither welcome nor is it binding. I have my letter authorizing me to carry out my duties right here. And the letter's signed by seven bishops and one federal court judge who has jurisdiction over the New Mexico Territory – does the name Judge Nathaniel Paul David ring any bells with you?"

Brett grunted. "Pulling all your guns on us, are you?"

"That's the only thing that's worked since I've been five."

"Well, baby sister, speaking of bishops, that's who I had a mind to ask to the prayer meeting with *Los Quinientos*. You've heard of the Bishop of Tucumcari, haven't you?"

Tommy stared at him, narrowing her eyes. "Always playing tricks on me, aren't you, Brett Daniel? There is no Bishop of Tucum – whatever you call it."

"Oh, but there is, baby sister."

"Stop calling me that."

"Tucumcari is east of here." Dianna had her hands on her hips. "It's just dry, empty country. There's a peak or mesa there called Tucumcari and nothing else."

"Hardly the sort of place for a bishop, is it?" mocked Tommy.

"How much time he spends on that mountain I can't say. But he goes there to pray and seek God's guidance. That's how he came to be called the Bishop of Tucumcari."

"Really."

"Yeah, really."

"He must be something of a fossil."

"He's a young man. Very intense. Very committed. He has no more use for women and marriage than you do for grooms and a wedding gown. But he knows how to defend the weak and the helpless. I believe he'd join us for our season of prayer."

"If he's a real person then what's his name?"

"Who knows? We've always called him Mesa. Mesa Tucumcari. The same way we've always called you Tommy."

"And what does he do, this Mesa Tucumcari, dear brother? He's surely no Methodist clergyman."

"He's as Methodist as you or I. The bishops back east employ him as a mender of fences, you know, someone who steps in when there's problems in one of our churches out west here. He always sets things right between a minister and his flock."

"How does he do that?"

"Prayer. Listening. Offering advice. Preaching a few healthy sermons."

"It sounds wonderful. No, really, it does. But how is a gentle man like your Mesa Tucumcari going to help us with hired killers from Old Mexico and Texas?"

"Shall I ask him to pay us a visit in Cazadora so you can find out?"

"Please."

Brett turned to Dianna. "Where would you like us to bury your men, Mrs. Charming?"

"Why, there is a spot with a few small trees a few minutes' walk east."

"Is your husband buried there?"

"No. He is in a spot by the Rio Oro with two other men – Dana's husband and a woman in town named Marianne Freeman."

Brett nodded. "I met her. A handsome woman who favors a gun."

"All three men stood up to Ahab Hawthorne. All three were killed there."

"I see."

"We have only buried a hired hand who was thrown from his horse. And a child I bore years ago who only lived a week."

"I'm very sorry, Mrs. Charming."

"It was a long time ago, Reverend David, but thank you just the same."

"Would you like your man laid to rest here or on your own ranch, Mrs. Fleming?"

Dana looked away. "Here among the men he fought and died with is fine."

The brothers put the bodies on their horses and walked the horses to the cemetery. Tommy dismounted and did the same. Reuben and Michael brought in the mules with their wagonload of lumber and placed the last two bodies on their mounts. Dianna fetched four shovels from the barn and the six graves were quickly dug, Tommy making sure she took one of the shovels for herself. After prayers, and a few words by Brett from a Bible in his saddlebag, the brothers returned to the barn and slung Hawthorne's men over their horses and walked them a quarter mile from the ranch before placing them together in a shallow grave. They said prayers over them as well but the grave was left unmarked.

"Lord have mercy," Brett whispered. "Christ have mercy."

Shortly after, Brett sent Michael and Scott back with Dana to her ranch to see how matters stood. Along with the others he repaired the windows that had been shot out in the kitchen, placing light cotton fabric that was almost transparent over the openings until they could get glass from town. Then Brett walked outside with Dianna and pointed west.

"That's the top of Lazarus there, isn't it?"

"I'm not sure."

Brett went over to his horse that was tethered near the house, removed a brass telescope from a saddlebag, and handed it to Dianna.

"Take a good look," he said to her.

He guided her hand till she was in the right place and rock steady.

"Yes, that's it," she suddenly said. "It's a bit of a mesa too, isn't it, with its flat top? I hardly look at it anymore I've lived here so long."

"I want to put a church right on top of that. So you can see it for miles around. A city that is set on a hill cannot be hidden."

"I like that idea. What are you going to call it?"

"We'll name it after the peak itself."

"I hope your use of the name is prophetic, Mr. David."

"I hope it is too. This land could benefit from a breath of new life. Please call me Brett."

"And please call me Dianna. You and your brothers saved our lives."

Brett smiled. "An honor. And then my sister snuck up and saved ours. She'll never let us forget it either."

Dianna smiled too. "Badger one another all you like. I have brothers and sisters back east too. We do much the same thing and we all love one another to death."

"I suspect that's a fairly accurate assessment of the David family as well."

"Being the only girl, Teresina must have felt surrounded most of her life."

"Maybe. But now it's the rest of us who feel surrounded by her."

They headed back to the ranch house together.

"When do you expect to start putting up this church, Mr. David – excuse me, I mean, Brett?"

"Tomorrow morning, crack of dawn."

"Just like that?"

"Just like that. When it's done we have to get your friend Marianne Freeman on her spread, safe and secure, and those other two women besides."

"What other two women?"

"They survived an attack on a wagon train. The attack sounds like the work of your friend Ahab Hawthorne again. They claim to have legal deed to property in this area. We need to get a house up around their heads as soon as possible. Is there anything left of your friend Marianne's ranch house?"

"No, Brett. Hawthorne's men burned it to the ground and drove off the cattle."

"So a lot of houses have to be raised up, not just church buildings. That's what I meant when I said the crack of dawn. We don't have any time to waste. My brothers and I will bunk in the barn, if you don't mind, then head out to Lazarus at first light."

"I do mind, Brett. I won't have your men sleeping in the barn. There's plenty of room in the house."

"Dianna – "

"I can be just as feisty as your sister, Brett, so don't push me too far. The house, not the barn. And Teresina will share my bed."

He smiled. "I was going to say you remind me of your friend, Marianne Freeman. And both of you remind me of my sister."

"Your sister is a beautiful and spirited woman. So that is a good thing, Brett Daniel."

Dana returned with Scott and Michael an hour later. Her ranch had not been attacked and her hired men had everything in hand so she had decided to help Dianna out. The two of them, along with Tommy, cooked up a meal of rice and beans and tortillas and everyone had an early night, Reuben and

Bobby standing guard first. Brett got the brothers out of bed at four and they took care of the ranch chores. After a breakfast of bacon and potatoes, that they helped cook alongside the women, the men headed west with the mules and wagonload of lumber and tools. After a short, sharp argument with Tommy, Brett permitted her to ride along while Michael stayed behind with Dianna and Dana. An hour after dark the men and Tommy returned, hungry and hoping to fill a wooden tub with water for baths. Tommy had the first bath and the others followed, all of them using the same water. Dianna and Dana had roasted a side of beef and the brothers dug in as if they hadn't eaten since the dawn of creation. Michael stayed up and kept watch over the ranch and remained behind with Dana and Dianna the next day as well. The third day the two ranch women decided they wanted to see for themselves what was happening at Lazarus Top and rode out with the whole crew, no one remaining at the ranch to keep an eye on things.

A foundation had been set in place on the top of the small mesa, the entire building had been framed, and that day the brothers started working on the roof. Tommy was nailing down a pine floor and Dana and Dianna took instructions from her and helped out. The men started work in their black clothes but soon stripped to their sleeveless white undershirts. Dianna tried to concentrate on what Tommy was telling her but found herself frequently glancing up to watch Brett and Reuben work. Tommy smiled her white smile.

"My brothers are pests," she said, "but they are certainly handsome pests."

Dianna looked down, aiming her hammer at a nail. "I didn't mean to stare."

"Stare all you like. None of them are spoken for. They move around too much."

"Don't any of them have any notion of settling in somewhere one day?"

"If they ever stick with one of their church plants, sure."

Dana finished banging in a nail and wiped her forehead with a bandana. "Warm work."

"You need to take a break now and then and look up," teased Dianna.

Dana smiled. "I've looked up plenty of times while you were looking down."

"Oh? Letting your eyes roam?"

"They don't roam too far. I favor Michael."

Dianna squinted upwards. "The brother with the curly dark hair who has been guarding our ranch the past couple of days."

"That's him. I like the way he walks."

Dianna laughed. "You like the way he walks?"

"And rides. And smiles. And talks."

"And looks at you?"

"He doesn't look at me."

"He sure does."

Tommy took a nail out from between her lips and held it upright on the corner of a floorboard. "Mikey likes fried chicken."

"Mikey?" repeated Dana.

"I use that name when I want to irritate him. Don't you use it. But he'd look kindly on the fried chicken."

"I'll remember that. Fried chicken tonight, Di? I have a recipe from a ranch woman in Cimarron."

Dianna smiled. "Sounds like the right thing to do. Are Reuben and Brett partial to fried chicken, Teresina?"

Tommy hammered her nail home. "They don't mind it. But thick steaks make the blood run in their veins."

"Well, I'd certainly like to make the blood run in their veins."

Tommy sat back on her heels and looked at Dianna. "A smile from a lovely woman has the same effect and it's easier."

Dianna reddened and dropped her eyes to the floor. "I reckon I'll try both then."

******

While the church building was going up at Lazarus Top, Adam David was teasing Noelle Saunders about calling him *dinkum*.

"That doesn't sound very good," he told her, setting down his cup of coffee. "I don't think we can be friends."

"Oh, mate." Noelle reached across the table and grabbed him by the wrist. "It's something good."

"How good can a word like that be?"

"Very good."

"Tell me what it means and let me decide for myself."

"It means, well, it means you're not false. You are something substantial, you know, real, genuine, true – all those things."

"Hmm. That does sound good. So you really think I'm *dinkum* after only knowing me for a few days?"

"I knew that after only knowing you for a few minutes."

"How's that?"

"You stood up to the sheriff and his five deputies for me."

Adam smiled. "It was the right thing to do."

"Well, keep on doing the right thing, mate."

"I'll try my best." He drained his coffee and stood up. "Speaking of sheriffs and deputies, I have a call to make." He unbuckled his gun belt. "Without these."

"What d'you mean?"

"I mean there's a time to laugh and a time to cry, a time to gather stones and a time to scatter them, as the Good Book says. And there's a time for the gun and a time where the gun needs to be set aside. I've been praying for those old boys and I'm going to try to make peace."

"Peace? Marianne says they're scoundrels through and through."

"Well, a lot of the people Jesus walked the land for were just like that. Will you mind that pistol for me?"

"Mind the pistol? I'm going with you."

"You're not going with me."

"Don't tell me what I'm going to do or not going to do, mate." Noelle stood up, eyes dark and flashing. "It's a free country."

Adam tried to fight back his smile. "Is that fact?"

"That's a fact. Now shouldn't your brothers be told about this scheme of yours?"

"We discussed it and prayed about it last night. Perhaps you should stay here and pack up. We'll be heading out to your claim right after lunch. Yours and Joyeux's and Marianne's. I understand they're quite close together."

"The sheriff won't let you do that."

Adam placed his black hat on his head. "That's what we're going to parley about. Coming?"

"I said I was, didn't I?"

They went out the door together and headed up the street side by side, Adam in black, Noelle in a light cotton dress speckled with blue flowers. Noelle was someone who prayed off and on, usually in church or at bedtime, but she found herself praying furiously as the sheriff's office got closer and closer, especially once she saw the five deputies, unshaven and scowling at passersby, lounging on the porch outside the office.

"What y'all want?" One of the deputies spat in the dirt by Adam's boots.

"I need to talk with Sheriff Westcott," Adam replied.

"He ain't in."

"I can see him through the window reading the newspaper."

"I'm saying he ain't in, preacher boy." The deputy glanced at Adam's waist. "You ain't wearing. How come? Gonna whack us to death with your Bible from here on in?"

"It's a heavy Bible, Simon. It might just do the trick."

"How'd you know my name?"

"It's what the others call you. Simon Hartstone. I know your family back in New York."

The deputy's face paled quickly. "What are you talking about?"

"It was just a hunch but I sent a telegram a couple of days ago when I heard your name. Got a reply yesterday afternoon. Turns out I was right. So I cabled your mother, Esmeralda. A fine Christian woman. She asked after you."

"You leave my mother out of this."

"I told her you were an outstanding peace officer. Would you like me to send her a different message?"

"I said to leave her out of this."

"Simon, my brothers and I are leaving Cazadora for a spell. I don't want anything to happen to the church while we're gone – not to the building or to the people."

"That has nothing to do with me."

"Sure it does. You're a deputy sheriff."

"That's a town matter. Go talk to the marshal. I deal with county matters."

"Well, now, I'd like to take it up with the marshal but he's dead. Folks tell me all five of you cut him down when he had his back to you and was window-shopping with his wife."

Simon slapped his hand to his holster. "That's a lie."

"A lot of people say otherwise."

"I don't care how many say it. They're all liars."

"The news is bound to reach your mother one day, Simon."

"Who's gonna tell her that? You?"

Adam shook his head. "Not me. My next telegram is going to be about how you protected a church from marauders and that you're a hero."

Simon's face went from white to a dark red. "You think so?"

"I'm counting on it. You've tossed your hand in with a bad bunch. But you know what the right thing to do is. That's how you were raised. That's how your mom raised all your brothers and sisters." Adam looked at the other deputies. "I reckon that's how your mommas raised all you men."

The deputies stared death at him but no one spoke.

"So if you boys will all work together," Adam went on, "I'm sure the church and its new steeple will be safe in my absence. Now, the other thing is, we're heading out to put this fine young lady here on her spread, her and two other women. That's county business. And I'd appreciate it if the five of you made sure their spreads weren't molested."

"Why, you're bold as brass," one of the other deputies sneered. "What makes you think we're gonna keep our hands off squatters?"

"Because they aren't squatters, Nick Harris."

The deputy's thick eyebrows knotted together. "You know too much."

"All their deeds are legitimate. I took the trouble to telegraph their contents to a federal judge back east and he let me know this morning each one of the deeds is fair and square."

"Who cares what a judge back east says? This is New Mexico, not Brooklyn."

"Well, now, it so happens this particular judge has jurisdiction over the New Mexico Territory."

"Santa Fe won't recognize his authority."

"You'd be surprised what Santa Fe will recognize when the Apache are on the rampage and your politicians need US cavalry as fast as they can get them. I hear tell Cazadora has been selected for a raid to teach the whites a lesson. Ever heard of Blood Lance, Mr. Harris? He has almost two hundred warriors. I wonder how long you could hold them off without federal cavalry at your backs? And they do more than scalp, these Apache. They favor burying deputies in anthills where the ants strip lost calves to the bone or strapping them to wagon wheels over nice, slow cooking fires."

"Adam!" Noelle's eyes were wide. "Really!"

Adam held up his hands. "The good news is God loves you and you can start over fresh today. Keep the church safe. Keep the womenfolk and the children safe. Keep the ranches in the county safe. Pin your badges on every morning for Jesus and plan to attend our worship service the next time we're in town. And no trouble will come near your tent."

"We work for Ahab Hawthorne," rumbled a deputy with a large stomach and an even larger red beard. "We sure don't work for God or one of his two bit employees."

"I'm sorry to hear that, Red Beard, because God is working for you."

"Oh, yeah?"

"Yeah. But you take your pick, Red Beard. God and a clean conscience or Ahab Hawthorne and a foot full of cactus spikes cutting right through fat and gristle as the Apache push them through."

"Adam!"

"It's all right, Noelle. I'm just helping these boys see the light. They can choose God and a saddlebag of good tomorrows. Or they can choose Ahab and a quick and nasty end. It's their call."

"You think it's gonna be that easy to get us to turn?" snarled a fourth deputy as skinny as a hoe handle. "An itty bitty sermon and a pretty boy smile?"

"I wish it would turn you, Hack. New Mexico won't be lawless forever. The army will come and stay for good. So will federal judges. So will the flag with a new star on it for the state of New Mexico. Change sides now while you still can."

"We're not interested in you or your God."

"He'll stay interested in you until the last moment, Hack. So will I. We may be enemies but I pray for my enemies, I don't just fight them. Do the right thing. Switch to God's side and ride for him. Leave Ahab Hawthorne in the dust. Leave him or you'll eat dust. I swear you will. A man reaps what he sows."

"I've had about enough religion to last me a year." The fifth deputy pushed himself off the wall of the office building and unholstered his pistol. "We need a good dance."

He cocked and fired at Adam's boots.

Adam didn't move.

The deputy kept firing, dirt and stones flying up around Adam's feet.

Still he didn't move.

The final shot went through the heel of Adam's black boot.

"That will be a costly repair," Adam said.

The door to the sheriff's office banged open.

"What in thunder are you doing, Blacksticks?" roared Teddy Westcott.

"Preacher here took up the offering. That was my ten percent."

Westcott glared at Blacksticks and Adam.

"What do you want?" he snapped at Adam.

Adam tipped his hat.

"Your boys can give you my message. I trust you to do what you were sworn in to do, Sheriff. Uphold the law. Not Ahab Hawthorne's law. Not even New Mexico law, so far as that goes. God's law, sir. The law all of you were taught in Sunday school. Keep it. It's not too late."

"It's way too late for us, preacher," growled Blacksticks.

"Never too late for anyone. Jesus rides in offering you all freedom. Take him up on it."

Adam walked away, heading back to Marianne's house.

Noelle ran after him and caught him by the arm. "You're crazy as a kookaburra, mate."

Adam's blood was up but he couldn't keep himself from smiling. "What's that? Something like a *dinkum*?"

"Just as good. You really don't know the meaning of fear, do you?"

"They wouldn't shoot an unarmed man. Not even them."

"Well, they came mighty close."

"I had to say what I had to say. The blood is on their heads if they decide to spurn it."

"What chance do you think there is that men like that will take what you said to heart?"

"I'd say fifty-fifty."

"Fifty-fifty? Even odds?"

"That's right. Especially when they think about the Apache riding down over the ridge with murder in their eyes."

"You're mad, mate. Now you have the Apache on our side."

"We're all made in God's image. Who knows how God might turn things around for you thanks to them?"

"Turn things around for me?"

"They're a sure bet to help you get and keep your ranch."

"The Apache?"

"Yes, ma'am."

"Oh, you *are* mad. And what have I told you about calling me *ma'am*?" She suddenly tugged him into a narrow alley piled high with wooden crates. "Come here."

"What are you going to do?" He was grinning like his brother Scott. "Spank me?"

"Yes, that's exactly what I'm going to do, mate." She pulled him into the shadows behind the crates and framed his face in both of her hands. "You are the bravest man I've ever met. And I get the distinct feeling that a lot of what you're doing is being done for me."

"Well, you need a home and a roof over your head. You need to feel safe. You need to feel secure."

"And you think it's your job to make sure that all happens, don't you?"

"God arranged for our paths to cross. I can't just – "

She kissed him quickly to get him to stop talking. When she pulled back the look on his face was such a mixture of surprise and happiness that she couldn't resist kissing him again. This time she went on for several minutes. She was rewarded when she felt his arms slide around her back and his strength bring her in closer.

"You're so beautiful," he whispered.

"Thanks, mate. I could say the same about you."

"We're not going to stop so soon, are we?"

She laughed. "No, we're not. Glad you're eager. It's been so long since I kissed a man I wasn't sure how I was doing."

"Better than a drink of cold water in a hot desert."

"That does sound awfully good. Would you like another drink, Reverend David?"

"I would."

Their lips came together. This time the grip of Adam's hands was stronger and his kiss took over from hers and burned down through her mouth and throat and into her chest. Always full of fight and the determination to get her own way, Noelle had the strange desire that she wanted him to hold her and carry her and take care of her, as if she were a child again playing by the big waves of the ocean and struggling with a feeling of fear. She had thought the expression *the lady sank into her lover's arms* to be ridiculous but now she felt like doing that very thing.

I've had to be strong and on my own for so many months why can't I just let go for a few minutes?

She did, and his arms took her weight easily. Her hands explored his back and felt the muscle moving under his shirt and the rich warmth of a body that matched his gentleness and softness perfectly. For the first time in a very long time she had a feeling of hope and excitement that the rest of her life could still be good and complete and blessed.

"Is that enough for you now?" he asked her quietly. "I don't want to wear out my welcome."

Her lips brushed against his. "Wear out your welcome? Mate, you've only just got in the door. Kiss me again, Adam David, and bring this woman back to life. Yes, go ahead, kiss me all day, if you like. Being loved like this is better than a thousand acres of the best land in New Mexico."

A Church Called Lazarus

July, 1866, the New Mexico Territory

"Whoa. Whoa, now."

The man hauled back on the reins and the wagon came to a stop. A hundred yards to his left he watched several men on a ladder and a roof wrestle with a tall wooden cross and place it on top of a white building.

"What are you stopping for?" asked his wife. "We won't have the morning cool forever. We need to get into town."

"Sally, those men are putting up a steeple."

The sun was just coming up behind them and she could see the cross clearly. "So they are. I haven't placed my eyes on a decent steeple since we left Boston."

The man steered the wagon left. "Let's take a closer look."

"Clayton, we don't have time for this."

"We surely do. Haven't we both been missing the praying and the preaching of a good church?"

"Yes, but the day heats up so fast here."

"Ten minutes, Sally. It won't kill us."

"What about Ahab Hawthorne, Clayton? Will he kill us? I'm sure he never gave them permission to put up a church on his land."

Clayton kept the horses headed towards the church. His only response to his wife's use of the name Ahab Hawthorne was to lean over and spit in the dust. The brothers on the ladder and on the roof turned to look at him as the wagon approached.

"Hello, there," he greeted the brothers. He was at the bottom of the small hill the church was perched upon. "Clayton Todd. My wife, Sally Todd. We have a small spread a few miles east of here. Heading into Cazadora for supplies."

The brothers nodded their heads.

"Pleased to meet you," Brett spoke up. "I know we look a little sunburned and worse for wear but we're employed by the Methodist Church. This meeting place will open its doors for its first service on Sunday."

"Four days. Have to be Methodist to show up? We were Presbyterians back east."

"Not at all. If you can sing a hymn or pray a prayer or have a yearning to feed your soul you're more than welcome."

"Does Mr. Hawthorne know about this?" asked Sally.

"He might," Brett replied. "Sheriff Westcott might have told him our plans."

"And he's going to allow you to put up a church on his land?"

"Well, it's not his land. The Methodist Church purchased Lazarus Top. We're counting on its location to draw people in from miles around."

"But we're all here on his sufferance, Reverend. All the people I know are. Unless they're squatters."

Dianna came out from behind the church building, a paintbrush in one hand, can of white paint in the other. "Who do you reckon are squatters, ma'am?"

"Why, anyone that didn't get Mr. Hawthorne's permission to settle here and buy their deed from him."

"You think he owns the whole county?"

Sally wasn't sure how to respond. "I — I don't know about that."

"Because my husband bought our deed from good people in Santa Fe and the officials there said it was all legal and fine. Then your friend Ahab Hawthorne came into the picture and said the deed was worthless. And he's trying to get Santa Fe to go along with him."

Sally's eyes flashed dark and light. "He's not my friend. He burned out neighbors of ours this spring. I just don't want trouble with him, that's all. So far we've stayed on his good side."

"I didn't know he had a good side."

"All God's creatures have a good side somewhere."

Reuben came down off the ladder. "Reuben David, ma'am. If it makes you feel any better, you should know all of us here decided an invitation ought to be sent to Mr. Hawthorne to attend the first service."

"What? You think he'll attend?"

"That's up to him. But the offer's been extended."

"Maybe he'll see the light." Clayton snapped his reins. "That would do him a world of good. It would do us all a world of good if Ahab Hawthorne knelt before the Almighty. We'll see you folk on Sunday. We'd best get into Cazadora before we're driving in a furnace."

Sally glanced back. "What time, Reverend?"

"Ten." Reuben wiped his arm over his forehead. "Give everyone time to finish up their chores. And it's well before the worst of the heat."

"We'll spread the word, Reverend."

"Much obliged, ma'am."

They all watched the wagon roll away, lifting dust from the ground.

"Reverend," teased Dianna.

Reuben smiled. "I never called myself that."

"But you didn't tell her to drop it either."

"Hold still." He took her chin in his hand. "You have something on the side of your face."

"What's that?" Dianna's eyes darted to the right. "If it's a spider get it off quick!"

He showed her his thumb. "Just a spot of white paint."

"Paint! You had me thinking it was something terrible!" She swatted his arm with her brush. "Now you can have some of it too!"

Reuben laughed. "Gimme that paintbrush."

"I won't. It's all I have to defend myself."

"It won't save you."

"Save me from what?"

Brett threw up his hands and he was laughing too. "Hold your horses! We need that paint for the walls, not Reuben's sunburn. And we have benches to nail together for Sunday morning. So let's get back at it." He smiled at Dianna. "But if you still want to paint Reuben white, you can do that during our *siesta*."

"I can't wait." Dianna smirked.

Reuben grinned. "Neither can I."

Dana rolled her eyes. "Oh oh, here we go."

"What?" Dianna slapped a streak of white on Dana's arm.

At one, just after lunch, everyone relaxed in the shade of a grove of Ponderosa Pines on Lazarus Top, about a hundred feet from the church. The horses were tethered under the trees by a small stream that made its way through the grove. Reuben helped Dianna to her feet.

"You're not going to walk me out into that heat, are you?" Dianna made a face.

"Only for a few minutes." He pointed. "Until we reach that tumble of boulders. That will give us shade."

She shaded her hands. "It will take us about ten minutes to get to it."

"It'll be worth it."

"Remind me again why we're doing this with a whole audience watching?"

"You covered me in paint."

"I didn't cover you."

"Close enough. Come on."

Reuben slung a canteen over one shoulder and picked up a lever action rifle with a long octagonal barrel and a brass frame.

"What do they call that?" she asked.

"A Winchester Yellowboy."

"I've never heard of Winchester."

"New company. I've got thirteen rounds of .44/40 ammo loaded into this."

"I have a friend in Cazadora who owns a Henry rifle."

"I know the friend. The Dutch woman. The Henry's a good rifle. But I can load the Yellowboy fast right through the side of the receiver – there's a gate here. You need one of these, Dianna."

"I do?"

"I recall you had a Civil War musket to hold off those gunslingers when I first rode up to your ranch. This Winchester will be a lot better. It's like having a dozen men."

They had walked off the hill and were making their way through the sage towards the boulders.

"Well," Dianna sighed, "I guess I'll need about that many to run the ranch after losing my boys. I can't afford them but I'm sure going to need help."

"An even dozen. Or a man who can work as hard as ten or twelve."

Half her mouth curled up in a smile. "And where am I going to find a man like that?"

"You won't have to look far."

"Whoa. What are you saying? I think this day is galloping away with me. And all because of a paint brush."

"I don't mean to make the day feel out of control for you."

They reached the boulders and sat down in their shade.

Dianna fanned her face with her hand. "Whew. That's better. Are you going to hold that rifle the whole time we're sitting here?"

"I am."

"Why, you could see anyone coming for miles."

"Not Apache. They'd spend two or three hours crawling through the sage to get you and me if they wanted us bad enough."

"I'm glad you told me that, Reuben Caleb. Now I feel perfectly relaxed. Can we go back to talking about white paint?"

Reuben smiled. "The thing is, after the service Sunday, everything changes. We pack up and move on. There are other churches to build."

"You're all leaving?"

"The rest of the crew will show up Saturday. That's the plan. They'll have the homestead for those three women up by now – three bedrooms and some corrals. A couple of us will stay here to run services and do the good work of God."

"Who?'

"That hasn't been decided yet. Brett will have it figured out by Sunday night."

"Might you – " Dianna hesitated. "Might you be one of them?"

"Depends." Reuben took off his black hat and laid it on the ground. "I know you favor my brother."

"What?" Dianna sat up. "Is that what you think?"

"I couldn't help but notice while we've been putting this church up day after day."

"Is that right? I'll let you in on a secret. I like green eyes as much or more than I like blue ones." Dianna looked at Reuben directly. "I am fond of your brother. But I'm fond of you too. In fact, I find you a little gentler and a lot more easy-going. So while I may have had one eye on Brett, I've had both on you."

Reuben flushed through his sunburned skin. "I don't know what to say to that."

"Try anyways."

He shrugged. "We travel a lot. Sometimes there are congregations; sometimes we start with a handful of folk, just like here. I see different women wherever we go. You got my attention, Dianna Charming."

"And how did I do that?"

"I admire your big heart. Your sweetness. Your feistiness. It all comes together very well."

"It does? My sass too?"

He grinned, the white of his teeth splitting open the dark burn of his face. "I wouldn't be without it. Of course your blond hair and good looks help temper the sass."

Now the flush was on Dianna's face. "It's been a long time since a man said such things to me."

"I guess you don't get off your ranch much."

"Not much."

"Otherwise you'd have a string of suitors lined up from here to Cazadora."

"Oh, I would not." Dianna tossed a handful of dirt at Reuben.

He ducked his head. "Hey."

She tossed some more dirt. "There's never a paint brush when you need one."

"No more of that now."

"They can't see us from where they are, can they?"

"No."

"So I feel like a tomboy today and I'm going to keep throwing."

He ducked his head again, put down his rifle, and pinned her arms to her side. "You're as bad as my sister."

"I'm much worse than Tommy." She wriggled. "Let me go."

"So I can wear more dirt in my hair? No, ma'am."

"Ooooh, was that on purpose? You know how I feel about the word *ma'am*."

"I won't use *ma'am* if you don't throw dirt again."

Dianna wriggled harder but couldn't break his grip. "We seem to have come a long way fast from polite nods and secret glances of the eyes."

"New Mexico has a way of doing that."

"New Mexico? Is that what's to blame?"

"The sky, the light, the air, the heat – yes, ma'am."

"There you go again. Why are you doing that?"

"I like to see the flash in your eyes," Reuben said.

"Flash?"

"Like summer lightning."

"Lightning? You'll see some lightning all right if you don't – "

His kiss was such a surprise to her that Dianna didn't realize he was no longer pinning back her arms. He took her face in his hands and his lips touched hers so rapidly and with so much heat she had a quick image in her head of his Winchester firing. She was going to laugh at this thought but found she couldn't laugh; it had been such a long time since any man had placed his lips on hers with such passion. So she did nothing. When his arms went around her she let them stay there. When his kisses burned against her throat and neck and ear, she let them. When his mouth covered hers, and she felt as hot as if they were out under the New Mexican sun, she laid back and enjoyed the heat. One black booted leg curled around him and her hands suddenly started going where they wanted

73

to go – the muscles of his back and shoulders, the beautiful strength of his chest and the hard flatness of his stomach, the dark shine of his hair.

"Don't stop," she said when he pulled back.

"I'm sorry, Dianna, I didn't want to come on so strong."

"But I want you to. I've felt so dried up and dead inside. Now it's like a fast and furious thunderstorm that fills all the *arroyos* with water and makes the desert flowers open." She traced a finger over his lips. "But tell me. Do you care for me or are you just a lonely man reaching out for a moment's comfort and pleasure?"

"I care for you enough to ask Brett to let me stay on at Lazarus Top as the pastor. That way I could see you a couple of times a week."

"A couple? I'd want to see your green eyes and handsome face every day."

"That suits me. Because I'd never get enough of your sweet face and strong arms and diamond hair."

Before she could reply, the kisses came again – rapid and fierce at first, just like before, then long and slow and deep, penetrating right into her blood. She wanted to cry out with happiness at the feelings tearing through her body. The fingers of both hands curled in his hair tighter and tighter. His only response was to kiss her more and to bring her in against his chest with greater strength. Her other booted leg twined around him.

"I have feelings for you," he whispered.

"I hope so," she whispered back.

"I've prayed about you. Read Bible verses."

"I'm glad to hear it. But we need more time. We both need more time."

Disappointment moved across his face. "So the kissing stops?"

She laughed. "I feel like spring inside, why would I want the kissing to stop?"

A sharp whistle pierced the air.

Her blond eyebrows came together. "Please tell me that's not your brother."

He ran his thumb over her cheekbones. "*Siesta*'s over. Time to build benches and finish painting."

"Do we have to go right away?"

"Hard to pretend we didn't hear a whistle like that."

"We can't see them from here." She kissed his eyes. "So maybe we can't hear them that well either. Don't you think we could get away with another few minutes?"

"Minutes? We could try."

"All right, let's try. Let's try our hardest."

Eight riders and two wagons drew up to Lazarus Top in the late afternoon light of Saturday, July 28th. Adam was riding beside Noelle; Marianne and Selah and Joyeux were right behind them, Luke had the back of the small column, and Joseph and Benjamin drove the wagons. Reuben was stripped to the waist and shingling the roof along with Scott and Michael. He shielded his eyes with the hand that was holding the hammer.

"Is this Ahab Hawthorne?' he called down.

Adam lifted his black hat off his head. "At your service."

"You come for some hellfire preaching, Ahab?"

"That's the only kind I like, Reverend."

"We'll be sure to dish it up with all the flames still wrapped around it."

Brett came out of the church. "What's all the hollering for?"

Reuben pointed. "Ahab Hawthorne is paying us a social visit."

Brett stared at the wagons and riders at the bottom of the knoll. "Is he?" His eyes roamed over their faces. Seeing Marianne, a slow smile began to make its way over his lips and he doffed his hat. "I'm glad to see you all again. I'm particularly glad to see you Marianne Freeman."

Marianne dropped her eyes. *I haven't been thinking about anything else, awake or asleep, except you, mister, so I'm glad you remembered my name.*

"Hello, Reverend David," she replied.

"Whooo, Reverend David." Scott squinted from the roof at Brett, his typically big grin even bigger. "She must set great store by you to hang your title on you like that."

Brett put his hands on his lips. "If Marianne says it, I'll live with it. Even if she doesn't have a gun in her hand."

"That was such a long time ago." Marianne looked up at him from the bottom of the hill, dust and sweat on her face. "Do you need to keep bringing it up?"

"I apologize. I guess I don't have as good a knack for funning with people as Scott does."

Scott tilted his hat back on his head. "God gives his creatures different gifts."

Brett beckoned with his hand. "Come on up. Bring yourselves and your horses into the trees." He nodded. "Welcome, Joyeux. Welcome, Noelle."

"Hello, sir," responded Joyeux.

"G'day, Brett," said Noelle. "We left a sweet homestead behind to come to church."

"Did you?"

"Oh, yes, indeed, mate. Your brothers did a magnificent job. A lovely house – trim, tight, and cozy."

"The house can't be very big."

"It's all we need for now," said Joyeux in her soft voice and soft accent. "It feels very Irish to me."

Marianne urged her paint stallion Arquero up the hill. "And very Dutch to me. It's sturdily built."

"Ha." Noelle grinned. "And very Aussie to me – nothing fancy, it just works."

Tommy came out of the church as the women rode up to the front door and dismounted. "How do? My name's Teresina David, sister to these critters, but you might as well call me Tommy. Welcome to Lazarus Top."

Joyeux extended her hand. "Joyeux McCain. I came over from Ireland."

"That's some horse you have there."

"Donegal's grand. A happy mix of Shire, Ardennes, and strawberry roan. I'll just get him in the shade. And he'll be needing some water."

"There's a stream," said Tommy.

Noelle took off her hat. "Noelle Saunders, Teresina. Australia. Hoping to make a fresh beginning in the New Mexico Territory."

She and Tommy shook hands.

Tommy saw the smile on her brother Adam's face. "I guess you're off to a good start, Noelle."

Noelle glanced at brother and sister quickly and laughed. "Oh, well, it's no great secret. He's fine. He's very fine."

Tommy slapped Adam on the leg as he sat in the saddle. "You see? I knew you'd amount to something if I prayed long enough and hard enough."

"I am forever in your debt."

"Are you? Then perhaps you can do the same for me."

Adam whistled. 'That would take a lot of prayer and fasting. Not sure I'm up to it. Maybe we could ask the whole congregation tomorrow."

"Let's not."

Marianne introduced her daughter. "This is Selah. The puppy is Spurs. And I am Marianne Freeman." She gripped Tommy's hand. "I'm very glad to meet you."

"Dutch, you said?" asked Tommy.

"*Ja*. My maiden name is Van Brewer. Freeman is my husband's name."

Tommy's face went dark. "They explained to me that all three of you were widows. Like Dianna and Dana. I'm so sorry."

"Thank you."

Dana popped out of the church door. "Marianne! You made it!"

The two women hugged.

"It's good to see you, very good," said Marianne, smiling. 'Where is Dianna?"

"She'll be out in a moment. She heard your voice but she's just finishing up with a bench, making it smooth for all the bottoms tomorrow." Dana shook the brown hair that fell in waves to her shoulders and small curls of wood drifted to the ground. "We are using carpenter's planes."

Michael looked out the door. "There you are. I wondered where you had vanished to."

Marianne watched a blush spread over Dana's face.

"Michael was helping me – helping us," Dana said.

Michael lifted his hat. "Mrs. Freeman."

"Reverend David."

"I prefer Michael."

"I prefer Marianne."

"All right. You win, Marianne."

"*Danke*. I like winning."

"Winning what?" Dianna squeezed past Michael, a plane in her hand, and wood shavings on her arms. "Marianne, it is so very good to see you. It's been ages."

They hugged and kissed each other on the cheek.

"Well, I think it has been a long time, much longer than we anticipated the last time we met by the Rio Oro," replied Marianne. "Our whole world has changed since then. Everything about our lives has changed."

Dianna laughed. "Oh, my dear, you have no idea."

Marianne arched a dark eyebrow. "I don't?"

Dianna took her friend by the arm. "Get your horses in the shade. Water them. Then come inside and help Dana and I plane. We'll chase Michael out." Dianna turned and smiled at Joyeux and Noelle. "Please join us. I want to make your acquaintance."

"I've never planed," protested Joyeux.

"Neither had I until two days ago."

Dana put her arm around Selah. "You too. All the ladies will squirrel away in the church. It will be the first meeting of the Lazarus Top Women's Missionary Society."

"What about my puppy Spurs?"

"Spurs can bring the message of encouragement and inspiration."

The church was finished at dusk. Brett gave a brief prayer then they all headed for the Charming Ranch for the night. Michael and Dana left the group and headed for her house on the Fleming spread to see how the hired hands were getting along. They intended to stay over.

"We'll be at the church by nine tomorrow morning," said Brett.

Michael nodded. "Dana and I'll be there."

"I hope things are exactly the way they should be at your ranch." Brett smiled at Dana. "If not, give us a shout and we'll be on our way."

"Thank you, Brett," she replied.

"Brother, it won't be anything my two hands can't deal with," promised Michael.

"Is that right?"

"Well, my two hands and God."

"Glad you brought him into the picture." Brett tugged on the brim of his hat. *"Vaya con Dios."*

"Gracias, hermano."

"Thank you, Brett," said Dana.

Tommy grinned. "Mind your p's and q's, Mikey. Big sister won't be there to get you out of a jam."

Michael laughed, tilting his hat back on his head. "Ha. The only jam I intend to get into is the jar at the breakfast table so's I can spread it on my toast. *Adios.*"

Dana nudged her sorrel mare Juniper to the left and Michael joined her. The sun was just resting on the tops of the Sangre de Cristo Mountains and the light was a mix of yellow, amber, copper, and gold. Michael reached over and rested a gloved hand on the fingers Dana had curled around her reins.

"I've been so busy hammering nails and sawing boards I haven't looked much at God's splendors."

Dana looked at the color of the sky. "I know what you mean. I never grow tired of it."

"Of course there are splendors and there are splendors." His green eyes glimmered with the sunset. "Hammering and sawing has its advantages if God wants you to see something else he made up sweet and fancy."

Dana felt the heat inching up from her neck to her face. "That's kind of you to say."

"A man has no idea where following God is going to take him. You think you're going to plant a few churches and move on. Then you start planting the churches and you fall head over heels down the ladder."

Dana's face burned. "Is that what happened?"

"Pretty much. I apologize. I guess this has all happened way too fast for you."

"Don't apologize. I like fast. Just like my friend Dianna."

"Really? How fast, Dana?"

"Full gallop. I have a lot of living to make up for. I've been lonely a long time."

Michael reined in his horse. "Full gallop?"

"That's what I said. With spurs."

He looked at her in astonishment. "That's the kind of thing I'd expect your friend Dianna to say. Not you."

Dana brought Juniper to a stop. "Why not?"

"You're quiet. Your smile is soft. Everything about you is gentle."

"Oh, Dianna is all those things too."

"Sure. And the next minute she's sizzling like the fuse on a stick of dynamite. Reuben latched onto a handful with her."

Dana leaned over from her saddle. "You may not know it, but so did you the moment you looked up from your nails and took an interest in me." Her black-gloved hand hooked around his neck and drew his head towards hers. Her lips were over his before he could say another word and she kept them there a long time. Finally she pulled away. "How's that for some sizzle, Reverend?"

His face was crimson. "I lost my breath."

"That was the idea. It's what I like to do when I kiss a man. I was afraid I'd be rusty."

"If that's rusty I'm in trouble."

Dana grinned. "You're not in trouble. You're in luck."

She leaned over and tugged his head towards hers again. The grip of her hand in her leather glove tightened and her lips pressed against his with more and more force and more and more heat. Then she drew back again.

"That's what's inside quiet women." Her gloved hand stroked the side of his face. "At least, that's what's inside this one." She patted his cheek. "Are you going to show me what you've got, preacher?"

"What I've got?"

"Kissing and hugging. That's all I'm talking about this side of the altar."

"The altar?"

"That's what I said."

"Are you thinking about marriage already?"

"A gal's always thinking about marriage after a couple of good kisses. Does that scare you off?"

He put his hand over the hand that was still on his cheek. "Are you trying to give me cold feet, Dana?"

"Not really. I'm just pushing you a little. Like I said, I want to see what you've got."

He glanced over his shoulder. "Looks like the crew is long gone."

"Yes, sir. Long gone. But I'm still here."

"What did you say about spurs?"

Dana laughed. "Why? Do you have any?"

In one swift movement he was off his horse, had her off her saddle and in his arms, and was giving her kisses so hard and fast her hat fell to the ground and she almost lost her grip on the reins in her hand.

"Michael," she murmured, her eyes closed.

"Hey, this is what I've got inside me."

His lips were on hers again, down her neck to the scoop of her shoulder, he tugged back the collar of her shirt and nipped her.

"Ow," she said.

"Did it hurt that much?"

"I'm more surprised is all."

"Didn't you say spurs?"

Still holding onto her reins she knocked his hat off and tangled her black-gloved fingers in his hair. "Yes, I did. You go right ahead, green eyes. And don't spare the horses."

He lifted her off the desert floor, his lips on her mouth and her throat, his teeth pressing gently into the soft warm skin of her shoulder, his arms squeezing all the air and words out of her so that she was left hanging onto his back, taking his kisses, feeling his strength, and beginning to believe she was a white feather spinning up and up in the copper and bronze of a New Mexican sunset.

"Where are we?" she finally asked.

"The same place where we started." His face was buried in the long waves of her gleaming brown hair.

"Are you sure?"

"Well, pretty lady, we are in the same physical location. Where we are now in terms of spirit and emotions, I can't properly say."

Gently he placed her on the ground.

She ran her gloved hands over his chest and smiled up into his face.

"Let's not hurry to the ranch house," she said.

"Let's not," he replied.

Notices had been put up in Cazadora about the church service at Lazarus Top. Brett hoped that ranchers who came in for supplies would read them and make their way to the church Sunday morning. Invitations had been sent to homesteads all over that part of the county as well, Adam and Joseph doing the lion's share after a day's work building the homestead for Noelle, Marianne, and Joyeux. Adam had been the one to mail a cordial welcome to Ahab Hawthorne's spread near Santa Fe.

"Noelle wrote most of it." Adam was standing with the others by the church on Sunday morning, watching the horizon. "I just signed it."

"On behalf of who?" asked Brett.

"The Methodist Church. And the Brothers."

"The brothers?"

"Capital T and capital B."

"You make us sound like some sort of family business."

"Aren't we?"

"I see dust. And three wagons in a row." Marianne pointed with the barrel of her Henry rifle.

Everyone squinted.

"Marianne." Brett was half-laughing. "I swear you have the eyes of a golden eagle."

She shrugged. "I have the eyes God gave me. There are two persons in the first wagon, six in the second, four in the last."

The humor had not disappeared from Brett's face or voice. "Can you tell me how many men and women and children? How old they are? What they had for breakfast?"

Marianne slid her dark eyes onto him. "Sure. Give me one more minute, Brett Daniel."

"I will." His eyes lingered on hers. "I will."

"I see them now." Reuben nodded. "Three wagons it is. And there's another coming up from the south, see?"

"Another wagon," agreed Michael, "and two riders in front of it."

Over the next half hour close to fifty settlers and ranchers – men, women, and children – made their way to the white church on Lazarus Top. The brothers welcomed them all and encouraged them to find a seat on one of the benches the ladies had planed smooth. Bobby handed out ragged hymnals and Luke prepared to lead the singing. Noelle sat with Adam, Dianna with Reuben, and Dana with Michael. Marianne shared a bench with her daughter Selah and the Irish woman Joyeux. Marianne stared at the backs of Dianna and Dana.

Everyone is pairing up. The widows are finding new love. All except me and Joyeux.

"Is there room for a spinster on this bench?" asked Tommy, sliding in beside Joyeux.

Joyeux cocked a scarlet eyebrow. "That's what you call yourself? A spinster?"

"That's the word for an unmarried woman. I admit bachelor sounds much better but the men have taken the term for themselves."

"There's many a single man glancing your way right now that wouldn't apply the word spinster to a fine lady such as yourself."

"I honestly haven't noticed, Joey. I'm not interested in finding a match for myself. For a flaming beauty like yourself now, or the flashing dark-eyed Marianne, that's another matter. I'm at your service."

"At our service, are you? Well, I've a soft spot for your brother Joseph, and Marianne is keen on Brett, so perhaps you can help with that."

"I am not keen on Brett," hissed Marianne.

Now Joyeux raised both eyebrows. "Of course you are."

"I haven't made up my mind about him at all. And I have no idea how he feels about me."

"No idea? Well, I can give you an idea. You've taken a fancy to him and he's taken a fancy to you."

"I haven't. And he hasn't."

"I can find out." Tommy was smiling. "I can certainly find out."

"I don't care," said Marianne.

"I care," responded Joyeux.

"Whether you care or not, my curiosity is piqued," replied Tommy. "I'll make some discreet inquiries after the service."

"Don't you dare!" snapped Marianne.

"Please dare," said Joyeux with a wink.

"Folks, I want to welcome you here this fine morning," announced Luke in a strong voice. "My name is Luke David and I'm an ordained minister with the Methodist Church in America. So are all my brothers who you see dressed in black and seated in various parts of the sanctuary or standing outside keeping an eye on things. This is the Lazarus Methodist Mission Church, the land it was built on is owned by the Methodist Church of America, and we dedicate the building and the land to the glory of God. We expect it to be here to bless all of you for many years to come. Brother Brett, will you open in prayer? Then I'd like us to sing *Nearer My God to Thee* and praise the good Lord."

"Amen," responded Brett. "Let's pray."

He bowed his head. Like the other men in the church building, Brett had already removed his hat. All the women and girls wore bonnets except Tommy who had taken off her black hat for the service.

Brett opened his mouth to begin when the door swung open.

A tall man wearing a gold paisley vest and a suit white as summer clouds entered. His hat was black and it was in his hand.

Whispers erupted throughout the sanctuary.

Hawthorne.

It's Ahab Hawthorne.

Now he'll see we're here.
There's going to be trouble.

Hawthorne, his lean, sun-browned face, with its trim beard, breaking into a perfect smile, lifted one hand as if to stop a rider. "I'm not here to collect rent or debate land claims. I want to welcome the Methodist Church to the county and worship God alongside all you good people. It's a fine building, isn't it? You can see it gracing Lazarus Top from miles away. Such a blessing. I have a number of my men with me, as well as Sheriff Westcott and his deputies from Cazadora. I hope there's room for them."

Brett nodded. "Yes, sir. There always seem to be seats available at the front in every Methodist church." He indicated several empty benches with his hand. "Please help yourself and welcome to the House of the Lord."

"Thank you kindly, Reverend."

Ahab Hawthorne walked down the center aisle to the front. Right through the door behind him came eight men, hats off, spurs jangling as they followed Hawthorne and took their seats on a bench beside him. Sheriff Teddy Westcott and his five deputies were next. Eyes darting from left to right, Westcott led his men to a bench across the aisle from Hawthorne. Blacksticks and Red Beard did not remove their hats. Hawthorne cast a sharp glance at them and their hats were off in an instant.

"We'll pray," said Brett.

Dianna and Marianne and Dana bowed their heads like everyone else but anger twisted its way through each of their chests.

You murdered our husbands.
You shot our ranch hands.
You burned us out.

They could not concentrate on Brett's prayer. Marianne forgot the words as soon as he spoke them. Her face burned and her heart was cold and dark.

I have my pistol in my belt. I could pull it out and shoot you in the back and call it God's justice.

But her hands remained in her lap.

"In Christ's name, amen," said Brett.

Luke began to sing in a clear, pure voice, holding a hymnal and beckoning with his free hand for the congregation to rise. Hawthorne was first to his feet, followed quickly by his men and Teddy Westcott and his deputies. For a moment, only Hawthorne and Luke were singing, as if they were performing a duet. Then the brothers were joining in, and Tommy and Joyeux and Marianne. Soon all the women and men were on their feet and singing with more and more strength.

Nearer, my God, to Thee, nearer to Thee
E'en though it be a cross that raiseth me
Still all my song shall be nearer, my God, to Thee
Nearer, my God, to Thee, nearer to Thee

Though like the wanderer, the sun gone down
Darkness be over me, my rest a stone
Yet in my dreams I'd be nearer, my God, to Thee
Nearer, my God, to Thee, nearer to Thee

There let the way appear steps unto heav'n
All that Thou sendest me in mercy giv'n
Angels to beckon me nearer, my God, to Thee
Nearer, my God, to Thee, nearer to Thee

Then with my waking thoughts bright with Thy praise
Out of my stony griefs Bethel I'll raise
So by my woes to be nearer, my God, to Thee
Nearer, my God, to Thee, nearer to Thee

Or if on joyful wing, cleaving the sky
Sun, moon, and stars forgot, upwards I fly
Still all my song shall be, nearer, my God, to Thee
Nearer, my God, to Thee, nearer to Thee

Once the hymn was finished, and everyone had sat down, Bobby and Scott passed their hats for the offering. A large wad of United States dollar bills dropped into Bobby's hat from

Ahab Hawthorne's hands. A number of settlers and ranchers put coins in the hats. Then Reuben preached from a large black Bible he held in front of him. The passage was from Joshua. He read the verses in a dramatic voice.

Now after the death of Moses the servant of the Lord it came to pass, that the Lord spake unto Joshua the son of Nun, Moses' minister, saying,

Moses my servant is dead; now therefore arise, go over this Jordan, thou, and all this people, unto the land which I do give to them, even to the children of Israel.

Every place that the sole of your foot shall tread upon, that have I given unto you, as I said unto Moses.

From the wilderness and this Lebanon even unto the great river, the river Euphrates, all the land of the Hittites, and unto the great sea toward the going down of the sun, shall be your coast.

There shall not any man be able to stand before thee all the days of thy life: as I was with Moses, so I will be with thee: I will not fail thee, nor forsake thee.

Be strong and of a good courage: for unto this people shalt thou divide for an inheritance the land, which I sware unto their fathers to give them.

Only be thou strong and very courageous, that thou mayest observe to do according to all the law, which Moses my servant commanded thee: turn not from it to the right hand or to the left, that thou mayest prosper withersoever thou goest.

This book of the law shall not depart out of thy mouth; but thou shalt meditate therein day and night, that thou mayest observe to do according to all that is written therein: for then thou shalt make thy way prosperous, and then thou shalt have good success.

Have not I commanded thee? Be strong and of a good courage; be not afraid, neither be thou dismayed: for the Lord thy God is with thee whithersoever thou goest.

As Reuben preached, he kept repeating the phrase, *Be strong and courageous,* and encouraging the people to trust God with their land, their crops, their livestock, and their future. Dianna felt a warmth go right through she was so proud of him. She glanced across the aisle at Ahab Hawthorne – was he uncomfortable? Was he squirming? She couldn't tell.

"We'll sing a final hymn," Reuben finally said, closing the Bible in his hands. "Then Brother Brett will close in prayer."

He sat down and Luke got up.

"Turn in your hymnals to *Amazing Grace*, please," Luke asked the congregation. "Let's stand together."

Tommy and Marianne and Joyeux beat Hawthorne to their feet and sang heartily from the first words. It sounded like they were trying to drown him out. By the end of the hymn the whole congregation was singing so loudly the windows were vibrating. Brett smiled when he stood up to close in prayer.

"That did my soul good," he said. "Your singing, Reuben's message, the very strong sense of God's presence in this place, it blessed me. I believe God is here to stay in New Mexico. To Christ be the glory. Amen."

Amen, said Ahab Hawthorne.

Amen, said the brothers.

Amen, said the widows and Tommy.

Amen and amen, echoed men and women in the congregation.

Brett lifted his hand in blessing. "Go in peace. We'll meet here again next Sunday. I hope all of you can linger with us a bit. We have some big pots of coffee to drink up. You'll find them under the trees and out of the sun. And there's lemonade for the children."

Hawthorne cleared his throat as people began to move towards the door. The shuffling stopped and eyes looked down or looked at him. He hooked his thumbs in his gun belt where two pearl handled revolvers were snug in their holsters.

"I was blessed as much as the good Reverend David was. Let me just say that godly churches are much needed in the New Mexico Territory. I know it will elevate the life of the people in a way that will hearten officials in Santa Fe. There have been, I admit, some hard times and some misunderstandings. Let me just say that I will always honor the deeds many of you purchased from me. As for those land claims that are disputed, I should like to declare an amnesty of thirty days. Come and see me and we'll set things right. There doesn't need to be further trouble. I don't wish to chastise any more of you or bring the law down on your heads. Have a coffee with me under the trees and we'll get everything straightened out."

Marianne saw Brett out of the corner of her eye but she could not stop herself. "The law! Are you the law? What gives you the right to shoot people in cold blood and burn their houses down around their ears?"

"No one was shot in cold blood," Hawthorne replied.

"What are you talking about?" shouted Dianna. "You killed my husband and Dana's and Marianne's down by the Rio Oro! All of them were shot in the back!"

"If that was done it was done without my knowledge."

"Of course it was done with your knowledge!" Dana's brown eyes were lit with fire and burned a sharp gold. "You've railroaded everyone in the county! You've railroaded everyone in New Mexico! No one pulls a gun without your permission! You should be in prison!" She pointed her finger at him. "Heaven knows how many people you've bullied in this church! We ought to all get ahold of you right now and string you up! That would be a good thing to do on a Sunday! That would be a truly righteous act!"

Hawthorne's eyes went black and a hand fell on the pearl handle of one of his revolvers. "No, that would be a mistake, ma'am. A mistake that anyone who laid a hand on me would pay for with their life. Maybe even their soul."

Marianne's pistol was suddenly in her hand. "The only soul that's going to be lost is yours!"

Brett shouted, "Marianne!"

Hawthorne and his men drew.

Sheriff Teddy Westcott put his six-gun to Marianne's head.

In a blink, all the brothers in the church had yanked their revolvers from their holsters. Four of their guns were on the sheriff and his deputies, another four on Hawthorne and his men.

"Not in a church, never in a church," warned Brett. "I swore to the Lord I would never harm a man in the House of God."

"That was your oath," seethed Hawthorne. He swung both his pistols on Brett. "It was not mine."

He cocked back the hammers on his guns.

The door flew open and banged against the wall. Benjamin ran in, a Yellowboy Winchester in his grip.

"Blood Lance just swept in from the west with sixty warriors, as far as I can count," he said. "We have maybe three minutes to get ready to fight back or get wiped out."

The Fight

Blood Lance!

Everyone in the church froze, their guns still pointed at one another.

Ahab Hawthorne didn't take his eyes off Marianne or her pistol, keeping both of his aimed at her. "Cana. See if what he's saying is true."

A tall man in black with golden hair and sharp gray eyes, pistol drawn, edged down the center aisle between the benches. He pushed past Benjamin and disappeared out the door but he was back in seconds.

"They're coming, Boss," he said. "Fast gallop. And they got rifles."

Brett was the first to holster his gun. "Women and children in the church. And half a dozen of the men with Winchesters. The others need to unharness the horses and put the wagons on their sides and make a wall."

Hawthorne hesitated. Then he slipped his pistols into their holsters.

"Put up your guns, boys," he ordered. 'We have something worse to deal with than widows and preachers." He made for the door. "You heard what the Reverend said. Let's unharness the teams and push those wagons over. Cana. Cavanaugh. Stay in the church and shoot from here. Bust out the windows before the Apache do it for us and send flying glass all over the room."

Brett was on Hawthorne's heels. "Reuben. Joseph. Adam. Stick with Tommy and the others and make your stand from here. No one gets the women and children. No one. Understand?"

"I don't need to stay in here," protested Tommy.

Brett's eyes were dark rock. "We need you in here. We need you to shoot from here. We need you to defend holy ground. Understood?"

Tommy backed down. "I've got it."

Glass began shattering as men used their rifle stocks to smash them open. Children and women began to scream. Joseph ran up to Joyeux and put a Yellowboy in her hands.

"Do you know how to use this?" he asked her.

"No, I don't," she answered as more glass broke with a crash.

"Work the lever to put fresh rounds in the breech. Use the sights to aim and make sure you aim low for the knees. That way if the barrel jerks up when you fire you'll still hit your target in the stomach or chest."

"I can't do that, Joseph."

Hard edges came into his boyish face. "This isn't a quick raid, Joey. They have more than fifty of the settlers here. The sheriff and his deputies. Hawthorne. They can wipe us all out in one blow. They'll surround us and keep firing until there's no one moving. Then burn the church and wagons down around our bodies. That's how they wage war. That's how they defend their land. The question for you is how you intend to defend your own."

"My own?"

"I look at you and I think of gentleness. I think of peace. I know you'd be the best mother in the world and there's twelve or fifteen kids here for you to mother. But even a she wolf knows when it's time to fight for her young. What are you going to do, Joey? Are you going to fight? Or let the children die?"

Joyeux stared at him a moment. Then she took the Winchester from his hands.

"I work the lever and it's ready to shoot?"

"That's right."

"What if I need more bullets?"

"Shout."

She half-smiled as men and women rushed past all around her. "All right, Joseph. I'll shout."

He smiled back. "Why not call me Joey too? Then we're a pair."

"Would you like to be a pair?"

"I would. But time kind of got away from me here and now we're in this mess."

"I like Joseph. But let's be Joey and Joey today." She moved a hand towards his smooth cheek, stopped, saw the soft color in his eyes, and reached all the way with her fingers to touch his face. "Thank you."

Rifles began to fire.

"They're coming up the hillside!" one of the settlers yelled.

Joseph took her by the arm. "Let's get to a window and do this fight together."

"All right. Joey."

Two of Hawthorne's men were already at the window Joseph led her towards. They were aiming and firing as rapidly as they could, gun smoke covering them in a thick cloud. Just as she and Joseph reached the men she glimpsed Apache warriors with red headbands gallop past the church, Winchesters just like hers flashing. Both of Hawthorne's men flew backwards, half their faces gone from a spray of bullets. She slapped a hand to her mouth and gagged.

"Steady," Joseph said in a low voice. "Steady. Let the other women tend to their bodies."

"I can't do this."

"You have to do this." He knelt by the window. "They were too exposed. Get down." Joyeux remained rooted to the spot. Joseph reached up, put a hand on her thin shoulder, and pushed her to her knees. "Shoot and duck. Shoot and duck."

Guns were going off all around the church, whether it was those of the Apache on the outside or those of the women and men inside. Joyeux saw Marianne crouched by the open door, a door already pockmarked with bullet holes, firing her Henry rifle. Right beside her were Noelle and Adam, both of them on their knees and working the levers on their Yellowboys as fast as they could. She saw Dana and Dianna at windows on the other side of the church, Reuben with Dianna, and Dana with Tommy, and all of them were shooting. The children, crying and moaning, had been herded into the middle of the sanctuary by Selah and their mothers sat in a circle around them. A girl looked at Joyeux, fear and hope struggling in her blue eyes.

All right, little one. Don't be afraid, little one. I am going to fight for you. We are all going to fight for you.

She worked the lever on her Winchester and threw it to her shoulder as she saw the others doing.

Uncertain how to aim, she squinted through the iron sights and along the barrel, caught a blur with her open eye, and fired. The barrel jumped up.

"Hold tight when you fire." Joseph tracked a warrior with his rifle. "Every shot has to count. If we run out of ammo before they do, we're dead."

Brett came running when there was a lull and threw himself through the church door. Another band of warriors raced up the slope firing their Winchesters and peppered the front of the church.

"Are you crazy?" Marianne shouted at him. "You could have been killed!"

Brett sat up, one arm full of canteens, the other full of saddlebags. "Had to make a try. Blood Lance isn't going to leave anytime soon. You'll need water in here. And ammunition. I pulled yours off of your horse."

"My horse! Is Arquero hurt?"

"No. The Apache tried to stampede the horses right off but we've got them tied tight to the trees. Now they're trying to shoot them but we have every horse down on the ground and out of sight. Blood Lance has only killed a couple so far. Your paint is all right." He tossed her saddlebag to her. "I reckon you have your revolver ammo in there too."

"Yes."

"What woman goes to church services with a Colt pistol at her waist and a Henry rifle on her shoulder?"

"The prudent Dutch kind. This is not Amsterdam. This is the American frontier."

He smiled. "Uh huh." He looked around the church. "Who's been shot?"

"Two of Hawthorne's men are dead. And one of the deputies. Reuben took a bullet in the shoulder. Dianna dressed it and you can see he's still firing."

"Did she get the bullet out?"

"Not yet. She said she would need flame to be sure her knife was clean as well as to cauterize the wound."

"All of you have your heads on tight. We'll have to get that bullet out before nightfall."

"You think they'll still be here?"

"No cavalry's going to rescue us, Marianne. Blood Lance'll be here for days. He'll try and stop up our water."

Ice cut at Marianne's spine. "Can he do that?"

Brett shrugged. "The stream emerges from underground on this knoll. Then it disappears again over the side and under the rocks. I guess if he knew where to get at a piece of it he could try and dam it or poison it."

"Is everyone all right out there?"

"There's a settler dead. Another two ranchers wounded."

"Are your wagons holding up?"

Brett nodded. "Their wood's thick. We've got them in a tight circle right up to the back of the church. But what worries me is the Apache are bound to use fire arrows soon. I don't know what will happen then."

The ice on her spine again. "Can't you put them out?"

"Depends on how many fires they start at once. If I were Blood Lance, and I felt I had to get back my land from us the way he does, I'd make sure I hit the wagons with three or four arrows each, all at the same time. And if the ranchers got those out, I'd be sure there were another two or three dozen arrows ready to fly the moment the white men thought they were safe. And I'd do it at night, just to make it harder to draw the water from the stream and throw it on the flames."

"So if he thinks like you, Brett, what are you going to do?"

Brett grinned as bullets slapped into the open door near them and Noelle fired rapidly in response. "You called me by my Christian name."

Guns going off in their ears, bullets thudding into the walls or whistling through the windows and door, warriors screeching as they raced past or shot at the church from behind the rocks, Marianne still found the presence of mind to blush up from her neck. "No, I didn't."

"Sounded like Brett."

"I'm sure I said Reverend."

"You might have said bet or fret or pet. But you sure didn't say Reverend, Marianne."

Wood chips came flying off the doorframe and they both ducked. Then they looked at each other and laughed.

"This is not a time for courting," Marianne said, still laughing.

"I think it's the perfect time. Especially since we might not live past two or three more days. I'd hate to miss out on what my brothers have been thanking God for."

"And what's that?"

"Love. Arms around me. A kiss. Maybe even two kisses."

Marianne felt the heat in her cheeks grow. "Two kisses?"

"Or one long one."

"Is that what you wish from me?"

"Before I die."

"Before you die? Who is going to die?"

"God knows. I don't. But he also knows, like I said, that I don't want to miss out. They tell me there's no kissing in heaven. That we're like the angels. So the kisses have to happen here."

Warmth moved through her whole body. "Suddenly the restrained and sober Brett Daniel David is so bold."

"No more time for restrained and sober. So I thought I'd try reckless for once in my life."

He reached up quickly with his hand, brought Marianne's head down before she realized what he was doing, and kissed her quickly. So much heat went into the kiss it was like touching her lips to a hot gun barrel as she blew smoke from its muzzle. Her mouth felt scorched. The sensation shot through her like a bullet. He pulled away and she thought for a moment she was going to fall to the floor.

"I've got to give out the ammo and the canteens," he said. "Watch yourself."

Her face flamed. "Watch myself from the Apache or from you?"

"Apache and Methodists are both dangerous in different ways."

The Apache were behind the rocks. Michael, peering out from the wheel of a wagon riddled with bullet holes, counted nine dead warriors and four horses scattered over the dirt. He had been to the other side of the circle of wagons and counted another seven dead as well as three horses.

"They still got plenty," grunted Hawthorne, who had been fighting beside Michael most of the afternoon.

'Why haven't they tried to set the church or wagons on fire?"

"Blood Lance'll get to it. He's waiting for dark." Hawthorne pulled out a gold pocket watch. "Couple of hours. His charge didn't work so now they'll snipe at us from the rocks. I expect he'll have a few of his men rooting around for another spot where the stream shows above ground. They'll block it up till we don't get more than a trickle. Then we'll have nothing to put the fires out with but blankets."

"Dry blankets won't do much."

"At least the ones we have today will be wet." Hawthorne jerked a thumb over his shoulder. "The boys soaked a few and they're hanging on the tree branches. Had 'em fill every wagon bucket and canteen and everything we could find that could hold a few drops. Just in case."

"Good thinking." Michael glanced at the church. "What if they set fire to the roof?"

"Someone goes up there on a couple of stacked barrels."

"The Apache'll pick him off."

"If they wait until dark it will work in our favor too."

Michael's eyes remained on the church.

"Your brother Brett can't make it back out till nightfall," said Hawthorne, following Michael's gaze. "He'd be too easy a target now."

"I wasn't thinking of him."

"I expect the women and children are all right."

"We don't know that."

"Is there someone you favor in there?"

"Maybe."

Hawthorne glanced around the circle and spotted the man he wanted. "Cana."

The blond man in black looked at Hawthorne. "Yeah, Boss."

"Think you can steal in one of those windows with more water for the kids?"

"Sure. But I won't be able to steal back out. The Apache'll draw a bead on that window."

"You don't need to come out right away. But I do want you to find out if a woman inside is all right."

"Why?"

Hawthorne smiled. "My shooting partner here needs to know. What's her name, Mike?"

Michael stared at Hawthorne in surprise and didn't respond for several seconds. "Dana. Dana Fleming."

Hawthorne nodded. "Cana, you find out how she is. Then you just dangle that hat of yours out the window. Any window. That'll mean she's doing fine."

"I got you, Boss."

Michael watched Cana scoop up three canteens and size up the closest window. Suddenly he ran up to the church wall, still crouching down behind the wagons, squeezed through a narrow opening between the last wagon and the church, sprang at a window, jumped, and shoved himself through it, legs wriggling. Bullets banged into the wall and Michael saw his boot heel go flying but Cana was in. A few of the ranchers, his brothers, and Hawthorne's men whistled and clapped. Michael kept his eye on the window. A minute went by. His throat tightened.

Suppose he never does put his hat out that window? Or any window?

All of a sudden the hat was there. Out and in the same window Cana had wrestled through. Bullets smacked the wall. Rifle barrels poked out and flamed as men and women inside the church fired back.

"There." Hawthorne smiled at Michael. "She's in one piece."

"You didn't need to do that, Mr. Hawthorne."

"Why not? If we're going to die together we might as well do one another a few favors."

"Kind of surprised a killer would do that sort of thing for a preacher."

Hawthorne narrowed his eyes. "Cana's no killer. Never did that kind of work. Just moves my cattle and runs the crew. I'm no killer either."

"So who does the killing? Santa Claus?"

"It's not what you think."

"Tell me what I should think."

"I run a lot less of the show than you imagine I do. I've never ordered a man shot in my life."

Michael frowned. "Who burns out the settlers? Who killed those widows' husbands?"

"Arrows!" Benjamin shouted, pointing with his finger.

Hawthorne got to his feet, head down. "Looks like Blood Lance isn't going to wait until sunset."

Four arrows, trailing sparks and smoke, arched up from the rocks. One landed short, sticking itself in the ground by the church door. Another embedded itself in a wall but the flame on its tip went out immediately. The other two struck the roof and a fire sprang up.

"Westcott!" cried Hawthorne. "Get one of your men up there!"

"I ain't going up there!" roared Blacksticks. "We already lost Nick taking on three Apache by himself!"

"Westcott!" Hawthorne's face was full of blood. "Get a man up there before the whole church goes up! Cana took the last risk!"

Westcott scowled. "It's enough risk just being here behind these wagons on account you wanted to show up at church."

"Westcott!"

Michael tugged off his hat and dropped his rifle. "Never mind. It's the brothers' turn. I'm going up. Cover me as best you can."

"Let me do it," argued Scott, a few feet away.

"I thought of it first. Just get up on that wagon and shoot straight."

Michael ran between the horses and grabbed one of the blankets. With the firing sporadic now most of them had calmed down but a few snorted and bared their teeth. Hawthorne had stacked two barrels on top of each other. He made a cradle with his hands, Michael glanced at him and planted a boot there, and Hawthorne shoved him upwards. Michael caught the rim of the top barrel, Hawthorne kept pushing, and finally he was on top. Michael could reach the roof with his hands. Blanket over his shoulders, he yanked himself up. Running at a crouch he reached the spreading flames and began to hit them with the soaking wet blanket. Bullets chipped the roof around his feet. He got the fire out and ran back the way he had come. He was just about to climb down when he heard someone yelling. Turning around he saw three more arrows hit the roof. Flames shot up.

"Crawl to the fire!" shouted Hawthorne. "Don't stand up!"

Michael dropped to all fours.

"We're going to go out and doing a little raiding ourselves." Hawthorne had both of his pistols in his hands. "We sure can't sit here all day and night and let them try and burn us up." He nodded at Westcott. "You first. Then me and my boys. And the preachers if they have the guts. We're going to give Blood Lance a bloody nose."

Westcott spat. "I ain't going out there. Let the church go up. The kids can jump out the windows."

"The Apache want your hair too."

"Then they can come in here and get it. I ain't gonna go out there and make it easy for them."

Hawthorne waved the barrel of one of his pistols. "Get going. Mike is up there on that roof and he needs us to draw off the Apache guns."

"I told you. I ain't – "

Hawthorne fired. The bullet cut open Westcott's shirtsleeve and blood sprayed from his shoulder. Westcott yelped and clamped a hand to the wound.

"Get moving or the next one opens up your stomach," growled Hawthorne.

"I'm bleeding."

"Not much. Go." Hawthorne waved his guns at the four deputies. "All of you. Slip out from between the wagons and jump over the edge of the hill. They won't be expecting it. Me and my boys'll be right behind you giving you cover fire."

Scott was smiling. "And so will the preachers. Shooting and praying, praying and shooting. Can't get better cover fire than that."

Slowly, led by Simon Hartstone, the deputies squeezed between two of the wagons one after another. As soon as they were out Hawthorne was right behind them.

"Open up!" he shouted, glancing back at the settlers and ranchers. "Open up with everything you've got!"

Michael was sprawled flat on the church roof when the guns erupted. Head down, he looked to his left and saw his brothers darting among the rocks while settlers and ranchers fired ahead of them. He could not see the Apache but bullets ricocheted off dirt and stones by Luke and Bobby and now and then he spotted gun flashes from hidden barrels. An arrow lodged in the wall of the church and flames gnawed at the white paint and wood. He used his elbows and knees to work himself to the edge and dangled the scorched blanket over the side but he could not reach the burning shaft. A shot clipped his ear. He cried out, put a hand on the cut skin, and jumped as another shot threw wood chips in his face. His legs buckled as he hit the ground. Rolling over twice he shook his head, saw flames spreading, heard children screaming, and sprang up, swatting the wall with the blanket. Gunfire cracked and snapped behind him as the men continued to hunt out the Apache scattered over the slope. A bullet drilled into his leg. He fell, got up, leaned against the church wall, and struck at the flames again and again.

Just another twenty seconds, God. Give me that.

He struck out with the blanket three more times and collapsed. The flames were out. Hawthorne scrambled up and got under one of his arms while Luke got under the other, they dragged him to his feet, and tumbled him through a window.

Hawthorne shouted, "He's bleeding! Patch him up!"

He and Luke pressed their backs against the church as shots splintered the wood all around them and fired back at the Apache behind the rocks with their guns, two pistols in Hawthorne's hands, a rifle in Luke's. Barrels that ranchers thrust out the window joined in, spitting flames and hurling bullets. Cana leaned out to get better aim with his Winchester, pumped the lever and pulled the trigger four times in the blink of an eye, and for the first time Luke actually saw one of the Apache warriors. He'd been hit in his bare chest, and he was flying backwards, his own Winchester spinning out of his hands and turning over and over.

"Get down to the rocks or jump through the window!" barked Cana. "Make your minds up quick!"

Luke and Hawthorne scrambled back among the rocks on the slope, firing as they went. Cana continued to work the lever on his Yellowboy and squeeze the trigger. A warrior leaped from behind a boulder and dove towards another but Cana's shots caught him in the air and when he landed he sprawled in the sand and stones and did not get up.

"Who taught you to shoot like that?"

Cana had pulled back from the window and was feeding fresh cartridges into the side gate of his rifle. He glanced at Tommy through the haze of gun smoke.

"My granddaddy," he answered. "He was killed in the war."

"I'm sorry to hear it." Tommy aimed out the window and fired twice. "But I guess that spares him the grief of watching a favorite grandson go bad."

"What are you talking about?"

"You work for Ahab Hawthorne, don't you?"

"I do, ma'am."

"He's treated people pretty rough in this county. I'd say you're one of the men who does his dirty work for him."

Cana kept loading his rifle. "I don't do dirty work, ma'am."

"What do you call it then?" Tommy fired a third time. "Lawful employment?"

Cana finished reloading and leaned against the wall. "Sounds to me like you want a fight."

"One fight at a time is enough, thank you. But it makes no sense to me why a fine looking man such as yourself has thrown his life away to take on the role of a desperado."

"Who says I have, ma'am?"

"I feel like a repeating rifle – you're one of Ahab Hawthorne's hired guns. That makes you pretty much an outlaw in my books."

"Sorry to hear it, ma'am."

"So am I. And stop calling me ma'am."

Cana looked out the window. "The firing's petering out. Sun's already going down. It'll be dark in half an hour. How much ammo do you have left?"

Tommy reached into the saddlebag Brett had tossed to her hours before. "Seventeen – eighteen – nineteen for the rifle. About three dozen for the pistol. I haven't used it much."

"That's good. We've chased them off the slope for now. But they'll come back with the darkness." He glanced at the children who were still sitting or lying with their hands covering their heads. "How are they?"

"Scared. But only a couple of them are hurt. Wood splinters, not bullets, I thank God."

"And your brother? The one they pushed through the window?"

"He's over in the corner. He's doing all right. Dana is tending to him. He put the fires out."

"I know that."

"So what are you and your Boss going to do now? Take off on your horses as soon as it's night?"

Cana leaned his rifle against the wall. "You have a poor opinion of us. As soon as it's dark I go out there and find a good hiding place. Blood Lance will send his warriors after us once we've had time to relax and grow tired and let our guard down. They'll crawl up here and try to slip into the church. Those of you who are in here need to keep your guns trained on the windows and shut the door tight and block it."

Tommy gave him a hard look. "I think you'll run."

He sat back and closed his eyes. "I reckon dawn will prove you right or wrong. It strikes me a woman like you doesn't think she's wrong much."

"I'm not."

"Meet me at sunup."

'Huh. You'll probably be all the way to Santa Fe by then with your tail between your legs."

Brett slipped out after dark, came back with an armload of blankets, and gave them to the mothers to wrap around the children. He made sure the women had guns on all the windows and then he got the men to follow him outside.

"We're going to be all over the slope and around the church," he told Marianne. "So don't worry. We'll get them before they get you."

"I am worried." She could barely see his face in the blackness. "Whether they try to crawl through the windows or not, that's one thing, but what makes you think they won't surprise you out there?"

"What Blood Lance will expect is to find us cowering in here or behind the wagons. Not ready to jump him from the rocks and bushes."

"They're going to be very quiet, Brett. You won't see them."

"We'll be very quiet too, Marianne. The advantage we have is we know they're coming and we'll be waiting. They don't think we'll be out there ready to ambush them."

"You hardly have any cartridges left. You told me that."

"They didn't have guns or cartridges in Bible days. There are other ways for a man to defend himself and the people he cares about."

Neither of them said anything for a moment. He took strands of her long curly hair in his hand and twisted them carefully around his fingers. They watched each other. Then he kissed her eyes and her hair.

"I'll see you in a few hours." His voice was soft. "We have a lot to talk about."

"*Ja,* we do. So try not to be late, Brett Daniel."

"Barricade the door once we're all out. Use the benches. Use the pulpit."

"Don't worry about that. Just watch out for yourself."

"None of us will come through the windows. Even if we get wounded men we won't thrust them through like we did with Michael. So if you see someone, Marianne, shoot. It will not be me or my brothers or Hawthorne and his hired guns or Teddy Westcott and what's left of his deputies. Shoot."

"I will, Brett Daniel."

"You have the children under your protection."

"I said I will and I meant it. I am the woman who is always pointing a gun at someone, isn't that what you said about me? So you needn't trouble yourself. If I must I will pull the trigger just as I did all afternoon. I am no nun, Reverend David."

His smile was a quick flash in the darkness. "I thank God for that. I must go. The Lord be with you."

He kissed her cheek and was gone.

"And also with you," she said quietly.

"There goes Brett." Joseph finished cramming his pockets with the twelve or thirteen bullets he had left. "Time for me to head out."

"I know that." Joyeux was holding onto his hand. "Do you have anything to tell me?"

He smiled. "I thought you were shy and withdrawn."

"When it suits me." She smiled back. "But everything changed when the Apache attacked. Now our lives are being lived at the pace of racehorses. So I ask you again, do you have anything to tell me?"

"The same things I've said all day while we fought side by side, Joey. You intrigue me. You excite me. You've captured me." He stroked her face with his fingers. "Do you think I'm falling in love with you?"

"That's not something for me to decide. Only you can know that."

"I might be able to give you an answer if I knew what love was supposed to feel like. Instead the day has brought danger and confusion and then there's you on top of it all. My mind is swirling."

"Am I In the middle of the swirl?"

"You're in there somewhere."

"Somewhere?" She sighed. "I've waited this long for a man to come back into my life. I suppose I can wait a little longer."

"It's not like I'm going away on a long journey, Joey. All I'm doing is walking out the door."

"You make it sound like you're going for a stroll in the park, Joseph. But it's dark out there. And the dark could kill you."

"Not me."

Joyeux watched Reuben embrace Dianna and half-run out of the church. Dana was arguing with Michael in as quiet a voice as she could but he pushed himself up off the floor, kissed her on the lips to stop her from arguing, and limped through the doorway, a Winchester in one hand. Joyeux was pretty sure it was Noelle in a corner, far away from everyone else, holding a man in her arms and kissing him as if she wouldn't see him again for a hundred years. When he broke away, and jumped out the closest window, the moon lit up his face, and she saw it was Adam.

Joseph was watching her. "Everyone else is having passionate farewells, is that what you're thinking?"

"I might be."

He took the hat off his head. "If we're racehorses then let's act like we're at the Derby in England." His movements were swift, his arms strong, his lips like sparks against hers. In a minute it was done and he released her to catch her breath and put his hat back on. "How was that?"

"It will do until I see you again, I think. But there had better be more where that came from. You can't kiss a woman like that and never return because that sort of kiss means you're serious. I'll be waiting for you."

"And I'll be back for you." He tugged on his hat brim. "God bless."

"May the stars be fair, the moon give you light, and if you must fight, may your aim be true, and I pray you spare no evil that may fall upon you or upon me or upon the children. And may the road rise up to meet you as well and the morning sun be warm on your face."

"Is that an Irish blessing?"

"After a fashion."

He and Cana left at the same time. Marianne and Dianna closed the door and began to push benches up against it. Noelle and Dana and Tommy pitched in to help and so did several of the ranching women.

They have more than enough. I have no desire in me to talk or joke so I will just settle in and guard my window.

Joyeux sat facing the open window and looking at the moon and stars. Other Irish blessings floated into her mind and she whispered them all. She checked to be sure her rifle was loaded and returned her gaze to a windowsill ripped up by bullets and a night sky flickering with stars the sliver of moon had not washed out.

Beware the knife, Michael. And the hands at your throat. Don't just be watching for the rifle or pistol. Do ye hear me? Hide well. Become the very stones, become the very desert. Be more Apache than the Apache.

"Reverend? Is that you?"

Brett raised his head slowly, knife in his hand.

"There are nine Reverends here, including my sister," he whispered. "Who's that?"

"Hawthorne."

"Ah. Thanks for the work you did today."

"The sheriff lost another deputy and I lost two of my men. But at least we got them and their arrows off the hill for a while."

"I'm sorry for the losses."

"Thank you. I take it your family made it through unscathed?"

"They did. Who do you have guarding the horses? And the water?"

"Cana. Your brother Luke. The settlers."

"Good. We shouldn't talk any further."

Hawthorne nodded. Brett could barely see Hawthorne's face and Hawthorne could barely see Brett's. Both had used soot from the fire on the church wall to blacken the skin on their heads and hands.

"I will move to the rocks just over there," said Hawthorne, pointing with one of his pistols.

107

"Do you have enough cartridges for your revolvers?"

"Only about ten."

"I trust you have a knife?"

Brett could not see it until Hawthorne put it in his hand. The blade had also been blackened with soot.

"It's like a sword it's so large," hissed Brett.

"Bowie used a knife just like it at the Alamo."

"It's a wonder the Mexicans didn't run at the sight of it."

Hawthorne tucked the blade back in his gun belt. "I'll head out. *Adios, Reverendo. Vaya con Dios.*"

"*Vaya con Dios.*"

Brett crawled to a different spot and blended into a small bush and a rugged boulder. His eyes wandered over the dark slope of the hill, moonlight and starlight trickling over the dirt and stones. Nothing moved. But Brett knew an Apache warrior might make one move every five or ten minutes. If you did not catch the move you would never see him.

Joyeux jumped.

A shot. Another shot.

She heard the children begin to whimper and their mothers hush them.

Her rifle was up and pointing at the stars in the window.

She knew the other widows and Tommy were doing the same, wherever they had positioned themselves.

The horses began to whinny, a few at first, but after half a minute many of them began to neigh and nicker.

More shots. Two, three, four.

The horses began to scream.

One thundered past her window.

She thanked God it wasn't Donegal.

The screaming of the horses continued.

Now there was rapid shooting.

A loud bang behind her.

She swung her head and saw Tommy leaning out the window about to shoot again.

In the second that took there was a man in her window frame.

She could not see his face.

Lord God Almighty and sweet Jesus the Son, save us!

She fired.

The man grunted but remained in the window.

She worked the lever and fired again.

He disappeared.

He is not in the church, is he? He cannot be in the church.

A hand clamped down over her mouth.

She let out a shriek but it was swiftly muffled.

The hand covered her nose now as well. It smelled of burnt meat.

Fairest Lord Jesus, what do I do?

She bit the hand with all her might.

The man only grunted and smacked her with his fist.

But her mouth was free for a second.

"Christ and all his holy angels above, help me!"

Bodies were suddenly all over and all over the man.

"Is that you, mate?" demanded Noelle and Joyeux felt a knife at her throat.

"God save Ireland, yes, I'm the mate. It's the other one who isn't."

The man growled as he tossed Dana and Dianna off his back. But he had no sooner done that before Marianne smashed her rifle stock into his face. He staggered backwards, reached out and grabbed her by her hair and pulled. She swung the rifle stock and hit him again. He gave another yank, a hard one, and she cried out but still tried to bring her rifle up, this time with her finger fumbling on the trigger.

"Don't shoot, Marianne!" shouted Tommy. "Heaven knows where the bullet will go! I have him!"

Joyeux, flat on the floor with blood darting into her mouth, watched Tommy jump on the man's back, tighten one arm around his neck, and drive a knife again and again into the man's side. He twisted and writhed and picked her off, hitting her twice and throwing her across the room. He stumbled forward three or four steps and Joyeux caught a glimpse of his eyes. He seemed to see her as well. Then his legs buckled and he collapsed.

Marianne crawled up to him, pressed the barrel of her pistol into his skull, and looked at his face.

"Apache," she said.

"That's good to know," responded Joyeux, lifting her head. "It's a fine thing it wasn't one of the brothers."

Marianne put her hand to his neck and her ear to his chest. "His heart's not beating. He's dead."

'That's also good to know, God rest his soul. I'd hate to have to wrestle him down again and bite his other hand."

The horses were quiet. There were no more gunshots. The women returned to their windows, including Tommy, who only had a few bruises and cuts, and Joyeux, who had no more than a small slash across her cheek and a torn lip. The pain did not bother her. What worried her for the next two hours was how she would be able to kiss properly with a wounded mouth.

Then the sky began to change in the east.

"Dawn," she whispered.

The light in the window was like pure gold it was so bright.

Don't attacks often take place at dawn? Michael, holy angel, defend us. I'm but flesh and blood and a teaspoon of sugar. I can't keep biting people all day as well as all night.

Gold filled the room minute by minute. The children were sleeping and many of the mothers were sleeping with them. The body of the Apache warrior lay under the window. They had covered him with a blanket. Joyeux stared at the window and stared at the body.

You fought for what you felt was yours. We fought for what we felt was ours. It has been this way on every continent and in every nation from the beginning of time and such clashes are not going to go away any time soon. Even though you were our foe in this battle, peace to you.

She glanced around the room. Her friends were crouched at various windows. Lines were on their faces and under their eyes. The violence of the night and the lack of sleep had drained them all. Now they waited to see if their men would return. But nothing was moving on the hilltop or in the desert landscape.

This is something that has also been with us from the beginning. Men go out to war and the women wait at home, hoping they will return. I pray the grim work of the night is

not a harbinger of dark news for the morning. My good God,
I think you are well aware that none of the widows are able
to bear another loss. Especially if it should come upon them
so quickly after they have met men they care about. And that
includes me. Lord, have mercy. Christ, have mercy.

Brett popped up at her window.

His hands were in the air.

"Don't shoot, Ireland," he said.

Marianne was across the church in a shot and he took her
in his arms.

"It's all right," he said. "We lost some horses and
Hawthorne lost a few more men but my brothers are fine."

"What's wrong with your face? What is all that on your
skin?"

"Soot. Don't worry. I'm fine."

Dianna, Dana, and Noelle quickly gathered around him
and Marianne.

"All of them?" demanded Dianna. "They are all alive?"

"Yes."

"Then where are they?" asked Dana. "Where's Michael?"

"They'll be along. We're moving cautiously. Blood Lance
may still be nearby even though he lost another five men last
night." He spotted the body. "Six. Did he get through the
window?"

Tommy was standing beside Joyeux. "For about two
minutes." Her face was pale and streaked with blood. "Where's
Hawthorne's man? Cana?"

"I don't know."

"You don't know?"

"We don't have a good idea where everyone is yet. Even
Bobby and Benjamin are still hiding, watching to see if any
warriors came up the hill this morning. But at least I know
where they're hunkered down."

A tall woman came over to them, smoothing down her hair
and her long dress. "What about our husbands? I pray to God
no more of them have been injured or killed."

Brett patted Marianne on the back and pulled gently away
though he kept one arm around her waist. "Some of your men
have been wounded, ma'am, but none seriously. The Apache

111

went for the horses and your men fought them off. Two horses were killed and two broke free. The others are safe thanks to your husbands."

"Donegal is not wounded, is he?" asked Joyeux.

"Your great Shire? I think he helped drive the Apache back, to tell you the truth. I'm certain he put the fear of God in them." Brett looked at Marianne. "How is your daughter? How is her puppy?"

"She remains fast asleep with the children and a great big thick blanket is pulled down over her head and the head of Spurs."

There was a thud and Reuben was in the room, entering through a window behind them.

"Do you mind opening the door up now?" he asked. "I don't think Michael is keen on dropping through a window with his gimpy leg."

"Reuben!" Dianna rushed over to him. 'They said you were all right."

He put his arms around her. "I am. No nicks, scars, cuts or bruises. The same man that left is the same man that returned."

There was a banging at the door. Dana and Joyeux and Noelle ran forward, tossing benches to the left and right as if they suddenly possessed the strength of ten men. The door flew open and Joseph and Michael made their way in, followed by Luke and Scott and Adam. Noelle cried out when she saw dried blood on Adam's sleeveless left arm.

"What's this?" she demanded.

"A scratch. It happened when I fell down the hill last night, Noelle."

"It didn't. I don't believe you. The cut is too deep."

"There may have been a knife there when I fell."

"A knife?"

"Look, I'm here, aren't I?"

Joseph cupped Joyeux's small white face in both of his sun-darkened hands. "Your Irish prayers did a great deal of good."

"It seems that way. Did the Lord grant you any visions?"

"Your old men shall dream dreams and your young men shall see visions? Is that it? I had visions of you. How's that?"

"Oh, I like that very much. What did I look like? All glistening and ethereal and properly angelic?"

"Actually, you looked the way you look right now, very lovely and very human. For which I am very grateful."

Dana kissed Michael on the lips. "Running out and playing the hero with that battered old leg of yours."

He kissed her back and gathered her close. "I didn't need to do much running. Just burrowed down into my hole and watched and waited."

"You didn't have to fight?"

"Only once. It happened very quickly and no running was involved at all."

"You make it sound like you were watering a horse or fitting a wheel on a wagon."

"I suppose it was a bit more hazardous than that."

"I want you to tell me everything."

"I will. After I've had something to eat and grabbed a few hours sleep. You must feel hungry and tired yourself, Dana."

"I'm not; I'm really not. Now that you're back I feel I could stay up for hours and just listen to you talk."

"If only I had the strength to stay up and do all the talking you want."

"We'll need to sleep and eat," Brett spoke up. "All of us, men, women, and children. But the men and women will have to do it in groups, one group guarding the church and horses, the other resting. And the horses will need fresh fodder. We have gleaned almost everything we could from the grasses on Lazarus Top."

"Do we have any food in our saddlebags or did we salvage any from the wagons?" asked Reuben.

"There's some," responded Brett.

"We have a little," answered the tall woman, "but we have given most of it to the children. There is plenty of coffee however."

Marianne smiled. "A man can get by a long time on coffee."

113

Brett nodded. "You're right about that." He saw Bobby come slowly into the church. "What's the matter with you? Are you hurt?"

"I'm right as rain in the body, brother, but not in the soul."

Everyone stopped talking and turned to watch him. He stood a few feet away and looked them over, one by one, his eyes finally resting on Marianne.

"What is it?" demanded Brett.

"I don't know what it is," replied Bobby. "I found Ahab Hawthorne stone dead at the bottom of the hill. He hadn't been scalped and he hadn't been cut up. What he had been was shot twice in the back at long range. I dug one bullet out of him." Bobby opened his hand and the bullet rested there. "That's from a .44 rimfire. Hawthorne was shot and killed by someone with a Henry rifle."

Betrayal

"You're the only one with a Henry rifle."

Sheriff Teddy Westcott walked into the church.

He had his gun out and he was aiming it at Marianne.

Brett's hand went to his holster.

Loud clicks filled the church.

Guns were aimed at the brothers from all directions.

"Don't do it." Westcott smiled. "Or maybe I should ask you to go ahead and do it. Then I'll be rid of all of you at once." He waggled his pistol at Brett and Marianne. "The woman's under arrest for murder. You preachers put your hardware on the floor, all of it. I still got three deputies and four of Hawthorne's men, enough to blow every one of you out of the saddle. You got cuffs, Blacksticks?"

"Yes, sir."

"Lock her onto the door handle."

"We still have Apache to fight." Brett barred Blacksticks from Marianne. "You're going to need us."

"I don't think so. Looks to me like Blood Lance has had enough. And I'm pretty sure his scouts have told him what's coming."

"What do you mean by that?"

"I guess you'll find out." Westcott waggled his pistol again. "Red Beard. Pick up their guns. Have the preachers sit in the corner on their hands. If they give you any trouble at all, shoot 'em. Get the guns off their women too and herd them over to the front of the church."

Red Beard grinned. "My pleasure."

Westcott caught Brett glancing through the open door.

"No help for you coming from outside, preacher man. I had a couple of Hawthorne's boys round up the rest of your crew. Here they come now."

Several of the brothers walked into the church, hands over their heads, two men with Winchesters right behind them, the rifle barrels in their backs.

Brett shook his head. "I sure hope you know what you're doing, Sheriff."

"Don't fret none, Reverend. Salvation is at hand. For me and my boys anyhow."

Blacksticks shoved past Brett, yanked Marianne to the door, and handcuffed her to its handle.

"There," he said to her. "You'll get a nice view of the cavalry thundering over the desert."

"Will it truly be cavalry?" she asked him.

"Well, our kind of cavalry."

"The way you have it set up, she'll be outside when we shut the door!" snapped Brett.

Westcott laughed. "That's right. If the Apache do launch another raid they can have her for free."

Brett's eyes went hard and cold. "*Vengeance is mine. I will repay, saith the Lord.*"

Westcott snorted. "You think you're God?"

"He's my employer. I do his bidding."

Westcott snorted again. "The only thing you'll be doing is walking barefoot through the desert in another hour. No water. No guns. I reckon you'll meet up with the good Lord long before I do."

Blacksticks pointed with the barrel of his revolver. "Will ya look at that?"

Marianne squinted in the bright desert light as Westcott came to the doorway.

"What're you looking at?" asked the Sheriff.

"One of Hawthorne's boys down there at the foot of the hill. He's holding an Apache warrior in his arms and just standing there."

Westcott shaded his eyes with his hand. "Who is it? I thought the rest of his men were dead."

"Guess not. Can't tell who it is from up here."

"What's he doing?"

Blacksticks shrugged. "Looks to me like he's waiting for the Apache to come and take the body off his hands."

"They'll kill him."

"Maybe. Maybe not. Them Indians have got their own ways."

Marianne could not tell if it was anyone she might recognize. The man was too far away and had his back to them. She spotted movement. The Apache lifted his head and raised one of his arms.

"The warrior is still alive," she said.

"What makes you say that?" demanded Westcott.

"I just saw him move."

The two men stared.

"She's right," mumbled Blacksticks. "That Injun's still got life in him."

"What's Hawthorne's boy playing at?" Westcott wiped his forehead with his arm. "Why doesn't he just kill the savage and skedaddle?"

As Marianne and the men watched, a dozen Apache suddenly emerged from the rocks and bushes as if they'd come right up from under the sand. Each of them had a gun trained on Hawthorne's man. It looked like they spoke with him a few moments. Then the Apache in the man's arms lifted his head again. Nothing happened for half a minute. Finally several of the Apache took the warrior from the white man's hands. One of them swung the stock of his rifle at the man's head and knocked him to the ground. Then they were gone.

"Crazy fool!" spat Westcott. "Did they think they were gonna hug and kiss and make up?"

"They didn't put a bullet in him," Blacksticks responded. "He'll make his way up here once he comes to."

"I don't want an Indian lover with our gang. Drill him as soon as he gets up here."

"Whatever you say."

Marianne lifted a dark eyebrow. "And you're arresting me for murder?"

Westcott grinned. "That's the benefit of being sheriff. You can't arrest yourself."

"You haven't even asked me if I shot Hawthorne."

"I don't have to ask. You hated his guts and you waited for your chance. All the noise and confusion of the fighting gave you a perfect opportunity."

Westcott leaned in close and she pulled her head as far away as she could.

"And you're the only one with a Henry rifle," he growled, his foul breath making her clap her free hand over her nose and mouth. "You had it in your hands during the whole fight, didn't you?"

"Of course I did."

"An open and shut case, as a lawyer might say. Of course, a few kisses might go a long way to changing your situation."

"I'd sooner kiss a snake."

"Well, that may happen soon enough. Give me some loving and you won't walk the desert till you die like your preacher friends."

She spit in his face. "I'll do the walk."

He slapped her with his six-gun. Blood streaked her mouth and cheek. "I reckon you'll change your tune once the sun heats things up even more and we pull the boots off your pretty little feet." He turned to Blacksticks. "Keep an eye out for that Injun lover. Soon as he gets in range, plug him."

"It's done." Blacksticks glanced up at the sun. Buzzards were circling the hilltop. "For that matter I could climb down there and do it now."

"Aren't you worried about the savages?"

"No. I may not have the eyes of this lady here but I picked out a plume of dust in the desert a couple of minutes ago. Riders are coming. A good bunch of them. Our friends, I reckon. The Apache won't want any part of that bunch."

"I guess not."

"Who are these men?" asked Marianne. "Cut throats who just broke out of prison like yourselves?"

"Why, they're clergymen," said Blacksticks. "Just like your boyfriend and his brothers."

"Clergymen?"

Westcott pulled out his pocket watch. "They're just about two full days late. They were supposed to be here on Saturday and sit in on the first service Sunday morning. It may be they had to do a little preaching and passing the plate on the way up here."

Marianne watched the plume of dust grow larger. "What denomination?'

"Methodist." Westcott put away his watch. "Blacksticks, let's make the most of this. Bring those brothers out here."

"What about the women?"

"Keep a gun on them. All of them. The homesteaders and their kids too. But I want to see the look on the brothers' faces."

"Those farmers and ranchers are gonna start trickling out from behind the wagons back of the church in a little while."

"Ignore 'em. First sign of trouble, shoot a few."

Blacksticks tugged on his hat brim. "You sure do like to keep things simple."

Westcott nodded. "That's always best." He stood watching the dust. "Can you make out the number of riders, ma'am?"

"Twenty-five? Thirty?"

"All dressed in black?"

"It's too hard to tell. It appears so."

Brett and Reuben came out into the sunlight with Hack, one of the deputies, just behind them with a shotgun.

"What's the occasion?" asked Brett.

"You'll find out soon enough," replied Westcott.

"You all right, Marianne?" Brett's eyes were on her face. "Beating up on women your idea of being a man, Sheriff?"

Westcott put his pistol on Brett. "She had it coming. You've all got it coming. You were a big man a few weeks ago, weren't you, preacher? Not so big now."

"Why do you still have her handcuffed to that door? Let her join the other ladies. You know she didn't shoot Hawthorne in the back."

"Now how would I know that?"

"You've seen how she acts and what she does. This is not a woman who kills in cold blood. She's a fighter, not a murderer."

"I'm surprised at you, preacher. You spend as much time around people as I do. You know they can do the things you least expect at the drop of a hat."

"Some can. Others stay true to what they are and what they believe."

"Well, the big surprise about men and women is that there are no surprises. Your lady said her prayers and shot the man who killed her husband clean through. Not hard to understand, is it? Not even hard to sympathize with. But the law is the law."

"You can say that?' demanded Brett. "With the kind of lawman you are?"

"Well." Westcott watched as the riders neared Lazarus Top. "Sometimes I'm on the right side of the law and other times the law is on the wrong side of me. That's all."

The rest of the brothers were brought out. They had their hands tied in front of them with rope.

"Welcome to the Grand Ball." Westcott waved his pistol. "Our guests of honor are about to arrive."

The features on Brett's face went sharp. "I know that man. Whatever you think is going to happen, Westcott, you're wrong. He's one of us, one of the Methodists. So are the men with him."

Westcott spat in the dust. "Is that a fact?"

"All right to come up, Sheriff Westcott?" called one of the riders when they reached the base of the hill.

"It is."

"You have water up there?"

"Plenty."

"Praise God."

The riders urged their horses up the knoll. Marianne found her eyes were on Brett, not the riders in black. She watched his whole body tighten as the men with their clerical collars reined in their mounts in front of the church. All the brothers seemed more tense, their arms and legs and faces rigid.

"Hello, Brett." A tall man bronzed by the sun smiled down at him. "How are you?"

Brett did not return the smile. 'Bishop. What's going on?"

120

"We planned to be here for the service. There was a delay. Some fences needed mending and some prayers needed to be prayed." The man looked over the cluster of brothers. "Reuben. Adam. Michael. Joseph. I hope I find you well."

"We're far from well, Bishop." Brett took a step forward. "Whatever you think this sheriff and his deputies are, you're wrong. Put your guns on them and cut my brothers loose."

The Bishop was still smiling. "Can't do it, Brett."

"Why not?"

"It wouldn't be right. They work for me."

"What?"

"Hawthorne's men. The Sheriff and his men. They're my work crew. Just like the boys riding with me today."

"Work crew? You're with the Methodist Church."

The Bishop nodded. "We sure are. And we work as hard for them as we do for ourselves." He glanced over at Marianne, lifting his black hat from his head. "I've forgotten my manners. The Bishop of Tucumcari, ma'am."

"You're the one they call Mesa Tucumcari," she replied. "They've mentioned you. But as a friend and fellow preacher. Not as an enemy."

"Enemy seems too strong a word. Let's just say that right now we have different theological interpretations on how to live out the Christian life."

"What are you talking about?" Brett took another step forward. "Have you gone crazy? These men that have us under their guns are no friends of God or the Methodist Church. I don't know what they've told you but you have things upside down and inside out, Bishop."

The Bishop shook his head.

"We came to bless the first service in this new Methodist Church. After that we were going to burn it down."

"Burn it down?"

The Bishop glanced at the church building. "But it looks like somebody tried to beat us to it."

"We had Apache trouble," said Westcott. "Blood Lance launched a raid."

"How many?"

"Fifty?"

"We saw sign. A lot more than fifty are on the move. Word is Chiricahua and Mescalero and Jicarrilla bands are working together." The Bishop walked his horse to one side of the church. "Quite a few bodies."

"We fought them off all Sunday and Sunday night."

"Did you lose many men?"

"Two of my deputies. Four of Hawthorne's men. Some homesteaders. And Hawthorne himself."

"Ahab's dead?"

"Shot through the back by this woman here. She blamed him for having her husband gunned down. He was a squatter."

"We were never squatters!" cried Marianne, trying to tug her hand free. "We bought our deed. Paid in silver. It was Hawthorne who said we had no right to work the land. He had his villains murder my husband. But I never shot Hawthorne in the back. I would not do it the way he did. If I had killed him it would have been face to face."

"Face to face, hmm?" Westcott holstered his pistol. "The bullets in Hawthorne were from a Henry rifle. And she's the only one with a Henry. By her own admission it never left her side, day or night."

"I didn't shoot him!"

The Bishop held up his hand. "It doesn't matter one way or the other. He was working for me and I'm still here. The plans go ahead even with Hawthorne in the grave."

"What plans?" demanded Brett.

"Burn out those who don't have deeds from Santa Fe Lands and Estates, my company. Use it for grazing beef cattle – the market is booming and prices are sky high. We'll have to put the torch to the houses of God here and in Cazadora too, Brother Brett. We don't want people settling in. We want the land for our herds."

"You work for the Methodist Church!"

"And myself. Don't worry. It's all work for God, as I see it."

"How can you say that?"

"There's a time for every season under heaven, isn't there? Well, this is my time. We'll plant a few churches up north closer to Santa Fe. But not down here, my oh-too-zealous Brother Brett. Not for a hundred years."

Westcott coughed. "What do you want to do with them?"

The Bishop leaned on his saddle horn. "Drive the homesteaders to Cazadora for now. We'll keep what cattle they have and light a match to their fences and cabins."

"I mean the preachers."

"Ah, the preachers. Well, you can see I have enough preachers with me here. The David brothers aren't really necessary anymore. Shoot them and throw their bodies into the church. Then burn it down. I'm sure they'd like to go that way." He smiled at Brett. "Isn't that right, Reverend David?"

"You had us fooled," replied Brett. "You had us fooled here and you have them fooled back east in Boston and New York. But no one fools God, Mesa. Not even clever devils like yourself."

The Bishop tipped his hat. "I take that as a compliment. Meanwhile the Apache provide me with a better explanation for the disappearance of the David brothers than I could ever have devised on my own. Wiped out. Massacred by Blood Lance. Burned alive in their new church. Martyrs to the cause of God and Christ. There will be statues and monuments, of course. I will pay for several myself, under the auspices of Santa Fe Lands and Estates and its board of directors. Your memory will be glorious. The work of God will experience a new surge of enthusiasm as your faith and heroism inspire hundreds of young men to advance the gospel in the West. Just not down here in this county, Brett. Everywhere else but down here."

"Who's taking Hawthorne's place?" asked Westcott.

"Why, you are, Sheriff. You must have known that. It must have flashed through your mind the moment they told you he was dead."

Westcott grinned. "I did kind of hope."

"Of course you did. And now your hopes are rewarded. So to your task, Sheriff. Order everyone out of the church. Put the bodies of the dead in it. All the dead. White, Apache, your deputies, Hawthorne. Get the David brothers to haul the corpses. Then put an end to the family. We'll water our horses and get the squatters in their wagons and on their way while you do your work."

"What about the woman?" asked Hack.

"This woman here? Send her to Cazadora with the others."

"No, I mean the one inside who's sister to these brothers."

The Bishop gave Brett a dark glance. "Are you telling me you dragged Teresina into this?"

"Whoever drags Tommy into anything? She came here on her own. The Church gave her papers and an ordination and everything."

"I didn't plan on that. I had no desire to kill her along with the rest of you."

"Then don't. Let her go to Cazadora with the other women."

"I can't. She's too smart. Too tough. She'll go to Boston and New York. Tell everyone the Bishop of Tucumcari is to blame."

"We're all too smart and too tough for you." Marianne glared at him. "So shoot all of us women and burn our bodies in the church along with the David brothers if that's the kind of man you are."

The Bishop took his canteen and sipped from it, swirling the water around in his mouth before spitting it out. "How many women are there just like you and Teresina?"

"At least half a dozen. For all I know, all the women ranchers and settlers are just like us. Are you going to murder every woman in the church?"

The Bishop sipped from the canteen and spat again. "If you force my hand."

"Just a minute," said Hack. "When I signed on as deputy I never signed on to start shooting women and burning their bodies."

"Shut up, Hack." Westcott hitched his gun belt higher on his pants. "Do what you're told and get the preachers to start picking up the bodies. I'll get the women out of the church." He stopped and glanced at the Bishop. "You want that sister out here or in there?"

The Bishop was silent for several moments, his face like iron. "Drive the others out. We'll take care of them. But the sister, leave her inside. Put a bullet in her after everyone else is gone."

"All right."

Brett rushed the Bishop and tried to drag him out of his saddle. The Bishop was expecting it and kicked Brett in the face as hard as he could with his boot and his spur. Marianne cried out as Brett staggered back, blood spreading through the fingers he clamped over his cheeks and mouth. The Bishop tugged a long barreled revolver out of his belt.

"I don't trust you, Brett. As soon as I turn my back I know you'll hatch a plan. The other eight are all I need to fetch bodies. You can go to heaven first and find out what it's like. Then come back and tell us what we have to look forward to after the rest of us die of old age."

"Why should he come back and tell you about heaven?" A voice cracked the air. "You ain't ever going there."

A gunshot.

The Bishop grunted and fell forward in the saddle.

The men with him slapped their hands to their holsters.

"Any man that draws, dies."

Three men pulled their pistols free. Three more shots cut the morning air. The men slid from their saddles onto the sand and dirt.

"Anyone else?"

Westcott lunged for Reuben, pressing his pistol against his skull. "I'll kill him!"

The gun blast and Westcott's howl were right on top of one another. The Sheriff fell to his knees, blood soaking his right sleeve.

"You clergymen on horseback. Unbuckle your gun belts. Anyone who goes for his pistol, I shoot. You other men with your guns on the brothers, drop them right now. If you try anything, I'll drill you. Hurry up. I'm an impatient man at the best of times."

Marianne could not see who the man was. She did not even know where he was. And by the confused looks on everyone else's faces, no one else knew where he was hiding either. There was gun smoke but a morning wind moving over the desert dispersed it so quickly she could not tell where the smoke had come from.

"I guess I'm out of patience."

The gun belts began to fall to the ground rapidly. So did the guns in the hands of the men who had them trained on the David brothers.

The man who'd been keeping his rifle on the women ran out of the church. "What's going on? Are the Apache back?"

Reuben punched him in the face and the man collapsed.

At the same moment one of the clergy spurred his horse. The man in hiding shot him out of the saddle. The horse galloped down the hill and away.

"All of you. Off your horses. Kick your gun belts to the side. Sit on the ground and sit on your hands. Same with you others. Kick your weapons aside and sit on your hands."

Reuben took a knife from the man he'd punched and began cutting the ropes on his brothers' wrists. They began to pick up the guns and arm themselves. Michael took the key from Blackstick's pocket and unlocked Marianne's handcuffs. She immediately ran towards Brett, tugged his fingers free of his face, and began to wipe at the cuts the spurs had made with the hem of her dress.

Adam hauled the Bishop out of his saddle. "He's dead. Right through the heart."

Michael looked towards the rocks. "Some straight shooting. Who are you, stranger?"

A tall man stood up. Blood was dried black and hard over his face like paint.

Tommy appeared in the church doorway with a Yellowboy in her hands. "Cana!"

He still had a Henry rifle aimed at the clergy.

"Good morning, Teresina."

He walked past her and the others. In a few moments he was standing over Sheriff Westcott.

"Recognize me, Sheriff?"

Westcott didn't raise his head.

"Remember shooting me last night? And Ahab Hawthorne who was right at my side? With a Henry rifle you threw down a hole in the rocks? I got it out."

Westcott spat blood and still wouldn't reply.

"You got that warrior too. It was Blood Lance. Did you know that? I lay beside him all night and he lay beside me. I

126

knew some Apache, he knew some English. We talked off and on. I had a canteen. We shared the water. You figured all three of us were dead, didn't you, Sheriff? But I pulled through. You didn't really put your bullets where they counted, not like you did with Hawthorne. I patched up Blood Lance with strips I tore from my shirt. Got his bleeding stopped. Kept him warm. Crazy thing, isn't it? I was supposed to be fighting Apache, not saving them. But you changed everything, stood the whole fight on its head for me. I guess you saw me give him back to his people?"

"Indian lover!" Westcott spat blood a second time.

Cana kicked him as hard as he could in the ribs. Westcott cursed and fell over on his side in the dirt.

"It would be better for you if you kept your mouth shut, Sheriff."

Cana lifted his head. "All of you get going. The devil's clergymen. You deputies. Hawthorne's boys. No guns. No horses. One canteen for every three men. You can keep your boots. But that's it. Get on your feet and get going."

"That's murder in this heat," whined Westcott.

"If you want to hole up somewheres out there and wait for night, you're welcome. But I'd start walking if I were you. Any of you still within gun range of Lazarus Top a quarter of an hour from now are going to feel the bite of this Henry."

"There's Apache out there."

"I hope so. Get going, Westcott." Cana looked around. "All of you. Get up and head down the hill. Reuben, fetch them some canteens, six or seven'll do the trick."

The women began to spill out of the church as men began to walk down the slope and out onto the desert. Scott and Bobby had gone around to the back, coaxing the settlers from behind the wagons, and the men joined their wives and children for the first time since Sunday morning. Michael and Joseph took the clergymen's horses to the stream to drink and while they were there they checked the other horses for wounds or bruises. A lot was going on all at once.

"Let me clean your face."

Cana was keeping an eye on the dozens of men streaming off Lazarus Top. "I'm all right, Tommy."

"You have a goose egg the size of my fist on the side of your head and blood caked on your skin that makes you look hideous."

"Maybe I am hideous."

"You're not." Tommy began to wipe at his face with a wet cloth. "What made you change your mind?"

"About what?"

"About riding with those men."

He lifted one shoulder in a shrug. "Fighting the Apache alongside all of you. Getting shot in the back by Westcott and left for dead. Keeping Blood Lance alive through a long, dark night. Listening to the Bishop's trash talk. All of it kind of changed me inside."

"I think you were already changing long before the Apache showed up."

"What makes you say that?"

"A man doesn't turn his whole life around in an instant. You had to be thinking along those lines already."

One side of his mouth lifted in a lopsided smile. "You're a preacher lady, aren't you?"

She scrubbed at a patch of dried blood on his neck. "Yes."

"You're used to people getting converted, isn't that right? So maybe I just saw the light."

She smiled and her eyes smiled with her lips. "Even converts at a revival meeting have had something ticking away at the back of their minds."

"Hmm."

She ran a hand over his back. "Where did the Sheriff's shots hit you?"

"One in the back of my arm. I dug the bullet out. The other high up on my shoulder. It went right through, never hit any bones. There wasn't a lot of blood."

"I have a flask of brandy on me. We'd better pour some on those wounds. Come around to the back of the church and we'll get that shirt off you."

"I'm all right. I need to keep an eye on those men."

"They're a quarter mile away now. And my brothers are watching them like hawks; you can be sure of that."

Reluctantly, Cana followed Tommy back to the wagons that were still on their sides and to the horses that were up and milling about. Her slender figure in a long black skirt, black blouse, and hat melted into the shadows under the trees.

"We have some privacy," she said, silver flask in her hand.

"Why do we need privacy?"

"So I can dress your wounds properly." She uncorked the flask and they could both smell the strong aroma of the brandy. "Please remove your shirt."

He hesitated, not sure what to do with the Henry rifle.

"You can lean it against a tree trunk, Cana. You certainly won't need to use it on me."

He placed the Henry, with its barrel pointing up, at the side of a tree and slowly began to unbutton his shirt. Tommy waited with the open flask, one hand on her hip.

"I'm glad you're not on fire," she said.

"My fingers are a little stiff."

"Really?" She drew close to him and undid the last two buttons herself. "It couldn't be that you're afraid of me, would it?"

"I'm not afraid of you."

"No?" She gently peeled off his black shirt. Her face was very close to his and her lips brushed his mouth. "Are you sure?"

"Of course I'm sure." But the words caught in his throat and he barely got them out.

"Turn around so I can get at the wounds."

He did as she asked.

Her fingers probed the hole in his shoulder first. He jumped at her touch.

"Relax." She used the quietest voice he had ever heard her use. "I'm not going to hurt you."

She poured brandy right into the wound.

He flinched.

"There's a lot of redness," she told him. "We need to stop the infection."

Her fingers played over the hole in the back of his arm. "This wound is bigger."

"I dug out the bullet with my knife."

"It's also very red."

She poured a larger dose of brandy into the wound than she had with the first one.

Again he flinched and grit his teeth but made no sound.

She patted his arm. "My brave man."

He heard a tearing sound.

"What are you doing?" he asked.

"We need to keep the dirt out of those bullet holes."

She was bent over and ripping cloth from the hem of her skirt.

"Don't do that," he protested. "You don't need to do that."

"Of course I need to do it."

"Use my shirt instead."

"Your shirt is filthy."

She used one strip on his arm, wrapping it snugly about the wound. The other she placed over the hole in his shoulder. She moved to the front to finish tying it off, her hands resting on his chest.

"How's that?" she asked.

"Good. Thanks."

"You're most welcome. Is there any discomfort?"

"Not much."

She was tall and only pushed herself up an inch on the toes of her black boots so that she could reach his mouth. His lips were cracked and swollen so she ran her tongue over them to moisten them before she placed her soft lips there. She took her time. Although she had a great deal she wanted to say to him with her kiss she was not urgent nor did she use all her strength. She let the kiss go on and on and was conscious of not wanting to hurt him or cause the cuts on his mouth to sting. Her hands found the cords of muscle on his back and gripped them, massaged them, dug into them. At the same time she moved her lips from his mouth, to the stubble on his cheek, to the lobe of his ear, and down to his throat where she tasted the salt of his exertions from the past day and night. She felt a deep sigh go through him, it made his chest shudder against hers, and his hands suddenly came over her back and the thin cotton of her blouse, removed her hat and dropped it to the ground, and unbound the hair she had plaited so carefully just an hour before. Then he took his face from hers so that he could bury it in her soft darkness.

"You smell like sage," he murmured.

"Do I?"

"And sunlight. And sand. And Ponderosa pine. It's a pretty heady mix."

She tried to reply but he seized her so tightly and ran his lips over her throat and neck so desperately she could only let out her air in a long slow way like a breeze making its way through desert willow and cottonwoods. At first she didn't even know what the sound was or where it was coming from. She thought somehow a colt or foal had gotten among the mares and geldings or that a pigeon or dove was in the pine branches. When she realized it was emerging from her chest and throat she threw her head back and closed her eyes and pushed her nails as far as she could into the naked skin of his back and shoulders.

You're lucky I'm a tomboy, I keep my nails short, otherwise I'd start the bleeding all over again. What's the natter with me? I'm always in control and now you're pulling me right out of myself. I'm losing my breath, my heart, everything.

"You're black and soft as a desert night," he said into her ear, "but you burn like the noonday sun. No man could ever get enough of you."

"I haven't had any men. I don't know what that means."

"It means you're all the good things in one body and one soul."

"Oh, don't be crazy, Cana. No person is that."

"You are." He kissed her hair and ears.

"You don't even know me."

But she smiled because she found she liked his words and he saw her smile and kept speaking them.

"It was life and death all day yesterday and all last night. I saw how you acted, how you fought, how you cared about the children and the other women. There was half a lifetime of getting to know you just in those few hours."

"You didn't see every part of me, Cana."

131

"Maybe not. But I'm seeing another part right now and it goes well with the first."

"How well?"

"I love the strength you have in your arms and shoulders. I love the velvet of your back and the hard rock of it too. Your stomach is flat and tight and smooth as stone. I know you're holding back on me with the kisses. I know it's because of the cuts on my lips. I don't want you to hold back. I've been alone most of my life. I've hardly ever touched a woman let alone been held by one as beautiful as you. Don't hold back anymore. Give me all of it."

She could not stop herself from laughing. "You make me sound so good."

"You are so good."

"I don't know if I can believe you."

"How do you want me to prove it?"

"I have no idea. I'm new to this woman loves man game. I know absolutely nothing about it."

"Well, then, if you won't kiss hard, I will."

"Cana – "

But flame was suddenly all over her mouth and down her throat, spreading through her chest and stomach and along her legs, burning, igniting, both pain and pleasure cutting into her and through her at the same time. She ran a hand over the hard flat of his stomach while the other gripped his gun belt and hung on.

"I'm on fire," she managed to say between kisses.

"Don't expect me to be the one to put it out," he replied in a voice that was rough and ragged and breathless.

"I don't want you to put it out. I've never been on fire before. I rather like it." She pulled back a moment and gave him a sly smile, her black eyebrows slanting inwards and her dark eyes crackling with light. "I want more of it."

Light and heat poured into her and soon she was giving every bit of it back, his face gripped by her strong hands, her legs wrapping themselves around his waist, her long hair covering him, her lips darting from his mouth, to his eyes, to his chest, her white teeth biting down sharply into his skin.

"Does that hurt?" she asked him.

"About a much as a bullet but it feels a whole lot better."

"I hope I haven't caused you any discomfort."

"Your beauty makes me forget about everything. I'm holding dark fire in my hands. I'm holding the desert night and all its stars."

"You and your words. Is that what the love game is all about? Men and their words?"

"They aren't words. I'm just comparing you to the earth and sky I see around me every day. And you come out on top."

"That's God's creation you're talking about."

"You *are* God's creation, Teresina."

"Teresina? Not Tommy?"

"I think both names suit you. But I like Teresina."

"And you like me as much as you like my name?"

He ran his thumb along the line of her cheekbone. "You'll think I'm making this up. But when I was lying there and bleeding among the rocks I thought of you. It felt good. Kept me warm. Kept me awake. I even mentioned you to Blood Lance."

"You did not."

"Yes, I did. He talked about his four wives and children. He asked me how many wives I had. None, I told him. He was astonished. *And you die without knowing a woman?* So I told him there was a woman like the night – the stars were her eyes, the crescent moon her lips, her feet were rooted in the desert and the rock. He seemed to like that."

"You said all this to an Apache chief?"

"Yes, I did. We both thought we were going to die."

"So you didn't mean it?"

"Of course I meant it. It put an ache right through me to think I never would hold you, never would kiss you, never have you as a wife. He called you *Sons-ee-ah-ray, Morning Star.* So I've called you that in my head over and over again as I kissed you."

"You're teasing me about all this. The way my brothers have teased me all my life."

"You're wrong." He kissed her gently on her dark eyebrows. "I'm not teasing at all. *Sons-ee-ah-ray.* I even saw the morning star as I sat among the rocks."

"You make me feel strange. Silvery and black and shining. You make me feel quite beautiful. I've never felt that way before. Oh, people have said I was attractive or pretty but I never felt anything. Now I feel so much and I feel like I have missed out on so much. Love me some more, Cana. Go right ahead. Love your Morning Star."

A half hour later they returned to the front of the church, Cana's shirt buttoned to the top. Graves were being dug and all the men were busy at it. Brett looked up at the two of them from a hole, a red slash on his face, and put aside his shovel.

"Where the blazes have you been?" he demanded, glaring at his sister.

She glared back. "Dressing his wounds."

"All this time?"

"He was shot twice."

"I could have done him up in one minute."

"And done a terrible job. At least my ministrations give him a decent chance of living until the next day."

Brett turned his hard blue eyes on Cana. "I don't appreciate any man dallying with my baby sister. But I appreciate least of all a man who rode with Ahab Hawthorne and was in the employ of the two-faced Methodist bishop I just covered with sand and stone."

Reuben was digging nearby. "You might recall he saved all our lives, brother."

Brett's eyes flamed at Reuben.

"And I don't think anyone could dally with Tommy and survive unless she cottoned to their company a whole lot," Michael spoke up.

Tommy's eyes blazed at Michael.

Cana cleared his throat. "The Apache would be more favorably disposed towards us if we treated their dead warriors with honor. We shouldn't place them underground. The bodies ought to be placed in crevasses in the rocks along with their weapons."

Brett squinted at him. "We need those weapons."

"No, we don't. With all the guns the deputies and clergy left behind we must have two or three for every man with plenty left over for the women. Bury the warriors with honor. It could save our lives. After all, the Apache are still out there."

Brett thought about it, looking at Cana. "You told Westcott you had Blood Lance beside you all night."

"That's right."

"Why didn't you slit his throat?"

"Because we weren't fighting each other anymore. We were fighting Westcott. And we were fighting death."

"Tell me something else. Did you do any killing for Hawthorne?"

"I swear to God I didn't."

"Burn any settlers out?"

"No."

"Then what were you good for?" demanded Brett.

"I guess I was kind of like his guard, his protector," responded Cana.

"Did you know about the Bishop of Tucumcari?"

"I knew about him. I never saw him until today."

"Was the Bishop the brains behind this whole idea of burning out settlers and moving people off their land?"

Cana shrugged. "The Bishop was over Hawthorne and Hawthorne was over Westcott. But I'm pretty sure there were other people over the Bishop. In Santa Fe and in Washington."

"Is that a fact?"

"That's a fact."

"Then answer me the big question, mister. If you knew so much corruption was going on, why did you stay with Hawthorne and the others? If you're such a good man, why did you keep hanging around?"

Cana did not answer.

Brett ran a hand over his mouth. "Are you sweet on my sister?"

"Yes."

"So why would a man of the cloth like me let you court a million dollar woman like my sister who's a minister of the Methodist Church to boot?"

Tommy's eyes went dark. "Brett."

Brett held up a hand. "I'm bound to ask. You don't think I've overstepped my jurisdiction do you, Cana?"

"No, I don't. If it was my kid sister I'd sure want to know."

"So then answer me the question."

Cana kept his eyes on Brett. "Hawthorne was my brother."

The digging around them stopped.

"I swore I'd keep him alive. I was always looking for the day he'd turn. We talked about it. But the money was too good for him to pass up. He stayed. So I stayed too. Once he was killed I had no reason to stick with the gang."

Brett's eyes were ice blue. "You let his murderer walk."

"I don't kill in cold blue. Not even a snake like Westcott."

"I doubt I could have let him take a step off this hilltop if he'd shot one of my brothers."

"He'll be back, Reverend."

"How can you be sure of that?"

"Because The Five Hundred are out there now. *Los Quinientos.* They'll come after us here just like the Apache did but they'll be worse than the Apache. They have cannon. And no code of honor, no values. They'll slaughter everyone. Take scalps. Burn the churches and all the homesteads. Drive everyone out of the county. Take their pay in silver and gold and disappear back into Old Mexico. That's who's coming for us next, Reverend. Hawthorne knew it. Westcott knew it. I wouldn't be surprised if the men we turned loose are squirreled away out there and waiting for them."

"When are they expected to arrive?" asked Brett.

"Any day. Any hour. For all we know they've got a scope trained on Lazarus Top right now and are planning to raid us tonight. So I suggest we take the bodies of the Apaches and place them in the rocks. It wouldn't do to have everyone mad at us at the same time."

Several of the brothers laughed.

A slow smile even spread across Brett's face.

He hauled himself out of the grave he was digging.

"I'll help you with the warriors. Adam. Michael. Joseph. Reuben. Give us a hand."

Tommy put a hand on Cana's arm. "I'm sorry about your brother."

"Everyone hated him, didn't they?"

"It's true we felt that way at the beginning. But I watched him do good things, kind things, during our fight with the Apache. He saved my brother Michael's life when he was up on that roof. No one felt the same way about your brother when the fight was over, not even Marianne. Dana told me she felt that the Bishop and his clergy were the ones that did the killing and burning out, not Hawthorne."

Cana nodded. "She's right. They attacked the wagon train Noelle and Joyeux were on as well. But the men who killed Dana's husband, and the husbands of Dianna Charming and Marianne Freeman, weren't sent by the Bishop. That was the work of *Los Quinientos*. Not all of them. Just a hand-picked crew of gunslingers. Including their leader. *El Satan Blanco, The White Satan*. My brother argued against it. He went up to Santa Fe and I had to wait outside a room where he had a shouting match with whoever was inside. I even had my gun out at one point and was going to crash through the door. They didn't listen to him. He was told to shut up and go about his business. When news came of the killings he was sick about it. I almost got him to turn then. But along came a Wells Fargo shipment addressed to Ahab Hawthorne with a strongbox full of gold coins – fifty thousand dollars' worth. So he tried to forget about the murders and carried on. And I stayed by his side."

"You loved him," she said.

"Yes, I did. But I don't think my love for him will make up for all the wrongdoing, even though I never pulled a trigger or lit a match."

"The Good Book says that love covers a multitude of sins. And God's mercy is great."

He half-smiled. "You really are something. Who'd have thought you could be so tenderhearted?"

"Shh." She put a finger to his lips. "Don't let my brothers hear you say that. I'll never hear the end of it."

"Not a word." He squeezed her shoulder. "I have to go and help them out."

"I know. Tell me something before you go."

"What's that?"

"Are you really sweet on me?"

His smile was full. "You bet I am."

"A big tough guy like you?"

"Yeah. A big tough guy like me."

"Meet me tonight by the stream?"

"Sure I will." He took in the beauty of her face and hair and figure. "But The Five Hundred could be about. Even the Apache. We'll have to kiss with both eyes open and rifles across our knees. It'll be dangerous."

"Am I worth it?"

The full smile again. "Yeah, you're worth it."

The bodies of the Apache were dropped carefully into fissures in the rocks. Cana marked each spot with a stick to which he tied the buried warrior's headscarf. Brett and the brothers prayed over the graves. After this a hearty lunch was prepared – the saddlebags of the clergymen who had ridden with the Bishop were full of jerky, bread, cheese, potatoes, carrots, and even chocolate, as well as lots of coffee. Then a few men stood watch while everyone else had a long *siesta* wherever they could find a scrap of shade. At sunset another meal was cooked and eaten. There was an hour of play for the children followed by a story from Scott that made everyone laugh despite the danger that surrounded Lazarus Top. Beds were made up inside the church for the second night in a row and Brett prayed a short but beautiful prayer that all the settlers were grateful for.

"Put men behind the wagons again," Brett told his brothers and Cana, "and out among the rocks. The women at the windows. Thanks to the Bishop we have plenty of guns and ammunition so if you see something suspicious, cut loose. You may not get a second chance."

"Do you think we'll get attacked tonight by The Five Hundred?" Reuben asked Cana.

"No telling. Maybe they're here, maybe they aren't. My hunch is that they won't come by night."

"Why not?"

"Because they're not afraid of anyone and they want people to see their faces and what they're doing."

"What about the Apache?" asked Adam. "The Bishop said something about different tribes working together."

Cana nodded. "Hawthorne had heard about it too. If three or four hundred Mescalero and Chiricahua decide to come after us it'll all be over pretty quickly."

"Let's pray they have bigger fish to fry."

"I'll join you in that prayer," Cana replied.

He met Tommy at the side of the church. She was watching two of the homesteader women as they knelt by their husbands' graves. Cana took his hat from his head.

"We don't need any more widows," whispered Tommy.

"No, we sure don't."

"I pray it's a quiet night."

"Amen."

"You're starting to sound like a preacher."

She took his hand and they walked to the trees and the stream where the horses were bedded down and the wagons on their sides in a rough circle. Settlers with guns peered at them.

"I guess they wonder why we're outside the wagons and not inside with them," said Cana.

"Because we want to watch for danger and kiss at the same time." Tommy arranged her skirt and sat on a patch of grass under a tall pine. She patted the grass beside her. "Here you go."

He settled next to her with his Henry. "Seems kind of crazy to go a-courting when men could be slithering through the rocks with knives in their hands to cut our throats."

"Oh, will you stop that?" She placed her Yellowboy across her knees. "I was perfectly composed until you used the word *slithering*."

"Well, that's – "

"Hush. Keep one eye on the rocks and one eye on me and we'll be all right."

"Yes, ma'am."

"Don't call me ma'am. Did you happen to see what my brothers were doing?"

"Adam and Noelle are at one window, Joyeux and Joseph at another, Dana and Michael at another, and Marianne and Brett at the open door. Dianna and Reuben took to the rocks."

"They're out in the rocks? It's so dangerous there."

"Reuben told me they like rocks and boulders. If you want to know all the details, I spotted where they hunkered down. That's not to say they won't move."

"And?"

"And what?"

"And what did you see?"

"She had his face in her hands and she was kissing the heck out of it. I don't think your brother has much of a chance against the Apache or The Five Hundred or Dianna Charming."

"I'm sure Reuben would rather die under her kisses than a hail of bullets or a swarm of arrows."

"I feel the same way."

"Do you?" Tommy cupped his face in her two strong hands. "How's this for a start?"

"It's a good start. I just wish the moon was up so I could see your pretty face better."

"You don't need to see my face when I'm kissing you."

"One eye on you, you said, the other on the slope."

"I did say that, didn't I?" She snuggled against him. "Suppose this was our last night on earth? Isn't this a splendid way to spend it?"

He put his lips against her hair. "I sure hope it isn't our last night on earth. I'd like to have a lot more of you than just a few hours in the morning and a few hours at night."

"Don't be greedy. All in God's good time."

"Well, I hope God's good time includes a lifetime with you."

"Is that how you feel? Just like that? A lifetime after a few hugs and kisses?"

"They were pretty special hugs and kisses."

"Yes, they were." Tommy suddenly gasped and drew back. "Cana!"

He lifted his rifle. "What's wrong?"

"Fires. Fires in the night."

He looked out over the desert. He could see flames blazing orange and white in three locations miles apart.

"It's the Five Hundred," he said. "They're starting with the ranches and homesteads."

As he spoke red flames burst up from a spot much closer to Lazarus Top.

Tommy put her fist to her mouth. "It could be the Apache."

"Maybe. But I'd put my money on *El Satan Blanco* and The Five Hundred. That's how they work. They like to do a dozen things at once."

"I thought they wanted people to see their faces."

"Oh, the settlers out there will see them all right. They'll see their faces in the light of a hundred fires. Just before they die."

"What about us?"

"They're saving daylight for us, Teresina. They want us to watch the burning all night and be afraid. Then they'll come in the morning or at noon and laugh as we try to shoot them all down. We won't be able to do it. The last thing they'll want you and I and your brothers and the widows to see is their faces. After that they'll kill us with our eyes wide open."

The Shadow of the Almighty

Smoke lay like a brown haze over the desert.

The sun was red within the haze as it rose in the sky.

Marianne opened her eyes, wondered where she was, remembered, glanced around for Brett as she sat up with her back to the church door, and saw him with his brothers. Three, four, seven, nine, she counted. They were all standing and looking at the long, low cloud of smoke that barely moved in the still air. Many of the men from the homesteads and ranches had joined them. And Cana.

"They burned us out," one rancher muttered. "I'll bet they didn't miss one homestead."

Brett stood with a Yellowboy in his hands. "I reckon not."

"If we'd been down there they'd have killed us all. Was it the Apache?"

"It wasn't the Apache. It was *Los Quinientos*, The Five Hundred." Brett looked at the rancher. "They'd have put half a dozen bullets in every man. The women and children they'd have sent to Cazadora."

"Unless the women fought back," Reuben spoke up.

Brett nodded. "Anybody that fights back they wipe out. Even kids."

"What kind of men are they?" groaned the rancher.

Adam took off his hat and wiped his forehead with the back of his arm. "Some say they aren't men. More like spirits or demons that move over the desert without the hooves of their horses ever touching the ground."

"What's gonna happen now?"

"They'll be along for us." Brett squinted out over the desert as the sun cleared the smoke and blazed yellow and white. "They'll be along."

"How many?"

"Hundred. Maybe two."

"How are we gonna fight off that many?"

Brett turned away and did not answer.

He came to Marianne, helped her to her feet, and kissed her gently on the lips. "I guess we have time for a decent meal for everyone."

"Will they come today? In the daylight?"

"I believe they will."

Dana Fleming and Dianna Charming were already helping Joyeux McCain and Noelle Saunders and the women from the homesteads get a good breakfast together. Meat was frying in pans and coffee brewing just outside the church door. The wood smoke from the cooking fires drifted white over Lazarus Top even as the brown smoke from the burned out homesteads sat unmoving on the desert floor. Every now and then, the ranching women turned tired and stricken faces towards the places where their homes had been. One murmured everything would have been all right if they'd never hitched up with the preachers and attended the church service. But her husband put an arm around her shoulders and explained the *desperadoes* had already been on their way to New Mexico long before they knew who was at the church service and who wasn't.

"They had every intention of doing what they did regardless of any church meeting on Lazarus Top," he said quietly. "The only difference is we would have been in our beds and they'd have set fire to our houses with all of us inside."

"We could have reasoned with them."

He shook his head and pointed with the barrel of the rifle in his hand. "Look at all the destruction. Those men never came to talk."

Joyeux wandered over to Joseph's side while everyone was eating and slipped her slender arm through his. "You're not eating."

"I have a coffee. That'll have to do."

"What's going to happen? Do you think they'll just charge the hill?"

"No. They have a funny ritual. Their leader will challenge our fastest man. If he loses they'll give us time to get out of the county instead of wiping us out."

"Do you think men like that would keep their word?"

"I don't know, Joey. Their leader has never lost a gunfight that I've heard about. So every task they've been given they've finished – they'll kill the men and let the women and children go."

"Please don't tell me you're the fastest man among your brothers."

"I'm not. Adam is."

"Noelle won't want to hear that."

Joseph sipped at his coffee. "I expect he won't tell her until he sees *El Satan Blanco* start riding this way with a bunch of his men. After all, The Five Hundred may do things differently now."

But ten minutes later Adam stood beside Noelle and watched half a dozen riders emerge from the brown haze and walk their horses towards Lazarus Top. Behind them, remaining at the foot of the hill, fifty riders sat on their horses and waited, rifles braced on their hips.

"What's this about?" she asked.

"It's about a duel," Adam told her.

"A duel? What duel? Whose duel?"

"Their leader against our fastest man."

"What?"

"They're supposed to let us walk out of here alive if our man beats him. But that's never happened."

"Who's supposed to go against their leader? Brett? Reuben?"

"Me."

"You?" Noelle dug her fingers into his arm. "You can't do that."

145

"I have to."

"We'll fight them. We'll shoot them out of their saddles."

"We do that and the whole gang'll ride down on us. There are fifty down there. Likely another hundred out in the desert. They won't leave anyone alive. At least this way there's a slim chance."

"They won't keep their word, Adam! You don't believe that!"

He took off her hat and kissed the top of her head. "All we can do is hope and pray. And I have to get my pistol out quick."

"Are you faster than their leader?"

"*El Satan Blanco?* I don't know."

"I'm not going to stand by and watch you get butchered."

"Maybe things will go our way, Noelle. Maybe we'll walk out of this alive."

"If you kill their leader they won't let any of us walk out of here alive."

"I guess we'll see." He smiled and kissed each of her eyes. "I love the fire I see in you."

"Please, Adam, don't go against him."

"If I don't everyone on this hilltop will be dead inside half an hour."

Brett came over to them. "You all right, brother?"

"I'm all right."

"I'm sorry," Brett said to Noelle.

"Don't let this happen, Brett."

"It's not our call. It's theirs."

"How do you know Cana's not faster?" she asked.

"He isn't." Brett was watching the six riders walk their horses up the slopes of Lazarus Top. "They went against each other three times at dawn while everyone else was asleep. Cana never cleared his holster once before Adam had his pistol out."

"Reverend David." A voice like stones rattling in a barrel came from the throat of a tall man with blond hair and pale skin and eyes that looked white. "All the Reverend Davids. It seems to me we've met before. But we've never enacted The Rite with any of you."

The six riders reined in their horses.

146

Sheriff Teddy Westcott was there as well as his deputy, Hack.

"No." Brett stared at the man. "Legend has it you'll let all these people walk if you lose."

"That's the legend." A laugh that sounded worse than his voice. "But the legend has never happened, Reverend. Only in people's dreams."

"Will your men honor it if you lose?"

"If I lose? The Second Coming will fill the skies before that happens."

"But your men will honor it? Or is honor something *Los Quinientos* never had?"

The pale man's eyes turned to ice.

"We have our own code." His voice was harsh. "Even the Mexican *banditos* and the Apache have their codes."

"Where do you want to do it?"

"Right here." The leader swung down from his horse. "You can herd the women folk and the kids into the church or let 'em watch. I expect they've all seen hangings."

"What's going on?" demanded one of the ranchers. "You burn down our homesteads and now you come for our blood?"

El Satan Blanco grinned. Even though everything about him was pale his teeth were dark. "That's right."

The man lifted his rifle. "What's to stop me from shooting you where you stand?"

There was a gun blast and the rancher spun around and dropped to the ground.

A young girl cried out and ran to him. "Papa!"

Blanco nodded up at Westcott. "Thanks, Sheriff."

"Just maintaining the law, sir."

"Glad of it." *Blanco* jerked at the body with his chin. "Get that mess out of here." He glanced around. "Who's challenging me? Let's get this over with."

"You see why I have to fight the monster?" Adam asked.

"Yes," Noelle replied.

He squeezed Noelle's hand. "I care for you."

"You care for me? That's all you're going to tell me right now?"

He smiled and ran his hand down the length of her hair. "I love you, Noelle. Is that what you wanted to hear?"

"Never mind what I wanted to hear. Just say what you mean."

"I do mean it." He turned away and walked towards The White Satan. "I'm ready anytime you are."

Satan snorted. "You? Not big brother Brett? What's your handle?"

"Adam."

"Are you number eight or nine in the family?"

"Seven."

"Lucky seven! Well, we'll see." Satan loosened each revolver in his black double holster rig. "Clear everybody out."

The brothers began to move men and women back towards the church. The children were taken inside and the door shut but faces soon appeared at the open windows.

"Are we doing this fair?" Adam asked. "I wing you and everyone has safe passage off this hill?"

Satan stared at him. "Wing me? You think you're going to wing me? I'm going to shoot you stone dead. If you think you have a chance try and do the same to me. I'll keep shooting so long as I'm breathing."

Adam stood still while Satan fidgeted with his gun belt and pistols once again. Westcott nodded to the riders with him to head off to the side. He took the reins of Satan's horse and led the gelding away.

"I don't understand any of this." Dana was standing by the church door with Dianna. "What is this perverse ritual this man feels he needs to perform in front of us?"

Dianna's eyes were dark. "I am praying like the wind and the more I pray the more I am sure of two things – the leader of The Five Hundred is a man who loves to kill. And Adam is not like any man he has ever faced before."

"Why don't we just shoot them? There are only six outlaws."

"The others would come for us. That's why those fifty are waiting at the bottom of the hill. Reuben told me there are a lot more out where we can't see them. Doing the gunfight there's a chance we'll survive."

"If Adam is faster."

"Yes. If Adam is faster."

"And if they keep their word."

Dianna nodded and folded her arms over her chest. "If." She looked down. "Should Adam get killed they'll kill all the men as well. But the women and children won't be harmed. That's what Reuben told me. That's how they do it."

Dana looked at Noelle standing nearby. "Poor girl."

"I went over to talk with her. But she wants to be alone."

"What can we say to her? We came here to help build a church and have a service and it's been like a bad twister out of Texas ever since."

"God help us. God help Adam."

Joyeux came up behind them. "There are chariots of fire all around us."

Dana and Dianna turned their heads to look at her.

"What?" asked Dana.

"You'll see."

The smoke of the cooking fires still moved about the church and the people crowded up against its walls. A puff of warm desert air made it snake around Adam and *El Satan Blanco*.

"I've never gone up against a preacher." *Blanco* smiled. "Appropriate though, isn't it? Satan versus God."

"I'm just a messenger," replied Adam quietly. "If this were God versus the devil you'd be dead by now."

Blanco laughed with his black teeth. "You got spunk; I'll give you that." He adjusted his belt one last time. "I'm going to pull both guns."

Adam shrugged. "One's all I need."

"I like to double my chances. It'll be over in a few seconds, kid. You won't feel a thing."

They looked at each other for several seconds.

The White Satan drew. Both guns were out quickly.

Adam had already fired twice before Satan squeezed the triggers.

Satan's pistols flashed and spewed smoke.

He went down.

So did Adam.

Satan writhed in the dust.

He looked up at Westcott as blood poured out of his mouth. "Kill them all."

Adam fired at Westcott as the sheriff drew his gun. Westcott grunted and dropped out of his saddle.

The other men with Westcott yanked their revolvers free and began to shoot at the men and women clustered at the front of the church.

There was a roar and a burst of gray gun smoke. A second roar followed right on top of it.

Three of the four gunslingers flew off their horses and crashed onto the hard earth and stone.

Hack held a double-barreled shotgun. Smoke curled from its muzzles.

El Satan Blanco glared up at him. "You'll die." He was hardly able to speak. "You'll all die."

His head dropped forward into the dirt.

"I can't ride with them no more." Hack let the shotgun fall and held up his hands. "I can't do what they do."

Noelle ran to Adam and tugged him over onto his back.

"Where were you hit?" She was yelling. "Where?"

"My leg. He got me good. Just let me bleed out."

"I am not going to let you bleed out!"

"They'll all be coming now. One hundred, two hundred. You need to get ready."

Brett knelt by him. "We'll be ready. Not much we can do. We only have so many guns. We could use yours."

"Tie me off then. But I don't make any promises."

"You made promises to me, mate." Noelle tore at the hem of her dress. "I'm going to tie you off so tight you'll never lose another drop of blood in your life."

"They fired at the people by the church."

Noelle began to twist the tourniquet above the bullet hole in his thigh. "They wounded one and nicked a couple of others. They only got off a few shots before that deputy unloaded the coach gun on them."

"Those fifty riders at the bottom of the hill, Brett – "

Brett nodded. "They're coming."

Rifles began to snap all around them.

"Get down and shoot at their horses!" Cana was shouting. "Shoot at their horses if you can't hit the men!"

Noelle crouched by Adam as he propped himself on one elbow and fired his pistol. When it emptied, she quickly reloaded it for him using the lead bullets in his shirt pocket. Brett knelt on his right knee, aiming and shooting his Winchester. The air was full of shouts and cries and dust and gunfire. Horse after horse, eyes rolling white in their heads, galloped past them, their saddles empty. One outlaw in a black sombrero fell at their feet, toppling from his saddle, lying in the dirt and not moving, the back of his head gone. Another rode right at them, teeth bared, pistol sparking. Noelle clapped a hand to her cheek as a bullet cut her cheek open. The outlaw suddenly slumped over his saddle and the horse twisted to the left, bucked, threw him, and raced away in a panic, its mouth white foam. After that Noelle could only see men riding down the hill.

"Stop firing!" yelled Reuben. "Stop firing and save your bullets!"

Brett stood up. "Fifty came up. About two dozen are heading down. They didn't expect to have thirty guns or more blasting at them."

"But they'll be back." Noelle was hoping Brett would disagree with her.

"Just like the Mexican troops at the Alamo, yes, they'll be back. Only there won't ten or twenty or fifty. They'll all come."

Marianne ran to Brett, Henry rifle in one hand, and threw an arm around his neck. "Thank God. I saw someone who looked like you go down."

He put his arm around her waist. "Not even a scratch. I hope you were under cover, Marianne, and not taking any risks."

"I wasn't hiding inside the church with the children, if that's what you mean."

"Where was Selah?"

"She was in the church with her puppy Spurs. She helped calm the girls and the boys."

"Do we have any wounded?"

"*Ja.* So many of your brothers are wounded." She quickly put a hand on his heart. "None of it is serious. But if you talk about taking risks, that is what your brothers do, Brett."

"Who's hit?"

"Michael. Joseph. Scott. Bobby. Luke. They are being taken care of."

"What about Tommy?"

"She's fine. Cana was shot in the arm. She is dressing that." Marianne glanced at Noelle and immediately dropped to her knees. "The whole side of your face is covered in blood!"

"No, no, a bullet cut my cheek, nothing more, yes, it's messy, but – "

Adam sat up, winced, and reached out his hand. "You didn't say a thing."

"Your leg is half shot off. Why should I say anything about a bullet that only grazed me?"

"Here." Adam gave his canteen to Marianne. "Please wash her face."

"I can do that for myself," said Noelle.

But Marianne was already sloshing water onto a cloth she had tugged from a pocket in her dress. "It is easier for me."

"There are probably others who have been shot dead."

"Yes, there are. But I can do nothing for them. So I will clean up your wound instead."

"Who's dead?" asked Brett.

"Two ranchers and one of the wives."

"Why wasn't she inside the church?"

"I wasn't inside the church. Neither were Dianna or Joyeux or Dana. The woman who was killed was firing a Winchester at the side of her husband. She knew how desperate the fight is that we are in. She understood how dangerous the outlaws are. So she chose to defend us. Honor that, Brett."

"Yes, of course I'll honor that." Brett looked around at the dead outlaws on the ground by the church or sprawled on the rocky slopes among dead horses. "Once the wounded are taken care of we need to gather the men, women, and children together. I have to speak with them."

"How long do you think we have, brother?" asked Adam.

"Half an hour. An hour. No more."

"What about the bodies?"

"We'll lay our own in the shade of the trees. We don't have time to deal with the others. It won't matter anyways. We don't have the means of holding off another attack, not one that will involve a hundred men or more."

"Is that what you're going to tell everyone?"

"No. I'm going to read the Bible to them. I'm going to pray. I'm going to tell them to spend the next hour of their lives with the ones who matter most to them."

"Sounds like a good idea for a worship service," said Marianne with a smile.

He smiled back through the dust caked on his face. "Well, I am a preacher. I intend to go with my boots on."

"Soldiers," spoke up Noelle. "What about soldiers or cavalry? Surely a hundred armed men can't just waltz across the border into New Mexico?"

Brett shook his head. "This isn't a federal jurisdiction. Just a territory. Sure, they've been requested before by Santa Fe. But, from the sounds of it, we have people in the government who want this county to stay grazing land. Some of them paid the outlaws to come here. No one's going to ride over the horizon to help us, Mrs. Saunders. In one of those books about the West they publish in Philadelphia or New York maybe. Not in real life."

"But your father is a federal court judge. I heard you say that. So why can't he order them in?"

"He has no idea what's going on here. He thinks we're planting churches. Only a handful of corrupt officials in Santa Fe know what's happening. And The Five Hundred."

"And the Apache." Adam closed his eyes and clutched his leg. "But there won't be five hundred, Noelle. They never had that many *banditos*. It was just a way to strike terror into people's hearts. But one or two hundred will be enough."

"So you're saying we're all done in then?"

"Yeah."

Brett walked towards the church. Marianne did a final wipe on Noelle's cheek, smiled at her, jumped up, and joined him.

"I don't suppose this is the sort of message they trained you to give in seminary," she said.

"No, it sure isn't."

"Have you already thought about what you're going to say?"

"Not a bit. Except I want to bless them and encourage them, not put any more fear than they already have into their hearts."

Marianne glanced towards the desert. It looked empty to her. "Perhaps they've gone away. After all, Adam killed their leader."

"Someone's already taken his place. They can't have it being said *Los Quinientos* was whipped by a bunch of preachers, and homesteaders, and women. They have to kill us."

"Surely we can hold them off. All of these people have proven they're able and willing to fight to protect their children and their right to live on this land."

Brett stopped walking and put his arm around her. "Look, you're right, they have proven that. They've tangled with the Apache and with a couple of dozen outlaws and they've had the faith and the courage to face up to those dangers. No one's taking that away from them. If we have to end it all right here I can't think of a finer group of people to head back to God with." He kissed her, looked into eyes that had both warmth for him and a trace of uncertainty and fear for what the next hour would bring, and kissed her again. "But we can't fight off an attack of one hundred or more men. Too many of us are wounded now, we've probably exhausted half of the fresh ammunition and powder we picked up off of the *desperados,* all they have to do is ride over us in waves from every direction. So now we have to die well. Like Jesus did. And the apostles. And all the first Christians the Roman Empire executed."

Marianne tilted her chin. "Barring a miracle."

"Barring a miracle." His blue eyes remained on her face. "My beauty. I would have liked a thousand years. Or if not a thousand, forty or fifty. I guess it comes down to just a few days and weeks." He played with a curl of her dark brown hair the way he liked to do. "I'll need your help."

"Me? What can I do?"

"Just read the Bible for me. For all of us. In a clear strong voice."

"Of course I can do that."

"Do you have a Bible in English? I don't know where mine ended up."

"*Ja*. I have one in English and one in Dutch."

"Psalm 91. That is what I would like you to read." He smiled. "That day on the trail when you pulled a gun on me, your Colt Navy Six, you wanted me to quote all sorts of Bible verses."

Her face reddened. "You wore a gun. Preachers don't usually wear guns."

"Was that the only reason?"

She hesitated.

"Since we are going to die anyways, why not?" she finally blurted. "You were too good looking to be a preacher. I didn't believe it."

"You mean God only makes ugly preachers?"

Her face grew even darker with blood. "*Ja,* that was the way I used to think. Though Marco is all right, he's sweet."

"And what am I?"

"Too much." Tears stabbed from her eyes. "Too much of everything. Goodness, ruggedness, holiness, handsomeness. Too much to lose." Her chin trembled. "They can send one hundred, two hundred, a thousand or more. I am going to fight them all and defeat them. I will call upon God for angels with swords of fire. I will call upon the Son of God to ride down through the sky on his white stallion. I will shout to the heavens. I am going to have a life with you that lasts longer than a few days and weeks."

"Is that right?"

"*Ja,* that's right."

"Were you like this back home in Holland?"

"No. I was much worse there. The wide open spaces of the American West agree with me."

He began to laugh.

"Do you find me so amusing?" snapped Marianne. "You don't think I can do what I say I am going to do?"

"Oh, heaven forbid I or God or anyone else got in your way, least of all the *desperadoes* themselves." Brett held her shoulders gently. "You stick by my side. Right to the end. I want to see you with every last moment the good Lord gives me."

"I will be there, Brett David. I have no intention of being anywhere else. And Selah will be with us too."

"That's the way it should be." He twisted a lock of her hair around his finger. "Let's talk to the people now. All right?"

"I just need to fetch my English Bible from the church."

Brett asked everyone to gather at the front of the church, for the boys and girls to sit with their mothers and fathers, for the men, women, and children to take all the water they needed, to finish off the jerky from the saddlebags they'd taken from the outlaws, to reload their rifles and pistols. While they did that he wanted to say a few things to them, just a few things.

"After that we ought to hear from God's Word." He smiled. "Hasn't this been the longest, wildest, noisiest Methodist church service you've ever been at?"

Though the anxiety and exhaustion pushed through the skin on their faces and around their eyes, the men and women laughed.

"But we've held together," Brett went on. "We've watched one another's backs. I'm sorry for those we've lost, and I'm sorry for the ranches that were set ablaze last night, but we've survived, and if we get the chance we'll rebuild every last one of them. I swear it. Did you ever see such clergymen as my brothers and me before? A hammer in one hand, a gun in the other, and a whole lot of Bible in-between? Every last one of those ranches is going back up. We just need a little more help from heaven."

The people did not laugh as loudly, some of them only smiled, but all eyes remained on Brett, standing in front of them in his dusty black preacher pants, a torn and soiled white shirt, a Yellowboy Winchester in his right hand.

"They'll come again. You know that. And they'll come with all their riders this time. We'll set ourselves up the same way we did with the Apache. Some inside the church with the children, some out, some at the back behind the wagons, some in the rocks. We'll distribute all the bullets and powder we have left. They won't take prisoners and they won't show mercy. So we'll fight to the end, whatever that end is. We'll go into it covered by prayer and by the Word. We'll go in ready to meet our God today or some other day and some other place fifty years from now. I wouldn't be a preacher worth my salt if I didn't bless you in the name of the Lord right now, you and your children, and give you the hope that, come what may, you'll be utterly and completely in the hands of God this morning."

Marianne was standing just behind him. She could feel strength moving over his brothers and Cana and women like Tommy and Dana and Joyeux and Noelle and Dianna. She could see the homesteaders lift their faces and tighten their grip on one another's hands and almost smile as they listened. Some closed their eyes and she saw their lips moving in prayer.

Thank you, Lord. Thank you for using Brett to put heart in these people. Come what may, we trust you. Yes, come what may, our lives and our souls are in your hands.

"I have a passage of Scripture I've always gone to whenever I've been between a rock and a hard place. It's never failed to lift my spirits and put my thoughts in the right place. I believe many of you know Psalm 91 and I believe the Lord Jesus will use it to put whatever it is you need from him in your mind and in the deepest part of yourself. Never mind the desert for a few minutes. Never mind the heat. Never mind what's going on at the bottom of this hill. Just listen to the eternal promises of God. May he bless you with the reading of his Word."

Brett stepped back so that Marianne was the center of attention.

The large black Bible was open in her hands.

She began to read.

He that dwelleth in the secret place of the most High shall abide under the shadow of the Almighty.

I will say of the Lord, He is my refuge and my fortress: my God; in him will I trust.

Surely he shall deliver thee from the snare of the fowler, and from the noisome pestilence.

He shall cover thee with his feathers, and under his wings shalt thou trust: his truth shall be thy shield and buckler.

Thou shalt not be afraid for the terror by night; nor for the arrow that flieth by day;

Nor for the pestilence that walketh in darkness; nor for the destruction that wasteth at noonday.

A thousand shall fall at thy side, and ten thousand at thy right hand; but it shall not come nigh thee.

Only with thine eyes shalt thou behold and see the reward of the wicked.

Because thou hast made the LORD, which is my refuge, even the most High, thy habitation;

There shall no evil befall thee, neither shall any plague come nigh thy dwelling.

For he shall give his angels charge over thee, to keep thee in all thy ways.

They shall bear thee up in their hands, lest thou dash thy foot against a stone.

Thou shalt tread upon the lion and adder: the young lion and the dragon shalt thou trample under feet.

Because he hath set his love upon me, therefore will I deliver him: I will set him on high, because he hath known my name.

He shall call upon me, and I will answer him: I will be with him in trouble; I will deliver him, and honor him.

With long life will I satisfy him, and show him my salvation.

"Amen," said Brett.

"Amen," said his brothers.

"Amen," said the men and women by the church.

Brett turned and looked out over the desert. Horses and riders were everywhere.

"It doesn't look so empty now, does it?" he asked Marianne.

"No. But I don't care. I am going to fight them."

"I don't doubt that." He set his rifle down and took her face in hjs hands. "One last kiss?"

"Of course you may have a kiss, Brett David, but it will not be the last one. I swear to God it will not."

All the Colors of Heaven

Dianna Charming glanced at the mounted men forming up in the desert. She tightened her grip on Reuben's arm.

"Don't try and send me into the church," she told him, "because I won't go."

"The children need to have adults in there protecting them."

"The mothers can do that. If this is the last I'm going to see of you on this earth I don't want to be watching from a distance, Reuben."

His arm went around her. "I feel the same way." He smiled. "We sure did have a wild and wooly courtship, didn't we?"

"A courtship? Is that what that was?"

"You'd never have so many fireworks for an ordinary Sunday-go-to-meeting relationship."

"Ah. So somewhere along the line, what with all the fireworks and excitement, I must have missed the proposal?"

"Must have. Shall I repeat it?"

"Please do."

But Brett barked out a command before Reuben could say anything else.

"Women and children into the church! The wounded too! Michael, Joseph, Cana, Adam, all of you, set yourselves up at the windows! If you're leg shot you can't move around quick enough out here! And we need some men behind the wagons out back!"

"Too late!" Adam, leaning on a broken rifle he was using as a crutch, pointed. "They're coming up in lines of twenty or thirty, one after another!"

"Get down!" Brett waved frantically with his arm. "Get the children down! Get ready to fire!"

Brett turned to Marianne who stood beside him with her Henry rifle. "There is a mercy in this. It'll be short and sweet. We won't last five minutes."

"The mothers are covering the children with their bodies."

"I see that. It won't matter. *Los Quininentos* will examine everyone after the shooting stops. Women, children, it makes no difference to them. They'll put an extra bullet in anyone who's still moving."

"And then the men who hired them will have all the land they need to graze their cattle."

"That's right. They'll be wealthy and buy their own children the finest clothes and food. Streets will be named after them in Santa Fe."

Marianne dropped to one knee and aimed her rifle. "Their names won't be written in heaven."

Bret began to fire his Yellowboy. "I reckon not."

Bullets kicked up dirt all around the church. A boy began to wail as blood streaked his face. The brothers were at corners of the church building, their pistols and Winchesters flashing, gun smoke making the desert air hazy. The first riders galloped through, hollering and screaming in Spanish, but every one of them was shot out of the saddle. The ranchers and homesteaders, both men and women, were aiming and firing at the next wave of men urging their horses up the slope but one rancher fell, then another, and Dana screamed as Michael was hit by several bullets and went sprawling in the dust.

I suppose it is over now. Marianne glimpsed Dana bending over Michael's body, tears cutting across her face. *I had thought you were going to do something extraordinary, Lord. I know not everyone escapes from the hands of desperate men but I thought you might do that for us. Sometimes people are saved and sometimes people are lost. It* was my hope our group here would be some of the ones you saved.

A bullet slammed into Marianne's shoulder and knocked her to the ground. She bit her lip from the stab of pain as blood trickled into her throat, making her cough and choke. For a moment she saw Brett's face and could tell his lips were moving, he was asking her something. After that it was dust and noise and horses and gunshots. She closed her eyes.

End it then, if that is your will. End it and let me see your better world. There is nothing more I can do here. Oh, Selah, if only you would hide, or take a horse and gallop away while everything is still in such a turmoil. But I know you will be protecting the children, you and Spurs, doing what little you can to defend the boys and girls. That is your spirit. That is what God will see.

"Something's happening."

It was Brett's voice.

His arm went under her shoulders. "Take a look."

He pushed a canteen against her lips. She drank and coughed.

Dust hung in the air as she glanced about through half-closed eyes.

Dead horses and dead men littered the ground.

"Where are the others?" she rasped. "There were so many."

Brett was kneeling beside her and holding her upright. "Look down the hill."

Her head was throbbing and she had to squint but she could make out a long line of riders cutting across the path of *Los Quinientos*. They were Apache. She could make out another line of riders behind The Five Hundred. More Apache.

"I don't understand," she said in a weak voice. "Why would the Apache stop them from attacking us?"

"I have no idea. Maybe they have an old score to settle. The Apache have them outnumbered three to one. This must be that large band of Chiricahua and Mescalero and Jicarrilla they said had come together." He went to lay her down again. "Let me look at that bullet hole while I have the chance."

"No. I must see what is happening."

"I'll tell you what's happening."

"No. I must see it for myself."

"My Lord, woman, but you are stubborn. You could be bleeding to death but you have to see the show."

"It is not about a show. It is about God."

"What about God?"

"If he will defend us."

"Using Apache?"

"So in the Bible the Lord used the Persians to defend his people and free them from captivity. Why may he not use Apache? *Thus saith the Lord to his anointed, to Cyrus, whose right hand I have holden, to subdue nations before him. For Jacob my servant's sake, and Israel mine elect, I have even called thee by name. I have surnamed thee, though thou hast not known me. I have raised you up in righteousness, and I will direct all your ways. You shall build my city, and you shall let go my captives, not for price or reward, saith the Lord of hosts.*"

Brett grunted. "You're as handy with a Bible as you are with a Henry rifle. Whether you're a prophet or not we'll soon find out."

He kept Marianne upright with his arm.

She watched, gritting her teeth from the pain of her shoulder wound and the bite of her headache, and in minutes the Apache had hemmed The Five Hundred in from the front and the back. There were a couple of wild shots from the *desperadoes*. Suddenly the Apache swooped and a shrill battle cry went up from hundreds of throats. Guns cracked and hatchets and clubs and knives slashed. Marianne closed her eyes and muttered a prayer.

You take no pleasure in the death of the wicked. I know that.

"I've seen enough," she said out loud.

Brett laid her back on the ground.

"Let me dress your wound," he said.

"*Go* ahead."

But Brett did nothing for several minutes as she lay there looking up at the rich blue of the New Mexican sky. She knew he was watching the uneven contest and she knew all the

162

others huddled on Lazarus Top and against the walls of the church were doing the same thing. Of course they were. They were astonished that it should be the Apache who were saving their lives.

Brett suddenly jumped to his feet.

"They're coming for us!"

He snapped his Winchester to his shoulder. "I knew it was too much to hope for. The Apache weren't protecting us. They were dealing with their enemy. Now it's our turn."

Marianne struggled to a sitting position.

Warriors were racing up the slope on horseback. Forty, fifty, sixty, she wasn't sure.

"Why aren't all of them attacking?" she asked.

"They don't need three hundred braves to deal with us."

Shots rang out from the ranchers and homesteaders.

"God help us!" screamed one of the women. "Death at the hands of those savages will be worse than a bullet from an outlaw's gun!"

Brett fired off a round. "From the frying pan into the fire. It's hopeless but I don't understand anything else except to fight to the end."

Cana ran to the edge of the hill so that everyone had to stop firing or hit him.

"Stop!" He faced the brothers and the ranchers. "Put down your guns!"

"Are you crazy?" Reuben tried to aim over Cana's head. "They'll skin us alive!"

"You think you can stop three hundred Apache when a hundred well-armed outlaws couldn't? Throw down your weapons and stop shooting!"

"I swear to God," growled Reuben. "Get out of the way or I'll shoot right through you."

"Blood Lance is leading them! None of his men are shooting! None of them have rifles out!" Cana turned towards the Apache, raised his Winchester high over his head in both hands so that everyone could see him silhouetted against the New Mexico sky. Then he threw it into the dust. "They won't harm us!"

"Won't harm us?" Adam was bracing himself against the wall of the church. "No one will be alive a minute from now if we don't fight back!"

"No one will be alive a minute from now if you do!" shouted Cana. "Blood Lance is coming! Put down your guns! Listen to me and we have a chance to live!"

Tommy was suddenly at his side.

"Didn't Cana save you from the Bishop of Tucumcari?" she cried. "Didn't he give Blood Lance his water that night they lay wounded?" She unbuckled her gun belt. "Trust him!"

Brett hesitated as the Apache swarmed over the edge of the slope.

None of the warriors had leveled their rifles.

They bristled with bows and arrows and hatchets but did not use them.

"Listen to Cana!" Brett dropped his Yellowboy. "Now!"

His brothers looked at him, glanced at the Apache riding in a tight circle around the church, and quickly laid their guns in the dirt. The ranchers and homesteaders were the last to put their guns down.

"It's madness!" shouted one rancher over the thundering hooves. "We've all gone *loco!* They'll slaughter us now for sure!"

Hooves struck the earth only feet from Marianne's head.

She spotted Dana and Michael crouched together in the swirling dust.

She thanked God that Selah, puppy in her arms, was with Noelle and Adam by the door of the church.

Joyeux had her arm around Joseph who was slumped against her side. Marianne could not tell if he was alive or dead.

The circling grew tighter and tighter.

She recognized Blood Lance from the time Cana had stood with the chief in his arms.

Blood Lance brought his horse to a stop inches from Cana and Tommy. Young warriors reined in on either side of him.

He raised his lance in his fist, brandishing it over his head, poised to throw.

Cana did not move. Neither did Tommy.

"Brett." Marianne tried to get up. "Brett."

"Easy. Don't so much as touch your Henry."

"They're going to kill Cana!"

"Cana knew the risk. Apache have their own ways. Pray. Don't do more than that."

The dust settled.

The Apache had them ringed on every side, their horses flecked with foam.

They were at a standstill and waiting like everyone else.

Blood Lance was as rigid as a rock, the lance clenched tightly in his grip, its point aimed at Cana's heart.

He hurled it.

The lance slammed into the ground at Cana's feet.

The chief wheeled his horse and galloped down the hill. His warriors followed him. At the bottom they joined the others and the whole group raced to the west. Behind them dead horses and dead men littered the desert. Buzzards were already wheeling in long slow glides, dropping lower and lower.

"Thank God." Brett dropped to one knee beside Marianne and gently hugged her. "Thank God and thank you."

November 1st, 1866, Tucumcari, the New Mexico Territory

The nine brothers rode their horses side by side in the slender light of a chill desert dawn.

On their right the large bulk of Mesa Tucumcari rose from the desert.

They were dressed in black from head to foot. The only white was their clerical collars. Even their skin had been darkened by the New Mexican sun and heat. Long black riding coats flapped around their legs and black hats were set firmly on their heads.

Four men were waiting for them. Two of the men were dressed just like the brothers even down to the clerical collars. The other two were dressed in gold vests and fancy ties. The taller of the men in gold vests tipped his hat.

165

"I am so glad you could meet us here," he said. "I was afraid you wouldn't come."

The nine brothers reined up.

"We said we'd come," Brett replied. "We're here."

"I'm Jonathan Metcalf of Santa Fe Lands and Estates. This gentleman beside me is Mr. Simmons of the Board of Directors. The clergymen are Reverend Hooker and Reverend Wright of the Methodist Church."

Bret rested both gloved hands on the horn of his saddle. "We're the David brothers. All ordained ministers in the Methodist Church. My name is Brett. I'm the eldest. I don't believe we've ever had the acquaintance of Reverends Hooker and Wright."

"Upstanding young servants of God, let me assure you. Chaplains to Mr. Simmons and myself and a host of others who do business with Santa Fe Lands and Estates."

"Glad to hear God's work is being done in the big city."

"Well, it's hardly New York or Boston but its day will come." Jonathan Metcalf coughed. "That's why we'd like to clear up this misunderstanding. After the massacre last summer you seem to have gotten it into your heads that certain people in Santa Fe, people of influence, had hired outlaws to drive out the ranchers and settlers in your county. The unfortunate outcome was the slaughter of dozens of Methodist clergymen along with scores of law-abiding citizens of Texas and the New Mexico Territory at the hands of Blood Lance and his savages."

"Mr. Metcalf," Brett replied, "there was a slaughter all right. It began with your Methodist clergymen, the late Bishop of Tucumcari, and your law-abiding citizens of Texas and New Mexico. They burned out all the ranches and homesteads in the county. After that they attacked a congregation at a Methodist church on Lazarus Top. The only thing that saved those churchgoers was an Apache attack against the men you hired to run everyone out."

Metcalf's face filled with blood. "We didn't hire anyone."

"Quite a few of them testified otherwise." Brett patted the breast pocket of his long black riding coat. "Things were said on Lazarus Top. Things were said by dying men the Apache left behind in the desert. We have it all down in writing with a number of signatures. In the hands of a good judge we can make a case against Santa Fe Lands and Estates. It so happens we know such a judge, one who has jurisdiction in the New Mexico Territory – our father, Nathaniel Paul David."

Metcalf tried to smile. "How do you know we don't have him in our pocket?"

Reuben's eyes flashed. "No one has our father in his pocket. Say it again and I'll kill you."

"Easy," murmured Brett.

Metcalf laughed. "Hot-headed men of the cloth. I came here to broker a gentleman's agreement. You leave the county and we give you good land elsewhere. I have a hunch it's not going to be easy to broker an agreement with any of you."

"There's a lot of blood to answer for, Metcalf. Men and women have been murdered, their livestock killed or stolen, children left as orphans. All while you sit up in Santa Fe getting private lessons in prayer from Reverends Hooker and Wright. Did they talk about washing away the stain of your sins? No human can do that for you, Metcalf. No one on God's green earth, Mr. Simmons. Only the Lord Jesus Christ can do that."

"I believe God came into our business dealings now and then."

"God's in it up to his elbows, Mr. Metcalf. But you have to decide how it's going to end. Let the people have the land that is rightfully theirs. Their cries have come to the ears of the Lord of Harvests. Buy the land you need for your herds elsewhere. There's room enough for everyone's dreams in New Mexico."

Metcalf shook his head. "Not for mine and the rest of the world's. Not for mine and every immigrant from Germany and England and Holland. Not for mine and every redskin who thinks his Indian God gave him this land to do nothing with except hunt and steal horses and cook rattlesnake. The time has come for judgment. Still, I'm sorry we couldn't have come to an agreement, Reverend David."

"There's still time."

"There isn't. We're fresh out of time. Just like the people you felt led to champion are out of land and out of hope."

"They're all back on their spreads. Fences up. Houses up."

"You've had a busy autumn. And the Apache have left you alone. Why is that?"

"Ask Blood Lance."

"Why ask? It's obvious. You helped him kill my men. There's an arrangement between you and the Apache. But one day the US cavalry will kill Blood Lance. Tomorrow the men riding up behind you will kill the homesteaders and squatters. And today I'll kill you."

Brett heard the horse hooves but did not turn his head. "There are other judges besides you and my father, Metcalf. Higher judges, as high as the heavens are above the earth."

Metcalf smiled. "That's not my theology." He glanced at Mesa Tucumcari. "Some say it's a Comanche word, *tukamukaru,* that means to lie in wait for someone. You should have taken it literally, Reverend. My boys have been here since the crack of dawn."

Brett and his brothers looked back. Twelve men in black with clerical collars had come around the high mesa on horseback and had sawed off shotguns leveled at their backs.

"You see, I have Aces and Kings." Metcalf tugged a pistol from under his gold vest. "Four of each. Plus four Jacks. There's no better hand. There's no higher judgment."

Brett stared at Metcalf, his blue eyes like hard, cold gemstones. "You forgot the Jokers. And the Deuces. It's especially important not to forget the Deuces when the Deuce is the wild card." He lifted his hat from his head. "Did your chaplains minister to you from the Book of James, Mr. Metcalf?"

Gunfire exploded from the top and sides of the mesa. Horses screamed and the twelve men with shotguns flew into the air at the same moment as if a huge hand had swiped them from their saddles with one blow.

Simmons pulled out his Navy Six and so did the two clergymen with them but the brothers already had their guns on them.

"Go to now, ye rich men, weep and howl for your miseries that shall come upon you," recited Brett from memory as the guns from the mesa continued to fire at the twelve preachers with their shotguns. *"Your riches are corrupted, and your garments are moth-eaten. Your gold and silver is cankered; and the rust of them shall be a witness against you, and shall eat your flesh as it were fire. Ye have heaped treasure together for the last days. Behold, the hire of the labourers who have reaped down your fields, which is of you kept back by fraud, crieth: and the cries of them which have reaped are entered into the ears of the Lord of Sabaoth. Ye have lived in pleasure on the earth, and been wanton; ye have nourished your hearts, as in a day of slaughter. Ye have condemned and killed the just; and he doth not resist you."*

Brett added, "Until now."

The shooting stopped.

Metcalf's cheeks were empty of color. "Getting me doesn't end it. Do you think the top men would come to parley with you out in the desert? It's bigger than you think, Reverend. I have men I answer to."

"And they'll answer to me." Brett holstered his gun. "We know what the Comanche word means too, Metcalf. We had our people here for two days camped out on that mountain. We've talked about Kings and Aces and Jokers and wild cards. But no one's mentioned the Queens. You made them widows. That was your biggest mistake."

Slowly a line of riders made its way down the side of the mesa. All of them carried rifles. All of them wore black. When they got closer Metcalf could see the first of them was a man but all the rest were women.

"Dianna Charming. Dana Fleming. Marianne Freeman." Brett kept his eyes on Metcalf. "You had their husbands cut down on the banks of the Rio Oro. Joyeux McCain and Noelle Saunders – you wiped out their wagon train and murdered the few friends they had. Sarah Godley, Nancy Harcourt, Serenity Shore, Tabitha Youngblood – The Five Hundred took their husbands from them forever at Lazarus Top. The man with these ladies is Cana. Your sheriff, Teddy Westcott, shot Cana's brother in the back when he was of no further use to you –

169

Ahab Hawthorne. The woman beside him is my sister. You won't get a chance to do her any harm. You'll be in prison the day she trades clergyman's black for a bride's white." Brett smiled. "I thank God all these ladies will be trading in widow's weeds for bridal gowns. That's something you won't be able to stop either. You're all going on a train trip east. Judge Nathaniel Paul David will be waiting for you there."

The nine widows rode between the brothers and Metcalf and his men. They reined in their horses.

Brett could not see the widows' eyes but he could see the eyes of Metcalf and Simmons. Long seconds went by. The two men could not meet the gaze of the women. They looked down. Even the men dressed as clergymen that rode with Metcalf and Simmons glanced away. The sun rose higher and lined everyone in sharp, bright edges.

"I'm not going to prison," muttered Metcalf, his head still down.

"I expect you will," Brett responded.

"I'm not going to dance in the air at the end of a rope."

"I expect you will," Brett answered again.

Metcalf's head snapped up in a sudden fury.

"Not before I take some of you with me!" he roared, lifting his pistol and aiming it at the women in front of him.

As soon as he raised his gun Simmons raised his and so did the men dressed as Methodist ministers.

None of the brothers could shoot past the widows.

But there was a burst of firing from the women. Gray smoke poured over them.

Metcalf and Simmons did not get their shots off before bullets knocked them off their horses and into the dirt.

The gunmen in clerical collars did not get a chance to fire. They tumbled dead onto the stones and sand.

Cana and Tommy had their pistols out but it was over before they squeezed the triggers.

The gun smoke drifted over all of them and slipped over the mesa and was gone.

Brett recognized Marianne's voice.

"Learn to do good. Seek judgment. Relieve the oppressed. Help the fatherless. Plead the widow's cause."

She turned her horse's head and faced him.

Her Navy Six was still in her hand.

Tears were silver in her eyes and on her cheeks.

All the widows turned their horses around.

Their faces were tired and broken.

The guns they held in their fists they held so tightly the skin was white as scraped bone at the knuckles.

"Is it over now?" asked Joyeux. "Is it over, Brett? Is it over, Joseph?"

Joseph nudged his horse forward, one arm still in a sling from the wounds of the summer before. "It is. Rest easy, love. Holster your gun."

"But the other men." Dianna's face glistened with the pain of her crying. "The powerful men he mentioned in Santa Fe."

Reuben walked his mount towards her until he could lay a hand gently on her arm. "That is something our father will deal with. He will gather the evidence. Find witnesses. Collect testimony. Tap the shoulders of the powerful men he knows in Washington. The days of the Santa Fe Ring and the cutthroats associated with Santa Fe Lands and Estates is coming to an end."

"More than that, he will tap the broad shoulders of the all-powerful and all mighty God." Dana looked for Michael in the line of brothers. "We all will."

Michael had dismounted. He walked to her side and she slid from the saddle into his arms and the hardness of her crying made her back and shoulders shake.

"So it's done then." Noelle struck at her eyes with her long fingers. "Our part is done."

"Your part is done so far as thieves and outlaws is concerned." Adam smiled at her. "Now it's time to wear white."

"Oh, mate, I can't wear white. I'm no virgin bride. Marrying you will be my second go at the bat."

"I don't care how many goes at the bat you've had. You're a bride. A bride God has chosen for a man who loves you. You all are. And you'll all wear white."

Noelle laughed, her fingers still swiping at the tears. "Is that right? And you're the Methodist bishop are you then? You can lay down the law?"

"I can. Can't I, Brett?"

Brett smiled. "You've earned it, Adam. We all have. If the ladies will agree to it, well, it shall be a wedding of the whitest and purest silks. No one shall lack for a gown the color of driven snow from Boston or Philadelphia or New York."

Marianne finally began to smile and all the women with her.

Luke, Benjamin, Scott, and Bobby moved their horses towards Nancy and Sarah and Serenity and Tabitha, light in their eyes, their smiles responding to the smiles on the faces of the four widows.

"And I?" Tommy had her fists on her hips. "I who have never been blessed by marriage before as my friends here have? What shall I wear?"

"Why, white of course," said Cana.

"Don't you think the color is getting redundant in this family?"

Cana took a length of her dark hair in his hand. "Not in my family. I have never married before and I am the only son left. Let me see you in white, my beauty, please, cover yourself in white, white as the New Mexico clouds."

Tommy laughed. "How can any woman say no to that, Cana Hawthorne?"

"And these?" Joyeux extended her hand to the men lying dead on the sand. "Shall they have shrouds of white?"

"They shall have a Christian burial," Brett replied. "As for white, their souls are in God's hands. I can say no more than that."

"Joey." Joseph leaned over from his saddle and put his good arm around Joyeux. "Let me think of you with your scarlet hair tumbling down over the white silk of your gown. Leave these other things behind now. The sun is lifting on a better day than I've ever known. Let's go ahead and let's be done with the darkness. I just want to think of you in white with the hair God gave you like fire on your shoulders. I just want to think of your beauty and your love."

Joyeux ran her fingers over his face. "Why, what's this? Have the David brothers and Cana all become poets? What's a woman to do? You'll charm us all."

"And so we should," said Brett. "*Woman is sacred. The woman a man loves is holy.*"

Surprise and delight made its way over Marianne's face. "Brett Daniel, you too? Another Shakespeare?"

He smiled. "Alexander Dumas actually. *The Count of Monte Cristo.* I've loved that story since I was a boy. And I've been waiting all this time to use those words in the right place and with the right person."

"And I am her?"

Brett nodded. "You are, my beauty. Praise God in his heaven, you are."

Christmas Eve, 1866, the New Mexico Territory
"Now are we ready to say our I do's?"

"For heaven's sakes, dear, you've had them standing for over an hour, please get on with it, after all they've been through I'm sure they are more than ready."

"Patience, Mrs. David. Much needed to be said." Judge Nathaniel Paul David swept his hand over the ten couples standing before him. "Why, this outdoes anything in Jane Austen. At the most she ended a story with a double wedding. Here we have a – "

"Nathaniel." Mrs. David, a tall woman in a burgundy gown, with dark hair pinned up handsomely on her head and interlaced with pearls, wrapped her arm around her equally tall and dark husband. "Here we have twenty young people eager to go on their honeymoons. Proceed with the I do's, make your pronouncement, and court is adjourned for the day."

"Very well."

Mrs. David remained standing with her husband while couple after couple finalized their vows. A wrought iron chandelier with dozens of candles burned over their heads, fashioned in the shape of a wagon wheel. The walls were freshly peeled logs and the few windows were small but covered in white lace curtains with intricate patterns. A fire spurted blue and green flames and died down in a massive fireplace of fieldstones. Women in silk gowns of various styles and lengths stood with their hands held by men of different heights and with varying degrees of sunburn and windburn on their faces. All the women were in a white that blazed under the light of the chandelier and all the men were in a black that stayed black as midnight regardless of the light that flared around them. Only the white of the men's shirts, buried under suit jackets and vests, gave back a glimmer of brightness.

"Don't smile so much," whispered Brett, teasing Marianne.

"Oh, why shouldn't I smile?" Marianne whispered back. "God has given me a new life." She hugged her daughter Selah who stood beside her in her own white gown, Spurs curled up at her feet. "My daughter and I are part of a family again."

Tabitha Youngblood, a veil covering what Luke called her "perfectly shaped face and eyes" glanced over at Marianne and Brett.

"Did you hear what they said?" she whispered.

"I did," Luke responded. "Shh. Dad's not finished."

"I'm in just as much in awe as she is. I am a widow for three months and you change my world by proposing to me."

"After helping build your cabin it seemed only right to make sure you weren't living in it alone."

"But where are you going to preach?"

"Shh. We've been through all that."

"It doesn't seem right."

"It's completely right. We'll take it a day at a time. God has a church for me."

"Where?"

"We can start one in our parlor, can't we?"

Judge David cleared his throat, one dark eye darting to Luke. "By the power invested in me as Federal Court judge, in particular by the power invested in me to act in that capacity in the New Mexico Territory, I now pronounce all of you husband and wife — and that includes my baby, Teresina. May God richly bless you all."

Reuben raised his eyebrows. "Can we kiss the brides, Dad?"

"Hmm? Of course, by all means, lift the veils and kiss the brides; do you need a directive for everything? And Teresina, please allow your husband to do the same for you without a fight."

"Thank you father," Tommy replied, "I will do that."

Cana drew back the veil and smiled. "I knew there was something beautiful under here waiting for me."

"Well, don't wait too much longer or she may vanish. I've never stood in one spot for so long for anything."

"So I'm worth it?"

She began to kiss him on the lips. "So far."

Reuben held Dianna close to his chest. "I've prayed for this day."

"Well, you didn't have to pray long, did you? Everything happened so fast my black boots are still back at Lazarus Top where I left them in the midst of all the excitement."

"We'll fetch them on our way out. Wouldn't do to have a wedding night without those black boots, would it?"

She laughed. "I reckon not. I'd scarcely know what to do with myself."

"Happy now, mate?" Noelle took Adam's face in her hands and kissed him with all her strength. "Got everything you wanted?"

"Pretty much. Need a honeymoon though. And a new leg."

"The leg will mend in good time. The honeymoon I can do something about right now however. Let's get on our horses and make tracks."

He cupped her chin in his hand. "You have so much beauty yet you're so strong. But it didn't come easy, did it?"

"Nothing ever comes easy, with God or without. But at least with God I get exactly what I need, whether I know it or not." She pinched his cheek. "In this case, I know it. I love you, mate."

"And, believe me, I thank God for that."

Joseph already had Joyeux out the door, half-running with her in his arms.

"Hey, now," she laughed. "Where's the fire?"

"In my heart."

"Is this what you do with me the moment you've got two good arms?"

"It's ten miles to our cabin and I wish we'd arrived there two hours ago."

"If we'd arrived there two hours ago we wouldn't have been married yet. Are we taking my great horse Donegal?"

"No, he's slower."

"Sure, aye, he's slower, but I can ride in your arms if we take him. Wouldn't you like that?"

"I would like that. All right, you've won my heart and my vote, Donegal it is."

"Oh, my, I hope getting my way will be as easy as that for the rest of our marriage."

Michael helped Dana up into her saddle. "How's that, my lovely? Are you going to be all right in that silk gown of yours?"

"I have to be all right. We all agreed we'd do this madcap ride to our honeymoon cabins in the gowns we were married in. We'll look like a pack of ghosts flitting through the desert."

"Good thing it's a warm night in December."

"Good thing we're in New Mexico and not New York."

Michael vaulted onto his horse. "Are you ready to go like the wind? You look so beautiful I can't wait another hour."

"It's Christmas Eve. Suppose someone slides down the chimney and spoils our fun?"

Michael grinned. "First thing I'm doing is starting a fire in the fireplace."

"I thought I'd be the first thing."

"Well, I'll start a fire with you first, if that's what pleases you, and then I'll go on from there."

Dana spurred her horse. "That is what pleases me! Let's go, Reverend! Your sermon from the Song of Songs needs to be preached tonight!"

But six riders were already ahead of them, three with their white gowns billowing out behind them like clouds moving swiftly along under the starlight. Dana and Michael could hear Scott shouting and laughing as his bride Serenity Shore pushed her horse past his and took the lead. To Serenity's left, Nancy Harcourt and Benjamin were neck and neck, and just beyond all of them, Sarah Godley and Bobby had settled into an easy gallop that ate up the desert miles. Watching from the doorway of the new cabin on Dianna Charming's ranch, now Dianna David, Judge Nathaniel David and his wife Ella watched the white and dark couples until the night was only sand and stars and warm breezes again.

"Ten cabins spread over fifty miles and every point of the compass." The judge smiled and drew on his cigar. "There will be so many churches hell won't find a home for a hundred seasons in these parts."

"I hope you're right," responded Ella. "I'm still worried about those hooligans in Santa Fe."

"Those hooligans in Santa Fe are no more. I've told you that. Two are in federal prison, one took ship to England, and the other three lit out for South America. We won't hear from any of them again."

"I wish the Apache had gone to South America with them."

The judge blew a stream of smoke into the desert night. "Why, this is their land, Ella. They're defending it just like I'll defend this ranch if trouble should come our way. But the truth of it is, Blood Lance is keeping to the Texas side and the other bands don't touch this county. That's the way it's been since Lazarus Top. So rest easy, my love. Save up your prayers for our youngsters who are starting their married lives tonight."

"Don't worry, I'm praying without ceasing."

The judge put his arm around her shoulders. "My dear, we've been praying without ceasing since they were in the womb. We've raised nine wild sons and one headstrong daughter who is equal to all nine boys put together. Now they are all off on their honeymoons and we can praise God for that. But after a quarter of a century it's high time for our second honeymoon, wouldn't you say?"

"What, Nathaniel? Right here?"

"The perfect place – a warm fire, soft candles, a feather bed and two feather pillows, a Yellowboy Winchester at my left hand, and the love of my life at my right. Stars thicker than snowflakes. A land where God can breathe. People would pay large amounts of cash to honeymoon safely in New Mexico. We are here for free."

Ella nestled into his arm. "A second honeymoon. Will we get up to watch the sunrise like we did after our first night together?"

"We will. It's a great thing to see the sky God paints at the start of a new day and a new world. It's always been one of his greatest gifts to allow us a fresh beginning over and over again. Shall I nudge you awake or shall you nudge me?"

She smiled and gazed at the white New Mexico stars. "The coffee I brew will get you up off that featherbed just fine, Nathaniel Paul David. I can hardly wait."

"For me? Or for God?"

"Why, both of you, my love. Tonight, you. In the morning, God. With that bright new sky of his and all the colors of heaven spread across it from one end of New Mexico to the other. A gal can't ask for more than that on her honeymoon."

The judge took a final draw on his cigar. "Nor can her man."

The End

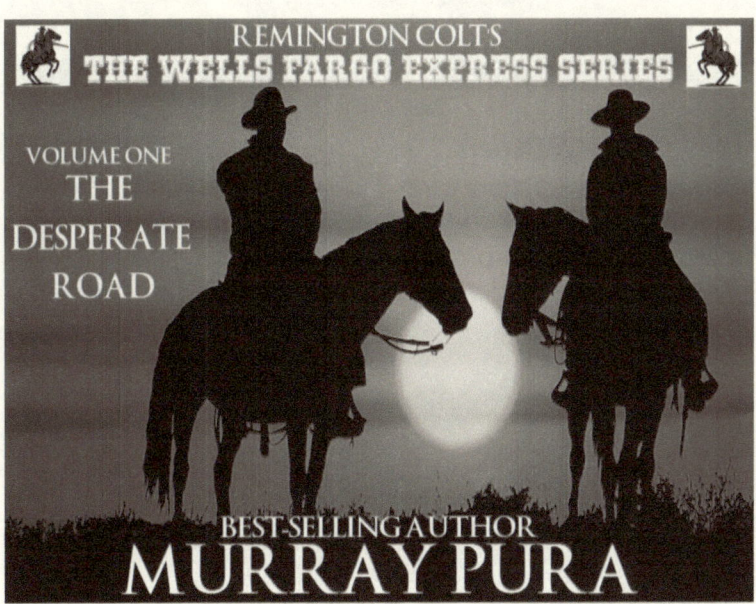

REMINGTON COLT'S
THE WELLS FARGO EXPRESS SERIES

VOLUME ONE
THE
DESPERATE
ROAD

BEST-SELLING AUTHOR
MURRAY PURA

for Glen Mickelson, cowboy

thanks for the friendship and support
I've enjoyed for so many years

Missouri, July, 1875

The bullet slammed into the stagecoach with a bang just above the elderly woman's head.

She began to scream.

Amos Dewery, derby hat on his head, black beard almost in the woman's face, leaned forward and squinted at the size of the hole. "Gotta be a .45. Excuse me, ma'am."

"Sure?" asked a lean man with his hat pulled down over his eyes and his arms folded over his chest.

"I use one myself."

There was more gunfire and the stagecoach swayed violently as the driver shouted at the horses and they began to move faster. A sound like a pistol shot made the woman scream more loudly. A lady in blue silk wearing a large blue hat with a broad brim looked at Amos.

"That was rather close," she said. "Can the bandits have caught up with us so quickly?"

Amos grunted. "The driver was cracking the whip."

"The whip? Are you sure?"

"I am." Amos brought out a large Bowie knife and began to sharpen it with a whetstone. "When they're close enough for me to use this you'll see me grab one by the beard and trim it for him."

There was more gunfire and another bullet cracked the wood paneling of the door closest to the older woman. She shrieked and fainted.

"I suppose you'll say it's a .45 again, Amos," murmured the man with the hat over his eyes.

"It is a .45, Holt."

"How's the coach holding up to the lead?"

"Pretty good."

"Make sure that gets in the report."

"Mm."

The young woman in blue narrowed her eyes. "You two seem to be very cavalier about this. What do you intend to do to defend us?"

BOOM!

"As little as possible," mumbled the man named Holt, hat still over his eyes and arms still folded over his chest. "They have a shotgun up there. That should take care of things."

More gunfire.

A shout from the driver. "Our shooter's hit!"

The lady stared at Holt and Amos. "Did you hear that?"

"What?" mumbled Holt. "The gunfire or the shout?"

Her face flushed. "When will you take this seriously? Do you expect me to fend off these cutthroats by myself while you two men just sit there?"

"You and the preacher could probably handle it."

The preacher was sitting between the older woman who had fainted and the younger woman in blue. His hands were resting on a large black Bible. He looked up in astonishment. "What, sir? I am not a man of violence, sir."

"Well, then, open your Bible and start preaching to those sinners, reverend. Just make sure you open to the passage where the cutout for your Colt Single Action Army starts."

"What?" The preacher's face went as white as his hair. "What?"

"How dare you bully that old gentleman!" snapped the woman. "Apologize to him at once! What sort of man are you?"

"The same sort of man who knows you have a Colt in your handbag. I noticed it when you took out a hanky after getting on board in Kansas."

Amos laughed and continued to hone his knife as the coach bounced over the road.

The woman's eyes and face looked like fire. Holt didn't see it because his hat remained where it was.

"How dare you!" she flared.

"If I were these robbers, ma'am, I wouldn't dare, not with the artillery you and the preacher have on you. You'll turn the pack of them into colanders in short order." Holt pulled his hat down lower. "You certainly don't need my help. Or that of my legal assistant, Mr. Amos Dewery."

Amos lifted his huge knife and turned it over and over in the sunlight that made its way into the coach. "Unless it's the Pittman Gang."

Holt smiled from underneath his hat brim. "Well, yes, if it's the Pittmans we can certainly lend Reverend Colt .45 and his sidekick Miss Colt .45 a hand."

The woman continued to glare hellfire at Holt while the preacher looked down at his thick Bible.

"I'm Benny Pittman! Pull up or we'll start shooting the horses! Pull up! All we want is the payroll! Y'all can keep your gold watches and diamond rings!"

The coach began to slow.

Holt finally lifted the brim of his hat. "Well, well, well, Uncle Benny."

Amos laid his knife on the seat and tugged a .45 Colt out from under the belt of his Levi Strauss and Company denim pants. "I'll take this window."

Holt slipped a large revolver from under his suit jacket. A distinctive steel web under the barrel set it apart from Amos' .45. "I've got this one. Perhaps Miss Colt will join in."

"I certainly will not!"

The white-haired preacher scowled and spat on the floor of the coach. "I started the cutout at Sodom and Gomorrah in Genesis. That's what I call my pistols – Sodom and Gomorrah. You didn't think there were two of 'em, did you, young man?"

Holt glanced at him in surprise. "No, I didn't."

"*Two are better than one,* the Good Book says, *because they have a good reward for their labor.*" The preacher brought out both revolvers and cocked them. They each had the small steel web under their barrels like Holt's. "Remington 1875s. Same as yours, young man. Similar to the 1858 I made use of during the war to put holes in all manner of Johnny Rebs."

Holt smiled. "Except our Remingtons fire .44 caliber cartridges."

The preacher smiled back. "An important exception."

"Well." The woman in blue glanced around her as the coach came to a stop. "A lady can't let the men have all the fun."

She opened her handbag and pulled out a short-barreled Colt .45 with gold engraving on the frame and barrel and cylinder.

Holt stared at it. "That's a custom job."

"Thank you, Mr. Holt, yes, it is."

He lifted his eyes from the gun to her face. "It's almost as pretty as you. But it falls short when it comes to the eyes, hair, face, and figure."

She smiled a sharp smile. "Why, thank you, sir. I'm relieved a gentleman has emerged in place of the absolute cad who held your seat a moment before."

Holt tipped his hat as riders approached the coach, bandanas over their noses and mouths. "Remington Holt, Mrs. –?"

"*Miss* Farr, Mr. Holt. *Miss* Celestial Farr. Is that what you were hoping to hear?"

"It is indeed. That's something worth fighting for."

Her smile sharpened and her blue eyes gleamed.

"I guess we changed our minds!" Benny Pittman, a red bandana over the lower half of his face, pointed his sixgun at the interior of the coach. "Seems the boys feel we could use a little loose change! Toss your rings and necklaces and pocket watches out the windows or we'll come in and get 'em!"

Remington Holt looked at Amos and the preacher and at Miss Farr. "Are we ready to dance?"

The preacher suddenly leaned over the older woman, who was still unconscious, thrust his two revolvers out the window, and opened fire, thundering at the top of his lungs: "*Then the Lord rained upon Sodom and upon Gomorrah brimstone and fire from the Lord out of heaven!*"

"Holy smokes!" Amos began to fire out the same window. "That's some way to start your sermon, reverend!"

Remington Holt and Celestial Farr began to shoot out their window at the same time. Benny Pittman flew backwards off his saddle, pistol firing wildly into the blue sky.

"My shot, I believe, Mr. Holt," she said as she continued to aim and fire her engraved .45.

"I believe you're right, Miss Farr. But I will take the henchman to his left."

"Be my guest. I have the right."

The coach quickly filled with smoke as the revolvers roared and spat flame. Several shots from the outlaws made their way into the coach again, shattering the door by the older woman, and tearing a derby hat off Amos Dewery's head. But in moments all the bandits were in the dust. The preacher fired the last shots, still screeching, *Brimstone and fire from the Lord out of heaven!*

The driver climbed down, stared at the outlaws, and stared at his passengers. "They're all dead."

"It looks that way," commented Remington Holt.

"You wiped out the Pittman Gang. A bunch of women and preachers and dandies."

"I ain't no dandy," growled Amos.

"He means me," said Remington.

"Why," the driver went on, "Wells Fargo has ten thousand a piece on these boys. Fifteen for Benny. That's sixty-five thousand dollars."

"That's ten for each of us and fifteen for you."

"What about the old lady?" asked Amos.

"She slept through it," grunted Remington as he reloaded his revolver. "Oh, heck, let her have five. She came the closest to getting killed out of all of us."

Amos stepped out of the coach. He was over six foot four in his dusty black boots. He tucked in his red and black flannel shirt and thrust his .45 back under his wide leather belt. Remington tossed his hat to him. Amos put his finger through the bullet hole and placed it back on top of his head. His black hair had fallen to his shoulders during the fight.

"Tuck your hair back up under your hat," said Remington. "Look presentable. You're a Wells Fargo employee."

"Hm. I have to get those bodies up on top first. Tie 'em down."

"I'll help."

Amos shook his head. "You'll just slow me down. This won't be no different than pitching firewood."

Remington sat back.

Celestial Farr arched an eyebrow. "Wells Fargo?"

"Yes, Miss Farr."

"Were you expecting trouble like this along your stage run?"

He nodded. "That's the reason Mr. Dewery and I are here. To fix problems. Though to be honest we didn't really expect the Pittman Gang."

"You're quite calm for someone who just shot and killed six men. Do you do this quite often, Mr. Holt?"

"I might ask the same thing of you. A beautiful young woman traveling on her own with an arm as a steady as a rock and a shot as deadly as a rattlesnake."

"That doesn't sound very flattering. I am an entertainer. I travel from city to city. Sometimes I have an escort but often I'm on my own between stops. A lady must be able to protect herself in these perilous times."

"It appears you're able to do that. May I ask what your entertainment involves?"

"I am a singer, Mr. Holt. A singer on her way to St. Louis to perform for President Grant."

Remington made a face. "Grant is in St. Louis?"

"All weekend. Is the president not to your liking?"

Remington shrugged. "I voted for Lincoln."

She laughed. "That makes you about ten years out of date. Though your clothing is quite 1870s. Well, you can always hope the next election will bring in the man you like."

Remington glanced down at his silk vest and string tie and his perfectly laundered white shirt with its gold cufflinks. "He's in his second term now, isn't he? So another election is years away."

"Perhaps. Where's home, Mr. Holt?"

"Cheyenne."

"Quite a ways to come for a few stage robbers. Are you stopping in St. Louis at all?"

"We are."

"Might I entice you to the show in President Grant's honor Saturday night? Even though you don't like him?"

"You might. I have a soft spot for blonde hair and blue eyes."

She gave him her full smile. "You can't be talking about our president. You must be talking about me. You really can be

186

gallant, can't you? Well, let's just say I have a soft spot for blonde hair and blue eyes too. Especially when it comes with a tall man from Wyoming."

The coach shook as Amos and the driver slung the bodies of the bandits on top of the stage.

Remington smirked. "Not as tall as Amos."

"I don't like my men that tall, Mr. Holt. You're just the right size."

The coach shook again.

"I'm pleased to hear that, Miss Farr."

"Celestial, please. People who have shared a close brush with death should not stand on formalities."

"My sentiments exactly."

She dug around in her handbag. As she did so she glanced at the preacher. "And how are you holding up, reverend? I fear we've been ignoring you."

He closed the top of his Bible. "I've just reloaded Sodom and Gomorrah and tucked them away until the next call to judgment. It's refreshing to serve righteousness, isn't it?"

Amos climbed back into the coach. "All done. We put some canvas over them. St. Louis in three hours, the driver says."

"How's the man riding shotgun?" asked Remington.

"Bullet went clean through his shoulder. He'll be all right."

"I'm so glad to hear that." Celestial brought two pieces of paper out of her bag. "These are tickets to the Saturday night gala in honor of the president. I do hope we'll see you there, Remington."

He took the tickets. "Nothing could give me greater pleasure."

The coach began to move forward.

Amos caught the preacher's eye and nodded. "Next time I'm in a religious mood I want to go to your church."

It was dark when they pulled into the depot in St. Louis but the city was blazing with gaslights. The preacher helped the older woman out of the coach and along the street. A man in top hat and cloak took Celestial's hand as she alighted and also picked up her luggage once the driver handed it down. She smiled back at Remington as she was led away.

"May I introduce my escort, Mr. Hamilton? Good night, Remington Holt. I hope to see you tomorrow night."

"I'll be there."

Hamilton turned his head, shot Remington a death look, and tightened his grip on Celestial Farr's arm.

"You're already married anyhow," Amos reminded him.

"She left me. Did you forget that part?"

"Were you ever divorced?"

"How should I know?" flared Remington. "I haven't heard from her in almost five years. For all I know she got her paperwork done in California and is living with some rich man in his fancy hacienda."

"Glad I never tied the knot."

Remington glared at him, his eyes a fiery blue in the lamplight. "Is that right? You seem mighty cozy with Elspeth Hartley back in Cheyenne. Even though you're twenty-three and she's forty-six."

Amos glared back. "She's just a neighbor, a good neighbor who takes care of things when I'm away doing work for you and Wells Fargo."

"She's interested in more than your goats."

Amos' hands turned into fists the size of small hams. "What are you saying, tinhorn?"

"Tinhorn?" retorted Remington, hand slipping inside his suit jacket to his shoulder holster.

The driver walked around the side of the coach with half a dozen police officers. "This is Mr. Dewery and this is Mr. Holt. They tell me they're agents with Wells Fargo. They helped apprehend the Pittman Gang."

"Let me see your badges," rumbled the sergeant.

Remington and Amos darted each other a final dark glance and yanked out billfolds. The sergeant examined their badges, smoothed both sides of his black moustache, then climbed to the top of the stage and peeled back the canvas. He whistled.

"That's Luke Pittman, all right. Never thought I'd see the day. What did you do, line them up for target practice? I've seen less holes in fishing nets."

He pulled up another head by the hair. "Bill Pittman. The brains behind the outfit they always said."

The sergeant jumped down and dusted off his hands. "It's up to Wells Fargo to settle the claims. But I'll vouch for you. Good work. You put this crew out of business permanently."

"We had help," replied Remington.

"Did we ever," added Amos. "A pistol packing preacher and the lady with the golden gun."

The sergeant stared at them. "What?"

Remington put his hands in the pockets of his pants. "Never mind."

"Well, we'll put the bodies on display for the night and the morning. With the president in town we can't do it any longer than that. St. Louis has to appear civilized. But it's important people see what happens to lawbreakers in the end. The wages of sin and all that."

Remington and Amos picked up their luggage and headed to a nearby hotel. Police had surrounded the building and the two men had to show their badges again and prove they had a valid reservation. Once inside, they went to the hotel restaurant and ordered steaks.

"I'm beat," said Amos.

"The food'll do you good. Wake you up. We still have to see the president."

"Can't it wait till morning?"

"No."

They tucked into the steaks once the waiter set them down and cleaned their plates off in a hurry, not because of the president but because they were hungry. They had barely finished before Amos nudged Remington and flicked his head towards the door.

"Pinkertons," he said in a low voice.

Remington glanced over. "Yeah. Robbie Scott himself. Who do you think he's looking for?"

Amos snorted. "You wanna bet your ten grand?"

"I don't. It doesn't matter now anyways. He's spotted us and here he comes."

The lean spidery man with the slim black moustache approached their table and leaned on it. "Well, well, well, Wells Fargo's pride and joy."

"What's the matter, Robbie?" asked Remington, popping the last bit of steak into his mouth. "Looking for work?"

"Oh, I've got work, more important work than riding the stage and spreading bloodshed from here to Kansas City. I protect the President of the United States. You two, on the other hand, instead of keeping the low profile we demanded of you, just blew the whole Pittman family out of their saddles. You pulled into the depot when? An hour ago? And all of St. Louis is already babbling about these two Wells Fargo agents who single-handedly put down six desperadoes. Is that what you call a low profile?"

"Couldn't be helped," replied Remington.

"They drew first," added Amos.

"It was kill or be killed," continued Remington. "Kind of like your job, Robbie. You know? The lead flying thick and fast?"

Amos drank off the rest of his beer and belched. "And it wasn't single-handed."

Robbie Scott's eyes became slits. "You two are clowns. Regular clowns from the backwoods of Wyoming. Why the president trusts you with such important work I'll never be able to fathom. The winner of the war reduced to relying on Silly and Willy to safeguard his political future and the future of our country."

"Well, he couldn't rely on you, could he, Robbie?" responded Remington. "You're too busy polishing his shoes and pressing his pants."

Scott took one end of his moustache into his mouth and began to chew on it. "I don't know why we waste our time. But President Grant wants to see you. Follow me to the top floor and try to keep your big mouths shut. I don't want anyone to think you two are with me."

The president was relaxing in a large chair in the grand suite when Robbie Scott knocked and came in. Seeing Remington and Amos, Grant got to his feet to shake their hands, a cigar in his mouth.

"Very good to see you, very good." Grant smiled through his beard. "Can I interest either of you in a good Cuban cigar?"

"I wouldn't mind," said Remington.

"I'd be grateful, sir," replied Amos.

Grant opened a wooden box and let them select their cigars. Then he snapped the lid shut and nodded at Scott. "Thank you. You may wait outside. Please send in Mr. Spencer."

Scott half-bowed. "As you wish, Mr. President."

Grant settled back in his chair after handing Remington a box of matches. "I understand you had quite a trip east. At first people were saying it was the James Gang. Then the Youngers. Finally the Pittmans. Which is it?"

"The Pittmans." Remington and Amos said the name at the same time.

"All six of them?"

"Yes, sir," said Amos.

"They weren't prepared to face five guns from four passengers, Mr. President," replied Remington. "They never saw it coming."

"Hm. Everyone on that stage was armed?"

"A preacher. A young beauty who will be singing at your gala tomorrow night." Remington drew on his cigar and leaned back, blowing out a stream of white smoke. "Lead was flying north and south and east and west. It was like Missionary Ridge at Chattanooga."

Grant laughed. "You and your men were foolhardy enough that day. Climbing up the slope with Minie balls falling on you like rain. But you never quit, did you? Even the Rebs had enough that day, watching you coming up and coming up those cliffs like spiders. Broke and ran. I hear some of them are running yet."

Remington smiled.

Grant smoked and eyed Amos. "And you were at Gettysburg with Meade."

"Yes, sir."

"With the Iron Brigade on Seminary Ridge."

"Yes, sir."

"You saved the day. The Army of Northern Virginia was on the field in full force long before the Army of the Potomac. If you hadn't fought like the hellions you were and slowed the Rebels down they'd have taken all the heights. It would have been Fredericksburg all over again for us. Outstanding work, Mr. Dewery."

"Thank you, sir."

The door opened and a man of medium height with sideburns and a large smile entered the room. "Mr. President."

"Tom." Grant waved the hand that held the cigar. "Our prodigals have found their way home again."

Remington and Amos got to their feet and shook Tom Spencer's hand.

"Hello, boys," he greeted them. "You're the toast of the town. The men who put Bill and Ben Pittman in the grave. Fortunately for our purposes the good citizens of St. Louis have your descriptions all wrong – two short men with red hair and beards, one with a limp, the other with an arm missing from the fight at Spotsylvania Court House."

"That's us," responded Remington.

"Cigar, Tom?" asked Grant.

"No, thank you, Mr. President." Spencer took a seat and steepled his fingers. "What news?"

Remington and Amos glanced at one another.

"Go ahead," prompted Amos.

Remington leaned forward, the cigar curling smoke from between the fingers of his right hand. "This group, oligarchy, cabal, whatever term you want to use for the men you asked us to investigate, well, they were not impressed with your re-election to a second term. They seem more determined than ever to ruin your administration and to rape the country, getting all the railroad and beef contracts and grabbing up all the land and the grazing rights they can bully out of everyone else. Amos and I had a set to with a group of them in Kansas. Two got away, three were killed, and we had one prisoner for about two hours. We managed to persuade him to tell us what he knew."

"What happened to him?" asked Spencer.

"He died of his wounds from the gunfight."

"I see."

Remington drew on his cigar. "He was KKK. They all were. To put it bluntly, they hate you, Mr. President. They hate you for being the general who licked Lee, the general who ended their dream of an independent Southern nation. They hate you for standing up to the KKK. The hate you for being a Yankee. They hate you for fighting corruption and trying to stonewall their schemes."

"That's a lot of hate," said Spencer.

"I've been hated before." Grant lit a fresh cigar. "What else? Do you have any names?"

"The gangs they hire to bully the ranchers and railroad men don't know who the big boys are. The prisoner called them The Bosses. That's the only name he could come up with a few minutes before his death when he had nothing to fear by telling us."

"Hm," mumbled Grant.

"Amos and I have had quite a few clashes with these people now. They have no intention of giving up. For some, it's this idea they lost the war but now they're going to rule their own nation regardless and have it exactly the way they would have run it under the Stars and Bars – they are adamant they are going to retain slavery and ignore the 13th Amendment. In fact, they look to the day they'll put a Southerner back in the White House. For the rest of the Bosses, well, they're true blue Yankees and all they're interested in is money and power no matter what it takes – fists, knives, gunfights, bribes, murder, buying off senators, blackmailing congressmen, torching hayfields. I wish I could say Amos and I were any closer to getting even one of the names of the men at the top. I can say this though – some of them are under the Capitol dome, some are high-ranking officers in the military, some are reverends and some are priests. And some are working hand in glove with you in the White House."

Grant continued to smoke, staring at Remington through the haze.

Spencer frowned. "If you know so little how can you be sure of all that?"

"We may not have names for you tonight. But we've talked to enough of their hired guns to put two and two together. We're dealing with whales here not minnows. We'll need a big net to catch them all and a strong one."

"We need harpoons," grunted Amos.

"Hm." Grant exhaled a lungful of white smoke.

Spencer stood up. "We're indebted to you both for your service to our country. The Pinkertons have stumbled upon one scrap of information for you that may prove useful."

Remington and Amos looked at each other.

"The Pinkertons? Really?" Remington glanced at the tip of his cigar. "What have they unearthed?"

"There seem to be levels or ranks in this organization. That is no great surprise, of course. But one of the ranks is that of assassins. The one Pinkertons caught and interrogated had this tattooed over his heart."

He handed Remington a sheet of paper. On it was a drawing of a snake.

Amos leaned over to look at it. "That's a Copperhead. You can tell by the markings."

Remington looked long and hard at the drawing. "Is it always over the heart?"

"No. He said no."

"Is he still a prisoner? Can I have access to him?"

"He died of his wounds."

"Who do they assassinate?"

"Well, it's a selective term, isn't it? Shooting a rancher would just be shooting a rancher. But killing a congressman or a railroad magnate would be an assassination to them. Remember Bisby?"

"Bisby? He was a junior senator, wasn't he? Didn't he get killed in a wagon wreck?"

"He did get killed in a wagon wreck. But this – Copperhead – he told Pinkertons that the assassins had arranged the crash. One of their own people engineered the whole accident and was driving the wagon loaded down with bricks that hit Bisby side on."

"What happened to their driver?"

"He was killed as well."

Remington placed his cigar in an ashtray. "You're telling me they're willing to engage in murder-suicides to carry out their agenda?"

"Apparently."

"That makes what they're doing more of a cause than a crime."

Spencer paced, hands in his pockets. "Isn't that what you've already suggested? That to some it's simply another way of having their Confederate States of America?" He stopped and faced Remington and Amos squarely. "The prisoner said the assassins all take an oath: *Sic semper tyrannis.*"

"Death to all tyrants." Remington picked up his cigar again but it had gone cold. "Isn't that what Booth shouted after he shot Lincoln?"

"So he claimed."

"After he shot an unarmed man in the back." Agitated, Remington pushed himself out of his chair. "Are we to see more of this Southern chivalry from these Copperheads?"

Hands still in his pockets, Spencer shrugged.

"Mr. President, we will do all that we can." Remington was practically standing at attention. "I hope we can see you in the White House for three or four terms."

Grant laughed and rose. "Two terms will be enough for me, Mr. Holt. After all, that's the equivalent of two consecutive civil wars. But I thank you all the same." He shook Remington's hand. "I'm grateful for your work. Keep us informed. But don't use the mail or the telegraph."

"No, sir."

"Mr. Dewery."

Amos got up and took the president's hand.

"I suppose you are back to Cheyenne in the morning?" asked Grant.

"Actually we were given tickets to attend the gala, Mr. President," said Remington. "So we will stay over Saturday night and leave after church Sunday morning."

"Ah, the gala. I promise to keep my speech short so the dancing can be as long as possible."

Remington grinned. "Thank you, sir."

But his grin was gone as he and Amos walked down to their room on the bottom floor, luggage in hand.

"Assassins! Oaths! *Sic semper tyrannis!* I'd rather deal with a bunch of money-grubbing crooks instead of a pack of fanatics!"

"I'm with you on that," Amos rumbled. "Better a thousand Pittmans than one Copperhead tattoo."

"Wouldn't it be something if we could find the man at the top of the heap and cut his head off? The whole snake would wither and die."

Amos patted the Bowie knife that hung in a fringed leather sheath from his belt. "I have just the tool to do it with."

When they were in their beds, and Amos had turned off the gas lamp, Remington asked, "What do you think of Celestial Farr?"

"I try not to think of her at all. You two are interested in each other so I don't want to get in the way."

"Don't you find her attractive?"

"A blind man would find her attractive."

"Where do you think she's from?"

"I caught a trace of an accent. Wouldn't hazard a guess."

"She's the kind of lady that drives a bad relationship far from a man's mind."

"I imagine she is."

"Do you think she'll dance with me?"

Amos turned over in his bed. "Why not? You smell like a flower shop and all women like flowers."

"There's a hard edge to her though."

"Won't stop her from dancing with a dandy. A woman is a woman. If she wants to shoot you she'll shoot you after she's had her dance."

"What do you think? Do you think there's a chance we could wind up together?"

"I'm falling asleep here, Rem."

"Even a small chance?"

"Small, large, there's a chance of some size. I'm in dreamland now, Rem. This is me sleep talking."

Long after Amos had begun to snore, Remington lay awake, hands under his head, turning Celestial Farr and her golden hair over and over in his mind. He thought of different phrases he might use when he saw her again. He wondered what her singing voice was like. He imagined how soft the skin on her hand or cheek was. Just before he fell asleep he felt her lips brush his and saw her blue eyes glitter like sun on the snow.

"Do you want a kiss?" she asked, teasing.

"More than breath itself."

"A long one or a short one, Wells Fargo man?"

"Kiss me through to Sunday morning."

She laughed like silver and gold. "All right, I think I can handle that. But there's something I need you to do for me before I start."

"What's that?"

But there was only her golden hair like perfume on his face and her fingers stroking his brow, soft as a summer breeze.

Amos and Remington went out for breakfast Saturday morning, walking by the dry goods store that had the Pittman brothers on display in their window, anxious to see if anyone recognized the two of them. But no one glanced at the pair twice. Three boys were counting all the bullet holes in the bodies, a photographer was setting up his camera, four or five men were murmuring the Pittmans had been captured and shot, making it murder, and one woman was reading out loud from her Bible to anyone who would listen. Underneath the bodies in their coffins was a hand printed banner with the words THE WAGES OF SIN IS DEATH ROMANS 6:23.

"You still feel like bacon and eggs?" Remington asked as the two of them walked away.

Amos shrugged, the derby with the bullet hole still perched on his head of long black hair. "Death happens every day. The rest of us have to eat."

Saturday passed quickly. They made arrangements with Wells Fargo to have their reward money deposited to special bank accounts in Washington, vouched for the others on the stagecoach who had contributed to the killing of the outlaws, got into a poker game and lost fifty dollars each, had a late lunch that served as an early supper, washed up in their room, and presented themselves at the gala smelling, Amos grumbled, "like teatime at the lady's missionary society."

"What does that smell like?"

"Like us."

"And it's not good?"

"Not if you're a man. But Celestial Farr may swoon so you might be in luck."

"You know, I dreamed about her last night."

"Rem, I don't want the details. Let's find a table and get something to drink."

"There you are! I'm so glad you two made it!"

Celestial Farr made her way towards them through the crowds of men and women and linked her arm though Remington's. "They're going to do some dancing first. Isn't that splendid?" She pouted. "You will give me a dance, won't you?"

"Of course I'll give you a dance," replied Remington. "I'll give you as many as you want."

"As many as I want? We could be here all night." She studied him. "I like the way you look tonight. And I adore your cologne."

"Why, thank you, Celestial."

Amos coughed.

"You look wonderful yourself," Remington continued. "That pale lemon yellow suits you."

"*Pale lemon yellow?* You're quite the poet, Remington Holt, and it appears I have quite the catch." She kissed him on the cheek. "Please join me at my table closer to the front you two."

She led them toward the stage and a table with yellow roses in a vase. Amos took a seat while Remington took to the floor as the band struck up a waltz.

"You're nimble on your feet," she said, leaning her head on his shoulder. "As nimble as you are with a gun."

"Nimbler."

"Are you really a Wells Fargo agent?"

"I really am."

"Where do you go from here?"

"Well, I thought we'd be heading back to Cheyenne in the morning. But I have a hunch we may be going north to Chicago."

"By stagecoach?"

"By train. Just this once. I haven't told Amos yet. He hates trains."

Her lips touched his ear. "Have you considered Europe? Or Mexico City? I have a performance season in the south and overseas. I could use a new bodyguard."

"What happened to Hamilton?"

She brushed her lips over his as they danced. "I had to let him go. Too much jealousy. I need more freedom than that. You're not jealous, are you, Remington?"

"Right now I'm not jealous of any man."

"You're sweet." Her lips hovered near his. "A woman doesn't kiss in public. But I'm a different sort of woman."

"I saw that in the stagecoach."

"I have other talents as well. Would you like to sample them?"

"In public? At the president's gala? Yes."

She smiled. "Rule breaker."

"That's me."

"I'd love to give you a kiss. Can you dance and kiss at the same time?"

"I have other talents too. That's one of them."

She laughed as they whirled over the floor between other couples. "All right. You've won a kiss. But before I do it I need you to promise me something."

"Do you know, I think I dreamed all this last night?"

"Truly?"

"Almost to the letter."

Her bare arms slipped from his back to his neck. "That sounds prophetic. Was it a good dream?"

"Very good. But confusing. You never told me what it was you wanted so I never got my kiss."

"Poor boy. Let's make real life better than the dream. I need you to be my bodyguard, Remington Holt. And I need you to be the best bodyguard in the world. I'm being followed everywhere I go and I fear my life is in danger."

"What? Why?"

"I don't know how much time we have before the president's speech. I will say it as quickly as I can. There is a secret group dedicated to the overthrow of the government. They know I know about them. They just don't know how much I know. I keep thinking they are going to shoot me. I believe the reason they don't is they'd rather abduct me and question me. I have to have protection from them, Remington. My revolver has only so many bullets and I don't have eyes in the back of my head. Will you do it?"

Remington gazed at her in surprise as they glided across the hall.

Her face darkened. "You don't believe me."

"I do believe you."

"Then why the face?"

"I didn't think anyone outside of Amos and myself and Pinkertons knew about The Bosses."

"So you do understand. You will protect me."

"Celestial, I – "

"Please, Remington, I need your help. We know so little about each other but I trust you. They've infiltrated Pinkertons and the White House."

"Pinkertons?"

"Yes. I never feel safe."

"I don't know what to say."

"Say yes. I can pay you four times what Wells Fargo is paying you. And I'm a much better employer than they could ever be." Her eyes had turned the softest blue he had ever seen. "I need you, Remington. I need you to keep me safe."

He ran his thumb over her cheek. "I'll do it."

"You will? Yes?"

"Yes."

"Oh, I'm so happy; I feel like you've given me my life back." She grasped his face in her hands and placed her lips against his. "American social rules and etiquette can go hang themselves."

She put her whole mouth and body into the kiss until Remington's head began to reel. Somehow he managed to continue to guide her over the dance floor. One kiss was followed by another and another. Then her lips were touching his ear again, and he felt her warm breath, and heard each whisper that came from her throat.

"No matter what happens tonight I need you to protect me. No matter who comes after me. No matter what you see. I need you to remain faithful and defend me. All right?"

"Celestial – "

"All right?"

"Of course. I've already promised to be your bodyguard, haven't I?"

"Ladies and gentlemen, the President of the United States."

The band stopped, the dancing stopped. Couples stood where they were and clapped.

Celestial glanced at Remington as he clapped heartily. "I thought you didn't like him."

He continued to clap. "You don't want to draw attention to ourselves do you?"

She smiled and clapped along with him. "No."

They returned to their table and sat with Amos. There was a decanter of red wine next to the yellow roses. Celestial poured herself a glass and sipped it as Grant made a speech about the future of America. Now and then she would slip her eyes onto Remington, blue eyes that were the color of the sea, deep and rich. Eventually she smiled and placed her hand over his.

Forever.

She mouthed the word to him.

Amos leaned over and spoke quietly into Remington's ear. "Moving along a little fast, aren't we?"

Remington whispered in Amos' ear. "She doesn't know slow and neither do I today. Look at her. Look at how beautiful she is."

"I'm looking. But she's not the Princess of Morocco, Rem. Take it easy, will you?"

"She's better than any Princess of Morocco."

"Ladies and gentlemen, we are now blessed with an aria from the lovely Celestial Farr who will soon be traveling overseas to begin her European tour. She will sing for us the popular song by Francs Scott Key, *The Star Spangled Banner*. Please join me in welcoming Miss Farr who will sing for President Grant."

As applause filled the hall Celestial got to her feet, smiling at everyone around her, and extended her elbow to Remington. "Please escort me onto the stage, my dear."

Surprised, Remington stood up. "You don't waste any time making use of your bodyguard, do you, Miss Farr?"

"Believe me; there's no time to waste, Mr. Holt."

Amos frowned up at them. "Bodyguard? What's this?"

Remington took her arm and glanced back at Amos. "I'll explain in a few minutes."

He walked Celestial up the steps to the stage as the clapping continued.

"Now leave me." She acknowledged her audience and the president who was seated on the stage with several of his officials. "Just remember what I said. No matter what happens, defend me, Remington."

"I don't think you need to be so alarmed."

"I know what I need to think. Don't leave the stage. Defend me."

"Of course I'll defend you. But you'll be fine." He fought back an urge to take her in his arms and kiss her again. "You look radiant, Celestial. I've never seen a woman shine the way you do."

Her smile grew and she turned her face towards his for a brief moment. "Thank you, Remington. You really are gallant, aren't you?"

He remained standing to one side of the stage as Celestial moved closer to the president and closer to the center. She faced the audience, a handkerchief that matched her dress in her fingers, and began to sing without the band or any sort of accompaniment.

O say can you see by the dawn's early light
What so proudly we hailed at the twilight's last gleaming,
Whose broad stripes and bright stars through the perilous fight

*O'er the ramparts we watched, were so gallantly
streaming?*
And the rockets' red glare, the bombs bursting in air,
Gave proof through the night that our flag was still there
O say does that star-spangled banner yet wave
O'er the land of the free and the home of the brave?

O thus be it ever, when freemen shall stand
Between their loved home and the war's desolation.
Blest with vict'ry and peace, may the Heav'n rescued land
*Praise the Power that hath made and preserved us a
nation!*
Then conquer we must, when our cause it is just,
And this be our motto: "In God is our trust."
And the star-spangled banner in triumph shall wave
O'er the land of the free and the home of the brave!

Her voice was so perfect, so pure, that Remington closed his eyes as she sang. He had never heard a woman sound so right, so in key, so heavenly. Her voice was an extension of her blue eyes and golden hair. She was a dream and suddenly everything she had asked of him seemed right. He would be her bodyguard. He would accompany her to Europe. He would be her lover as well as her protector. Remington was so caught up in her voice and his plans that he never saw it coming.

"Seize that woman! Seize her!"

He opened his eyes, startled to see a body of men bursting into the hall. He recognized Robbie Scott and several of the Pinkerton agents right away. Leading them was the man who had been Celestial Farr's escort and bodyguard the night before, the man she had called Hamilton. Running towards the stage he pointed at her with a black walking stick.

"Seize her, I tell you! She's going to shoot the president!"

Celestial pulled her revolver out from under her hooped skirt, the Colt with the gold engraving on its barrel, cylinder, and frame, and shot Hamilton twice. Women began to scream and throw themselves under the tables while both men and women jammed the doorway, rushing to get out of the hall. Celestial fired a third time, knocking down a Pinkerton agent who had reached the stage, then swung her Colt on Amos, who was tugging his .45 out of his belt and fighting his way through the shrieking and shouting mob of people. Changing her mind, she put the gun on President Grant who rose swiftly to his feet to face her. Amos' pistol was clear of his belt.

"Shoot him!" cried Celestial to Remington. "Shoot Amos! Shoot the Pinkerton men! You swore you'd defend me! You promised you'd protect me! They're in league with the devil! Even the president is in league with wicked men!"

The Remington .44 was in his hand. He saw Robbie Scott and the Pinkerton agents lifting their pistols. One had a shotgun he was raising to his shoulder. Amos was bringing his .45 up to fire.

His gun barrel moved from the stage to the Pinkertons and back to the stage.

"*Celestial!*" he suddenly shouted. "*Sic semper tyrannis!*"

She spun around, the revolver leveled at him.

Her eyes were the hardest blue he had ever seen.

Then, for a moment, they became as soft as the summer sky.

He fired three times. All three bullets hit her in the heart. She flew backwards and fell by the president's feet. Grant's officials hustled him through a door behind them. The Pinkertons scrambled onto the stage as the screaming and yelling grew louder. Remington walked to the far side of the stage and sat down, still holding his .44.

"She would've killed him." He saw the polished boots and recognized Robbie Scott's voice. "None of us could have got a shot off fast enough." There was a pause. "Good work." The boots were gone.

The hall was empty. Without thinking, Remington ejected the shell casings and reloaded his gun with cartridges from his shoulder holster. Then he continued to hold the .44 in his hand. Amos sat down beside him.

"It happened too fast between the two of you," Amos said.

"I know that."

"She was setting you up."

"I know that too."

"Grant would like to express his gratitude to you personally."

"Did you find a tattoo?" Remington asked.

"What?"

"The tattoo. Did she have one?"

"Yeah. She did."

"Where was it?"

Amos did not answer for a moment. "There wasn't much left of the tattoo. It was over her heart."

"She could have shot me first, Amos. Why didn't she?"

"I don't know."

"Her eyes turned the softest shade of blue right before I killed her."

Amos was silent.

"She was beautiful. Easy on the eyes. Nice laugh. Brave. Noble. Voice like an angel. How come the Copperhead tattoo?"

"It was her cause. Like you said last night."

Remington stood up. "I don't feel like sleeping. I don't feel like eating. You think maybe I can sit in a church for an hour? You think there's one open?"

"I guess there is."

"After that I want to get on a stagecoach. I don't care where it's going so long as it's heading west. You think we can do that? Head back where the mountains are high and the land is wide open and something makes sense?"

"I guess we can."

Amos got to his feet and stood beside Remington. "Let's get you a coffee. Before we sit in the dark with the angels. Before we climb aboard a Wells Fargo stage and head back to God's Country. A big cup of coffee. Hot and black."

Remington put his .44 into his shoulder holster and looked out over the empty hall. "Yeah. I'd like that. I'd like that a lot."

www.ingramcontent.com/pod-product-compliance
Lightning Source LLC
Chambersburg PA
CBHW031419250626
47155CB00004B/1546